Rehears

Real World

Robin Lindsay Wilson

LEAF BY LEAF

Published by Leaf by Leaf
an imprint of Cinnamon Press
Meirion House
Tanygrisiau
Blaenau Ffestiniog
Gwynedd, LL413SU
www.cinnamonpress.com

The right of Robin Lindsay Wilson to be identified as author of this work
has been asserted by him in accordance with the Copyright, Designs and
Patent Act,1988. © 2020 Robin Lindsay Wilson ISBN: 978-1-78864-908-7

British Library Cataloguing in Publication Data. A CIP record for this
book can be obtained from the British Library.

Designed and typeset in Garamond by Cinnamon Press. Cover design by
Adam Craig © Adam Craig from original drawing © The Trustees of the
British Museum.

Cinnamon Press is represented by Inpress and by the Books Council of
Wales.

Foreword

I began writing these mini monologues, as training exercises for the students I was teaching to be actors, at Queen Margaret University, Edinburgh. The speeches were used to stimulate participants into exploring characters and situations.

Within each little monologue, I embedded repetition, hesitation and a range of punctuation. I hoped to focus a performer's attention upon applying each comma, exclamation mark, ellipsis, dash, question mark and full stop. I also tried to provide a range of verbs, adverbs and adjectives for students to play with. Semester after semester, for over five years, I found these narratives to be effective at improving each student's ability to lift language off the page and to give it spontaneous expression.

I must admit however, that some stories got away from me and decided to find their own journeys and endings! Words which began under my control, bolted down strange twisted paths, to unknown places. A few of these tales were too long to use in class. But the shorter ones became popular with students who had a liking for the mysterious and the bizarre.

At some point during my teaching, I happened to read *Hold Me!* by Jules Feiffer. Feiffer's flexible, but clearly defined and dynamic structure, provided a way to knit my collection of random pieces into a coherent single work. By creating narratives themed by a single subject, as he did,

I could build links across my uneven, contradictory and diverse material.

However, while I used his book as a model, I tried to be original. Where he introduced dances, I introduced blues songs. I also created the animal speeches, and the ramshackle poems or lists. They bonded the work and created a rhythm while providing some strong images. Both devices helped lift the book away from the prosaic and logical into a more fantastical and poetic way of interpreting experience and the human condition.

Towards the end of writing these pieces, I chanced across the prose of Lydia Davis. She was the winner of the Man Booker International Prize in 2013. Some of her short stories only lasted a paragraph, or a single sentence. This encouraged me to think that my condensed speeches might double as stories in their own right. Her work gave me the courage to fancy that there might be a slightly wider audience for these speeches beyond that of colleges, universities and acting programmes.

As the title of this book suggests, much of *Rehearsals for the Real World* is related to the craft of character acting. Each little speech is spoken by a unique individual. I wrote some of the characters with a male bias, and some were written from a female perspective, but, as the characters were played out in workshops, this distinction proved mostly irrelevant. Gender was shown to be adaptable and fluid. I have not indicated the bias of the person speaking at the beginning of any passage for this reason.

I disclaim any responsibility for the opinions the characters express. Although they insisted on being heard, they do not speak for me. I am pleased that quite frequently, as soon as one character has expressed one point of view, another character pops up to propose very different values.

I only apologise for the work not fitting easily into any category or genre of writing. But—well... I suppose I like it that way. I enjoy being spoken to openly and directly by odd individuals who argue with each other and themselves.

Whether you use this book as an assortment of acting pieces, or as short fiction you can dip into on a commuter journey, I hope you find something to divert and entertain you!

Robin Lindsay Wilson

To all the students who became my teachers

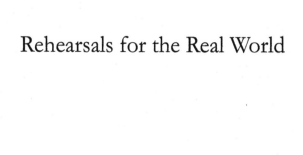

Rehearsals for the Real World

BEST PROGNOSIS BLUES

I'm going to sing you a song about protracted illness. Incurable disease. Misery, and then agonising death. It will make you feel a whole lot better.

MONKEY MAN

Question! What is civilization? Answer. A couple of friends. A child to rear. Spare cash. Leisure time. Some self-worth. A bit of reflection on what life is all about. Question. When did it start? Answer. When people had some friends round to share their fire. A couple of spare cowry shells. Time to idle before the next task. Some confidence. Some contemplation on what life is all about. Summery. It started before fire was controlled. It started as soon as children were born and demanded prolonged attention. It started as soon as friendships were made. It started after eating a successful hunt. It started with the first generous impulse. It started with a liar caught out and then laughter. It started with an old woman telling a story... There has been civilization forever.

THE REAL HISTORY OF MANKIND

Civilization started with masturbation. Without masturbation there would be no civilization. Masturbation requires time out. Time not struggling to survive. Masturbation requires imagery, mental pictures, substitutions for the real thing and the understanding that these fantasies are not to be acted upon. Masturbation is the sublimation of the real thing—the withdrawing of a potentially disruptive action into the self. Masturbation, therefore, removes potentially violent lustful chaotic desires from troubling society. It helps maintain rules, boundaries, taboos. The history of civilization is the history of masturbation. Could artists and writers have created those beautiful objects, paintings and manuscripts if they were constantly hunting for sex? Of course not. It's obvious that the most prolific artists were the best wankers! The continuing development of civilization is fundamentally dependent on the practice of self-gratification. Not what your parents told you. Not what schoolbooks told you. Not what religion told you... I've lost the thread... no—the thought's gone—time to help civilization advance—!

IMAGINE

My religion is the most difficult religion in the whole world. It is the oldest religion. It is the most mentally exhausting. It is the most emotionally draining. My religion says that you should imagine yourself walking in the shoes of your enemy. My religion asks me to imagine myself walking in the shoes of the stranger, the other, the bully, the outsider, the refugee, the thief, the beggar, the whore, the liar, the hypocrite, the warmonger, the boaster, the zealot, the betrayer, the well poisoner, the fool. Did I tell you that in the excoriating truth, there is also the gift of grace? My religion only has one commandment. You shall imagine your neighbour, as you imagine your self.

ALL YOU NEED IS LOVE

I love love. I love everything about love. I love sharing dumb movies. The pet names. The silly tacky little gifts. Waiting all day for you to arrive. The sound of your footsteps. The sound of your voice. The smell behind your ear. Your terrible taste in music. Your inability to spell. The clumsy way you haul a jumper off. The way you leave your dirty pants in the bathroom. I love it all. I love love. That's why I put up with your betrayal.

LIFE STORIES

Why didn't you tell me? Why did you tell him? We—I thought we told each other everything. Everything about our lives. You know all my stories. You know me. But—but —you were with him, not long—just long enough to tell a story about yourself that you never told me. You gave him a bit of yourself you kept back from me. Maybe you thought I would not accept... But you told him, and he told me. He knew I didn't know. He enjoyed telling me but pretended he didn't. He told me because he wanted me to accept him with you. I don't. Tell me another story. I don't know you. Tell me another story. Who are you? Tell me another story about who you really are.

PROMISE

I'm pregnant. If it is possible to feel twenty things all at once—that's how I feel. Delighted. Terrified. A heartbeat between them. Suddenly, I want there to be a God to keep the life inside safe. Suddenly, I feel inadequate. My mind, my ability, my resources and my protection, don't seem enough. Only my heart. My big fat heart!

IS IT IN MY HEAD?

I thought of extravagant things. I wanted to rush off into jungles and sultry nightclubs. Leave with a door slam. Nothing behind, nothing forward. The lonely glory of one-night stands. I thought of putting myself in harm's way. I had urges for wild, cruel things. Not because I was wild, or cruel. But I could not detect myself thinking. I could not hear myself think unless I exaggerated. If I challenged and pushed there was an echo of a faint something... If I was just quiet and still, there was nothing there. Nothing underneath it all. No love of ordinary things.

IN PLACE OF LOVE

My fear of love didn't stop me from having a lot of sex. Uninhibited. Let's just go that way sex. Sex that had a life of its own. Every encounter a redefinition of who I might be. A chance to exist as a new sensation. I've never had bad sex. Only periods of no sex, when I was no one. Just a ghost looking—looking... But when I was flesh—flesh exploring, I was always grateful. Too grateful sometimes to remember my own body. But my giving borrowed from my taking and the balance always tipped towards release. Every act found its own satisfaction... Satisfaction in the mechanics of satisfaction... Nothing to do with love. The love I have for my own body... My fear of love... Two very different things... Both making me unlovable.

BLUE MOON

I have not opened my house to the moon. I have not bowed to it formally. I have not opened my wardrobe and let the moon inspect my street clothes. I have not presented the moon with the scent of lilies in a crystal vase. I have not slid back the cutlery drawer and let the moon sip from my spoons and cut with my knives. I have not invited the moon into my bed to discover me naked. But tonight, when the sun goes out, I will open all the doors of my life to moonlight's howl. My hall will flood with silver. The moon will kiss my forehead. My heart will empty of shouting. My prayer will be changed forever.

CHARACTER CHOICES

I'm going to be a star.
I'm going to be the best actor in the world.
I'm going to win fifteen Oscars.
I'm going to break all the box office records.
I'm going to create unforgettable characters.
But people will still see it's me.
But I'm pretending to be somebody else.
And I'm so brilliant at being believable they will be completely convinced.
But I want them to see it's me.
What's the point if they don't see it's me?

ANOTHER OPENING, ANOTHER SHOW

My friend is a struggling actor. I've seen him in a profit share thing and a couple of community shows that he 'facilitated'. Now and then we go to the movies together. Discuss the film over a drink after. I can't stand John Boyega, he said one week. I was surprised. I hate Daniel Radcliffe; he exploded another time. I had to watch what I said. I'd see him in another poorly attended sullen production. Talking after, he'd say how awful Chris Hemsworth was and how Robert Pattinson couldn't act at all. I gradually stopped going to see my friend's shows. There were less of them as time went on anyway. But I always enjoyed going to the cinema with my other friends, or on my own. Bradley Cooper is my favourite. What a hunk!

EXPERT TEXTPERT

I'm communicating all the time—everything that happens to me. I have all the latest apps on all the latest devises. Costs a fortune. Tweeting. Texting. Emailing. Phoning. Blogging. Skyping. Whatsapping. I'm always busy. I'm always in touch. I'm a brilliant communicator. I tell everybody everything. I have over a million friends. I'm on 'send' 24/7. Nothing happens to me.

LOVE IN VAIN

I look good. You look good. Together we look super-good! We turn heads. People want to be us. We are glamorous. Everyone envies our cool—elegance, élan, sexiness! I don't particularly like you, you aren't too keen on me. If you want to end it—I will understand. Fine! I just think we should stay together because, well—together we look—come on—we look—we look sensational! Everyone wants to fuck our brains out, and we are so—so only into each other. Unavailable. Let's drive them mad, let's give them heartache and fever by only gazing with longing at each other. Let's laugh on each other's necks, like we have dirty secrets. When we fondle thighs and breasts, let's make them sick with lust. Let's break their hearts. Isn't that what we both want really?

RELIEF

I found some sticks. They are big enough. We could put a plastic cover over. The people over there on the plain have got plastic. They have been here the longest. But we have only been here three days. The camp has run out of plastic. We have a little rice from the trucks. There is just enough for the children. I can walk to the waterpipe. A mile is nothing when the water is clean and good. I have a plastic container. It has a red lid that snaps shut. I am happy with this container. I am happy the flood did not kill us. We are safe in this camp. If only we had a plastic sheet to cover our heads from the rain, we would have everything. Perhaps tomorrow the plastic will be given.

ABSENT

I am an elephant. I remember when the world was born. I remember the sky being born. I remember fire being born. I remember death being born. I remember you being born. I remember being unborn. I remember not being here. I remember you not being here. That was worse.

THAT'S NO WAY TO SAY GOODBYE

We let each other go. Just like that—walked out of each other's lives. One day we were sitting chatting about moving in together. The next day we were in the same cafe, at the same table, saying that maybe we should wait. And later that day—seventeen minutes later, we came to the simultaneous realisation that neither of us had the energy —inclination—impulse—interest, to take it, us—our relationship further. So, we finished our coffees—your latte, my cappuccino. I insisted on paying. You tipped the same amount. We stood up, gathered our jackets. You almost forgot your bag—and we air kissed. I held the door open for you, and we spoke over each other, about what we were doing with the rest of the day. Then we looked away— simultaneously looked away. Simultaneously decided not to linger. Simultaneously walked away. I wonder if right now, you are simultaneously wondering, if we should have just spent a moment longer noticing how simultaneous we were together.

AMBITION

I want to be a lion tamer, because my name is Timothy. I want to ride motorbikes through flaming blades of steel, because I'm the middle child of five sisters. I want to swim with sharks, because I live with my mother. I want my mother to swim with sharks without the safety cage, and with a pound of raw beef chained to her neck, because I still live with my mother! I want to skydive because I've got no hair on my chest. I want to be a safecracker, because I'm a junior clerk in an accountant's office. I want to be a tightrope-walker way up between skyscrapers, because there is no significant 'other' in my life. There is no significant 'other' in my life, because I still live with my mother! I want to be a murderer because... I want to be a... I want to be murderer, because my mother won't let me... I want to be a... I want to be!

SMOOTH OPERATOR

My recipe for a good life is to always speak to foreigners. In fact, don't bother with your neighbours, or locals. They know you too well. Focus on people from other countries who can't really understand you. Look lively—look bright —look receptive—responsive—that makes you attractive. Speak a bit of French—Bonjour, tu veux boire un verre? Speak a bit of German—Hallo, mocheten sie einen drink? Most of all, speak a bit of Spanish—Hola, quieres un trago? Mix in a bit of something else—Hej, chcesz wypic drinka? And you will be popular and have friends all over the world. You will be welcomed, be given hospitality— entertainment—company—laughter—sex. They fill in the missing words for you. They translate you into who they want you to be. They have no idea that in your own country you are such a total loser!

SHIPBUILDING

I built a boat. It was something to do. Get my hands out of my pockets. Useful. A boat. In my shed. A boat where the Volvo used to be. A keel. Like a whale's jawbone. Then a boat—plank by plank. Oak. Nail by nail. From scratch. Working on it on my own. Getting it wrong. Hammering the planks back off. A boat with strange long rectangular gaps in it. Then the years went by and the planks slowly found their places and settled. My hands got rough. The boat became smooth, polished, gleaming—complete. Ready for the sea. I'm frightened of the sea. Terrified. But I've built a boat to sail through that. I can't swim. But I've built a boat because…

UNDER PRESSURE

It was truth or dare. So, I said—'dare!' I had to take my top off—get my breasts out. I wouldn't do it. Rickie—we all call him Dickie. Dick had got his dicky out. So, they were in a raunchy party mood. Benny began the chant 'Get them out! Get them out!' I'm not modest but—I didn't like the way they wanted it—mean—and Benny… Well, Benny could see I was nearly in tears. So, he turned it round —'Truth then!' That was the only other option. I looked him in the eye. Swallowed hard. Then I heard my voice say —'I love you Benny Turkali.' There was a pause. I felt the ground open up under me. Then Benny said—'Get your tits out!' They all started to chant again. So, I got my tits out. By then I didn't care.

LEADERSHIP QUALITIES

I am a block. I respond partially, never wholeheartedly. I respond too late. Sometimes I don't respond at all. I don't listen. I hear, but I don't listen. I've got cement between my ears. In a meeting I will repeat what you said, seconds after you said it, and I will think that an original idea has just occurred to me. I'm a beat behind. My skin is one layer thicker than yours. I cannot turn easily. I am not flexible. I am only aware of the things directly in front of me. I talk louder than most people. I have strength in my upper body. I have strength in my voice. It gets me promoted. People turn around me. I am the axis. Other people bend and flex while I stomp ahead. They resent it but they comply. They wait for me to fall, but I have authority. These big heavy hands, and this thick neck and fat head, give me authority. I use it to destroy.

CLOWN

I react too much. I'm always giving more than I get. I'm sensitive to other people's needs. I give them what they want. It makes them want me. I'm a puppy dog wagging its tail. Even if you are mean to me, I'm wired to smile. I feel that insult. I will remember the slight, but when I meet you again, I will offer my hand. It's automatic. It's not who I am. And if you are fooled, I despise you. And if you can detect what I really am, I'm afraid of you. What I would really like is to have the confidence to ignore you. I am about to ignore you. But—are you all right with that?

GAMES PEOPLE PLAY

I love you most of the time, but sometimes I don't love you. I like being with you, but now and then, I don't want you in my life. I want you when you're not around. But when you are, I get restless, bored. I'm so inconsistent. How can I make a commitment to you when I feel so contradictory? I don't know what to do. The minute I moved in with you, I would want to move out. The second we were married, I'd want a divorce. I obviously don't know my own mind. You'll have to tell me what to do. And I'll have to hate you for telling me.

CREEP

I don't belong here. I have an alternative heart. If I was bright enough, I'd have an alternative film running in my head. But I'm a follower. Not a leader. I'm an alternative follower. I can see right through the straight world. There's nothing really there. But everything alternative is a cliché copied from a cliché. I don't want eyeliner. I don't want to shave my hair up one side. I don't want deadpan. I don't want Doc Martin's. I don't want piercing. I don't want nerd. I don't want geek. I don't want Emo. If I was a leader I'd invent something brilliantly arty and alternative. Something shocking. I'm only smart enough to disagree. My alternative is waiting. Waiting for someone like you to disagree with me.

CUPID

I went into the card shop, rushing at the last minute—all the overtime I'm doing. So, suddenly I was standing there with a bag of M & S microwaveable meal deals, staring at these rows of cards. Red glittering hearts, 3D hearts, upside down hearts, cracked hearts, hearts struck by arrows, hearts held by blue patchwork bears. Commercial—chu-ching! But then, I saw something else. Expressions of love. For wives, husbands, boyfriends, girlfriends, babes, hunks, acquaintances, the un-noticed, the near-at-hand, the long way off, the married, the partnered, the loose ends, the misfits, the strangers, the yearning, the yearning, the yearning. So much love. Okay, I'm going to say it—I burst into tears. I sobbed out loud. People looked. I fled the shop. I'm sorry, dear. That's why I didn't get you a card. I didn't forget. Honest.

SEIZE THE DAY

I'm being made redundant next week. I can't wait. It's going to be brilliant! Brilliant! I'll have time to do it all. Get fit. Join a gym. Climb mountains. Kayaking. Do the West Highland Way. Travel. See St. Kilda. Dolphin and whale watching. Meet up with my friends. It's going to be magnificent. Time to get on with the good things in life. Sharing it with the people I care about. Sharing it with—ah! All my mates will be at work. All my family will be at—oh! Oh shit!

SUGAR DADDY

He gives me things. That's why I stay. He gives me nice things. I like nice things. He gives me expensive things. I don't love him. But I stay. Because it is lovely having beautiful things. Love isn't everything. Anyway, you can grow to love someone, someone who loves giving you everything you want. Yes please, to a whole lot more love!

ALL DOWN THE LINE

I put everything off to another day. Today I learned that it is a syndrome. It is a recognised form of behaviour. *Brinkmanship*. I thought I was the only one who tried to pull the rug out from under myself. Who thought I had to fail at all the easy moments because it would be too 'ordinary' to succeed. Who was doomed to fail until I saved myself on the last chimes of midnight. Then a beat before the announcement of loser, the loser shows his genius... With a single stroke of effort, of willpower, of whim, of panic, of imagination—he is free! It's a syndrome with its roots in vanity. The pride generating it fuels every kind of lie. Including the lie that out of certain failure you alone can conjure up the talent to make anyone care.

TARGET SETTING

I'm going to get out of bed.
I'm going to put on my clothes.
I'm going to go to work.
No, I'm going to phone in sick.
No, I'm going to do my work.

I'm going to reach my target.
I'm going to exceed my target.
No, I'm going to stay here and play computer games.
I'm going to fail.
I'm going back to sleep.
No, I'm going to have a shower.
I'm going to catch the train.
No, I'm going to have a little rest.
I'm going to dream my favourite dream.
Where I'm at work.
Where I achieve all my project targets, and then run out of targets.
I'm going to dream my favourite dream, where I get promotion. Get a huge salary raise. But win the lottery. And never work again!

THE GAP

I'm waiting for my life to begin. Inside, I'm already spring sap, but outside its winter. Inside, I'm already famous, driving a red convertible and waving to fans. Outside, I'm still living with my parents and catching the bus to college. Inside I'm making films. Inside I'm alive. Brimming with hello! Hi! I'm great! You're great! Let's make summer right here, right now! Outside, it's mist—it's rain in my face. It's the careless indifferent insult of the north. Inside, I'm already a genius. Outside, I can't even spell, or add up. The difference between them—inside and outside—the time between them—inside and outside—makes me want to explode! Turn inside out with a fucking great BANG!

OPENING TIME

Let's go to the pub! Let's make a circle of good company. We'll take our turn to buy rounds and pass ourselves off as open and generous. Let's go down to the pub where we can play with our opinions, as if our opinions mattered. We'll listen in order to tell our side of the mystery. Let's go down to the pub, and exaggerate our friendships, as if we hid nothing from each other. Let's go down to the pub, where we can loosely join, and with new arrivals and alliances, loosely re-form. And then drift away unravelling, without fault or obligation. Let's go down to the pub, to laugh at our striving, to laugh at our emptiness. Let's go down to the pub to fall in love with each other.

WORD POWER

Rigorous, incisive, determined. That's what I want to be. Clear thinking. Cognitive. Goal driven. Focused. Rested. Healthy. Thin. Confident. Rigorous, incisive, determined. If I say the right words out loud—if I make them my mantra —rigorous, incisive, determined—that's what I will be! Rigorous, incisive, determined. The more I say it—the more I will move towards it. Rigorous, incisive, determined. I can feel it coming. Rigorous, incisive, determined. I feel I'm leaving slapdash, muddled, lazy, behind. Hello— rigorous, incisive, determined! Goodbye—slapdash, muddled, lazy. Goodbye... Hullo...

MIND OVER MATTER

You can explain everything, every action. You can explain every comment. Every frown, every hesitation, delay, silence—justified. You live your life logically. There's no difference between your inner life and your outer life. You even rationalise your dreams. How can I live with that? You know everything about yourself. You've explained every dark corner of yourself, to yourself. There's no such thing as a whim, a hunch, a gut feeling—an irrational impulse. You never surprise or confuse yourself. No mystery. You do what you say you'll do—nothing more—nothing less… NO! You don't know yourself at all! I have no idea who you are. I have no idea who I'm saying goodbye to.

HAPPY EVER AFTER

Today I saw Sally again for the first time in four years. She looked exactly the same. She could have just got out of my bed. We could've just parted with a kiss. There she was with a shopping bag, looking in windows, stepping aside for baby-buggies, living her life, absorbed in a world without me. So, I followed her. She went to the butcher's and bought a chicken. At the fruit stall she turned a pear in her hand, then tried another, but didn't buy. She pressed the zebra crossing button but didn't wait, (she never waited!) She talked to a woman she knew and laughed, then looked at her watch. She broke away smiling and waving and making the 'phone' sign. I watched her go. I just stood there as she went. All that life happening to her without me. Without a thought, a memory, a trace of me in it. Fully functional without me. Full of all that moment to moment life. Sally, without me. Loved by the world. Gone. But not. *Me* gone.

GLOOMY MONDAY

Sometimes I'm sad for no reason. I just get sad. Nothing sets it off. It could be a bright sunny day—I'm just down. But these days you can't be sad. You're not allowed to be sad. It's abnormal, it's forbidden. You must be clinically depressed, chronically depressed. You must have the wrong hormone levels. You have to go to the doctor because you're sad. It's an illness that requires treatment with pills of different colours. You are not sad. You are sick with disassociation. You're unbalanced with stress. You're traumatised with suppressed memories of abuse! You're psychologically a nut job! You, my friend, are in the abyss. No... I'm sad. Just sad. I'm sad because... because... because... sometimes it's time to be sad. That's all. I'll get over it.

PRODIGY

I was going down and then I had this great teacher in my last year at school. Mrs. Grieves was brilliant. She inspired me to aim for the sky. Turned me on to museums, art galleries, science, travel, and—and—and even classical music. I know! I soared out of that school with all her passion fuelling me. And it worked. The best colleges wanted me. I had my pick of universities. Then they wanted my research. I was a success. My future was bright. But the enthusiasm was borrowed. I began to run out of Mrs Grieves. Her vision dulled. I became distracted and careless. I couldn't be bothered working, or thinking, or enthusing. I wore out the spirit she gave me. Like a spent rocket, I fell back to earth. Back to my original self. Back to exactly what my parents thought of me.

STANDING IN THE SHADOWS

I try so hard to be good. I try so hard to be nice. But it's not getting through to people. I smile so much my jaw aches, but when I see myself in the photo, it's a very average smile. I push my kindness forward. I make such a big effort to buy gifts, to remember birthdays, anniversaries, rounds of drinks. To be sensitive, supportive, willing. But I don't break through. My behaviour is just what's expected —just the norm. It is just what everybody else does—does better. I'm the trier who you don't notice trying. That doesn't mean my trying doesn't cost me. It costs me— sleepless nights, wasted holidays, time off work, exertion, inconvenience, putting myself out. But despite my best efforts I make no impact. I am not significant. I do nothing memorable. Everyone else must be making an even bigger effort all the time. The responses that I thought were just natural, just easy... Shit! What an incredible investment everyone else is making! I've just realised!

MOVING ON

I'm sorry for you. Why don't you want me to be sorry for you? Do you think you don't deserve it? Is it because you feel that everything that's happened to you is your own fault? Well, it is your own fault. That's why I feel so sorry for you. Although it's your own fault I don't blame you. I love you. The part of yourself that you condemn, that you hate—I love that part of you too. So, don't hate yourself. Just feel sorry for yourself. And let me feel sorry for you. I'll show you how. You will feel better. It's not an excuse. Being sorry is not an excuse. You did wrong. But don't be cruel to yourself. Let's be sorry. We will do it together. And find a little mercy.

UGLY CUPID

I run a dating agency for the unpleasant. Unpleasant people want to go out with pleasant, good natured people. Not necessarily good looking but definitely smiley. That's not possible obviously. Unpleasant people can only be matched to other unpleasant people. The art, my art, is to disguise how deeply repellent both parties are to each other. I tried using confidence building techniques but the more confidence my clients gained, the nastier they became. What turned things round was flattery. Flattery transforms. Flattery changes the clammy little worm into the bright butterfly. It creates a fantasy that the grub wants to reach for. Tries to achieve. While they struggle to become it— they pay their fees! Result!

HAPPINESS BLUES

I'm going to sing a happy song about sunshine, love and butterflies. It's going to ignore anything negative. All of life's little niggles and annoyances and petty irritations, will be left out. It's a smiley song. In this song I will be concentrating on joy and flowers. This song is about my ex... who never saw the butterflies and left me for a cockroach.

GO NOW

I don't want you anymore. You irritate me. I'm bored. I don't like you. We have different values. You bring out the worst in me. Let's agree to differ and go our separate ways. I don't want your opinion, or your advice. I don't need your contribution to make my affairs run smoothly. I don't need your governance to keep me healthy, or safe. I'm an adult, not a child. You are full of your own self-importance. You boast and serve yourself. You bully all of my friends. I'm weak. That's why I've put up with it. You are company, that's all. It was you, or long lonely nights by myself. You're not love. Just misery talking to itself… I'm stronger now. Bye!

ULTIMATUM

I'm going to stand up to him! I'm going to stare him down. He'll get the shock of his life. I'm not frightened anymore. I used to be so scared that he'd walk out—take off. Leave me with the kids. Leave us to fend for ourselves. I used to think the worst thing in the world would be him abandoning us. Now…Now I don't care. He'll see that in my face. He can go. We'll manage, somehow. At least we'll be at peace. If he wants to stay, it will only be on my terms. I've grown up. It's time for him to decide if he wants to be an adult too.

FRAGILE

I'm broken now. You finally did it. Feels all jagged and scrunchy inside. When I move all the smashed-up bits of me sound like dropped cups and saucers. You did a good job. Not a dream left. Not a trace of self-respect. But, if I had to be broken, I'm glad I was broken by you. Not the world, not an enemy, not myself. You broke me. Now when I reach across the empty bed the children hear crockery scraping against itself. When I get up to look for you at the window, the neighbours hear porcelain and bone china tumbling to the floor. So loud in the still night. So loud. So much love—broken.

MARCHING ORDERS

You spoil everything. Everywhere we go, you spoil it. We always set off sunny and then when we get to the cinema your face is, like, very fizzy fizz! Or in the middle of a party you suddenly hate me. Picnics end in tears. An evening with friends has invisible tripwires stretched across the living room. I thought it was me. You wanted me to think it was me. Well, I'm normal. I know I'm normal—so it's not me. And if it's not me—it's you! So—right here, right now, I'm giving you your big moment for a final huff puff and rant —because it's time for you to fuck right off out of my life! Go!

WISH FULFILMENT

I wish I was taller. And faster. And smarter. And funnier. And richer. And had a bigger cock. I wish I was someone else. I wish I was someone else who didn't wish they were someone else. Like...? I don't know anyone like that. Someone taller and smarter and funnier, or—oh! wait a minute—I know someone with a bigger cock! But he's a cunt! He's not rich, or tall, or smart, or funny. But he's got a bigger cock. But he's still a cunt! I guess you've got to give up asking for the impossible. Who cares about being faster, and taller, and richer, and smarter, if you've got a big cock? I don't. I wish I was Simon Hughes. He's a real cunt!

PATH OF LEAST RESISTANCE

My advice, when you get into an argument, is to lose the argument as quickly as possible. The less you invest in the argument, the less you lose. So, say the most idiotic thing, give the worst evidence to back up your claim, and walk away with a grin. Let your rival think you are a fool. Let the bully believe you are weak. Convince your opposition that you couldn't care less. Let your enemies find out that there is no value in winning. Give up petty power to the petty minded. They will never suspect that all their victories are your idle gifts and that your instant defeat masks a hidden implacable revenge.

ACCENTUATE THE POSITIVE

I want to pursue happiness.
I want the time to pursue happiness.
I want the money to pursue happiness.
I want the confidence to pursue happiness.
I want permission to pursue happiness.
I want to know how to pursue happiness.
I want to know what happiness is.
Can I ever be happy?
Maybe I should pursue something else, something achievable...
Like... unhappiness.

MORAL JUDGMENT

I don't believe in right and wrong, or the simplicity of good and bad. There is no such thing as evil, or wickedness. That's stupid. You see, everything changes. Everything is in flux. So, how do I know right from wrong? The answer couldn't be more simple. It all comes down to fear. If I'm frightened of doing it, (whatever it is), it's wrong. And if I'm not frightened of doing it, (if I feel like doing it), it's right! People should let fear into their lives. Everyone should embrace their fear. In this mad world, of confusion and complexity, and moral equivocation, I am never uncertain about what action to take. I allow fear to govern my entire life. Because I have given myself up wholly to fear, I have discovered that I am always right.

LITTLE WARS

I betrayed my family. Their values. Customs. Beliefs. They think that. I wear Western clothes. I eat in KFC, Subway, McDonalds. I'm accused because I don't pray. They say I'm not part of the family. I'm not one of them. I love them. They hate me. I am family. They should be like me. I'm not a prisoner of old-fashioned village traditions and superstitions. That doesn't make me a traitor. That just makes me modern. I'm not a sinner. I can still believe in God and wear jeans. I'm a virgin. I'm not sleeping around. I just like to show off what God gave me. But they say I'm a disgrace. I've brought them dishonour. They don't speak to me. They won't let me go out. They won't let me go to school. They've taken my iPhone. I'm frightened. I'm going to run away. I'm going to shag myself stupid!

SANCTUARY

I'm strange because I like dogs *and* cats. They know I love
them more than anything. They come to me. They find me.
I've got a special empathy. I can understand what they are
thinking. It's not always about food, not a bit, oh no! I
speak to Harold—that's my little Westie. He speaks back.
He thinks that I'm a dog too. My children think I'm mad.
They have stopped coming to see me. They don't like cats.
Not cats without a pedigree anyway. It costs a fortune, in
Whiskas and Chum, to feed all my strays. My children have
got good jobs. None of them put their hands in their
pockets. Even when all the animals are screaming. Every
uncared for dog and cat on the planet—screaming!
Screaming!

RUBY TUESDAY

I loved you because you were unconventional. You
followed your own lights. Did whatever you wanted to do.
Super confident. Bold. Dangerous. You stood out from the
crowd. Dazzled. Spoke your mind. Partied like you had
totally lost it. You were free. A free spirit. I wanted to be
part of it. I loved that energy in you. You drove like there
was no one else on the road. Thrilling. Self-destructive. I
wanted to protect you. I realise now that you are actually
crazy. You have abandoned yourself. Thrown yourself away.
You don't know who you are. You are lost. So— so—how
can I find you? You don't love yourself. How can I love
you? You have to have love for yourself, for me to love you.
Without love you are totally insane.

CHARITY BEGINS...

Oh fuck, what are we going to do?! I mean—fuck! People are dying. Don't you care? What about the refugees? What about the babies with malnutrition? How can you be so heartless? You could fucking make a fucking difference! Why don't you put your fucking hand in your tight pockets and change one little fucking life? You think it's their own fault somehow, is that it? They deserve it for being poor, or living in an earthquake zone, or for being fucking different from you! What's wrong with you? Shame on you. I can't understand you. You don't think you can make a difference, is that it? Where to fucking start? Oh really? I'll tell you where to start! Fucking start with the first poor person you fucking see. Start with the Big Issue seller. Start with the fucking tramp raking through the fucking High Street bins. Start anywhere with anything! But fucking start! Start with your fucking family! Fucking START!

I'M NOT IN LOVE

I do not want to be in love. I don't want to feel my heart being pulled out of my chest. I don't want the sleepless nights thinking about you. My life is just fine as it is. My girlfriend is lovely. I don't want to be in love with you. I don't want the trouble. I don't want the fever. I don't want the need. The need to look at you. The need to make you laugh. I don't want the little death when you don't laugh— when you look away—look at someone else. I don't want the pain. I don't want the torture. I can make myself not love you... I can do it... Oh fucking shit! Too late. I love you. I love you. I love you!

DIVISION OF THE SPOILS

Do you want to keep all that stuff we bought together? All this stuff, that belonged to who we were together, stays the same. Stays, exactly the same, even though we've split. Would we have bought any of it on our own? Maybe two separate people (with good taste) merged into a married entity thingy with very bad compromise taste. And now we're back to being single—what if we don't really want any of it? All that purchasing. And now we don't care. We don't care. So, all our stuff just goes... goes away... disperses somewhere... Charity shops. What does it matter? All those things that were placed in rooms by us—what we agreed were good, tasteful, even artistic—nothing to keep it there now! We are not those people today. Not an *us*. But the vases and lamps and ornaments we pretended to like—they live on. All our bits and pieces drifting to other lover's conceits and homes.

IT'S ALL TOO MUCH

You are it! My everything. You mean everything to me. I love you so much. I love your cute little face and squishy little nose. So much! I couldn't bear to be without you. If anything happened to you—Oh God! I couldn't go on. I'm so happy when I'm with you. I'm so happy that I feel I don't deserve all this happiness. I think something dreadful is going to happen to you. I imagine you getting run over. I imagine you falling in the shower, stumbling off a cliff—all sorts of terrible accidents and horrific injuries. That's why I can't drive you anymore. I keep thinking I'm going to crash the car and kill you. I imagine your hair all bloody and matted. I imagine your face all—ahhhh! What's wrong with me? I don't understand. Don't I love you enough? Don't I love you enough? Don't I love you enough to keep you safe?

ALL TOMORROWS PARTIES

It's the getting ready I remember, not the thing I'm getting ready for. It's the girls coming over early, and us all checking out our accessories, and necklines, and having just a little something to get us into the party mood. That's the best bit. The looking forward to it. Not the party itself. It's the chat before you go. Who's going to be there? Who's going to be there with who? With what?! That's the fun. That's when you've got mates and feel the closest. The jokes and the giggles—without any pressure. I laughed until the tears rolled down my cheeks. Shame we had to go to the party at all—that's how I always felt. I wanted to hold all my friends prisoner, never let them leave. Keep them just for myself. Be the party. Be the party girl who never went to the party.

SLAVE TO LOVE

I gaze at him with adoration, like an imbecile, when he's not looking. I break into a beaming grin when he looks my way. I try to anticipate his every wish. I place cups of tea in front of him, that he doesn't want. I make breakfasts, and snacks, he doesn't touch. I hover over his shoulder just in case, just in case—there's anything—anything wanted. Love has made me irritating. I'm constantly trying to stroke his hair—irritating! Touch his skin—irritating! I would be irritated, if I did it to me. My love is driving him away. If only I loved him less—I think he would love me more. I'm ruining everything. I plead. I simper. I abase myself. Love is making me ashamed. Love is making me sick. I don't recognise myself. Love is making me a stranger. A stranger to love!

CARELESS LOVE

Because my mate Tommy fell in love with her, I fell in love with her. Because he said she was the most beautiful girl in the whole world, that's what she became to me. Because he wanted her, I wanted her. Because he did everything he could to try and get her, I tried to do everything I could to get her, but secretly, slyly. When she and Tommy moved in together, I was beside myself. I thought my heart would explode into mist and red atoms. I'd wait outside in my dad's car just trying to catch glimpses of her shape against Tommy's blinds. Then after a few months Tommy said he didn't like her anymore. He was going to tell her to shift herself out. And the funny thing is, right then and there, when he said that—I didn't love her anymore either. My love just flew away. I saw the weakness in her that he saw. But the thing that's even funnier is, I think she is falling in love with me. I'm sure. I can feel it. I bet she thinks loving me will make Tommy love her again. But that's not working. Last night coming home on the bus after band practice, Tommy said he loved me. It feels good. It feels good to have love and not give it back.

BLIND SUMMIT

I can't imagine what you've been through. I've tried to. Every night I lie awake and I think about what happened. I think through every moment of what I did. I wanted to meet you. I want to say how sorry... I was the one driving. I was the one trying to find Capital FM on the radio. I took my eye off the... I will never stop thinking about your... loss. I will never stop being horrified. I know it doesn't equate to your—I know it's not enough... What more— what more can I do? I'm so sorry. Please. Please say something to me. I dream of your little boy... Darren. Ahh! Every night. I see him every time I shut my eyes— Darren in his car seat. Please speak to me. Shout at me. Hit me. Anything! Let me grieve too. I caused it! I caused it! Let me grieve for your son too! Please... Help me.

FREE FALLIN'

Your face was incredibly sad, that's why I stopped. You were looking down into the river. It flashed through my mind that you were going to—disappear. You looked so emptied, so broken. I fell in love with you at once. I fell in love with your tragedy. Your tears were beautiful. We talked. I talked you back from the brink. I held you. Day after day I listened. I dried your eyes. I lay with you. I gave you something else to love. Now your eyes are clear. The hurt has gone. Your face is open. I changed your story. I gave it a happy ending. I gave it a smile. Now I walk the city all night, looking for figures poised on bridges. Looking for faces to fall into. I've stepped over the edge.

OH, WHAT A BEAUTIFUL MORNIN'

He said he left me because I sang around the flat all the time. I sang around the flat all the time because of his bland impassive face. I sang songs I didn't even know. I made up the words. I liked the sound—cheery. When I looked at that set expressionless face I thought, I don't know what's going on behind those grey eyes. He might be thinking of leaving me. So, I sang longer and louder. He left. I was right... I don't need to sing any more. But I still do. The habit is there. I sing show tunes now. I go to all the musicals that come to town. I know all the words. A musical has more life than a big blank scone of a face! Musicals are true. They are documentaries of a better life.

AFTER THE RESCUE

I dated Little Red Riding Hood. Met her at a cinema in town where they only screened Romcoms and jeopardy. The movie was scary. I expected her to clutch onto me. I expected her to need a reassuring hug. But she shook all over in the dark when I tried to hold her hand. She watched the credits roll and become small and just logos until the lights went up. I offered to buy her a drink, but she said she wasn't thirsty. I offered to walk her home, but she said no. You're just a sheep, she said. You're just a lamb. Stop pretending. Stop dressing up in wolves' clothing. Then she ran off to the deep dark woods. And her house was in the opposite direction.

LOVE MINUS ZERO

I'm attracted to you, but when I'm with you I have no opinions. No interest in my friends. I'm late for everything. I let things slide. I stare out of windows. I'm not thinking of anything. I think I'm going to lose my job and I don't care. My mother says I'm wasting away—just skin and bones. Her voice is so small and far away. I don't care about anything but you. You don't really care about me. You just want me to spend money on you and run after you. I know you're using me. I don't mind. It doesn't matter. The only thing that gives me energy—life—is seeing you. I see you less and less. You stay out late. You know it hurts me. You don't care! And that makes you strong. Desirable. My stomach churns when I hear your footsteps coming up the stairs. My love for you is all I have left. Love! What a magnificent thing to blame!

THE BLUES AND THEN SOME

I'm going to sing you a song about oppression. About injustice, and the long weary struggle for basic human rights and freedom. I'm going to sing a song about cruelty. Indignity. Humiliation. Abuse of power. Poverty and disease. Starvation. Ethnic Cleansing. War. Invasion. And waking up in the morning feeling like death. Sing along if you know it.

KIDULTHOOD

I don't want to grow up. I don't want responsibility and blame. I don't want to be a wage slave. I don't want to grow old. So, I'm not doing it. I'm going to stay a child. I'm going to stay simple minded. I refuse to weigh up complex rock-and-a-hard-place options. I refuse to spend my working life seeking out the maximum benefit outcome and the least damage limitation result. I renounce the world of leadership stress and adult heart attack anxiety. I'm going back to primary colours, rainbows, and wonder at the trails of snails. I'm going to play my days away. Play! Play! PLAY! Who's going to play with me? Who's coming out to play?

SLEEPING WITH THE ENEMY

She arrived at my doorstep with a black eye. It took until three in the morning for her to tell me the whole story. I invited her to stay for as long as she liked. If he phoned, I was to say that I hadn't heard from her. The next evening when I came home from work, as I was making a carbonara, she told me how being in the Paras made him psychotic. I checked the locks then poured the pasta. He phoned the next day and knew that she was there. I pretended she wasn't, but she took the phone out of my hand and sobbed into his ear. All that night I tried my best to persuade her to leave the bastard. I thought my shelter made her my friend. I thought her need made her my friend. When I returned from work the next day with extra fish and new potatoes, she was gone. I rang her but there was no answer. After that when I saw her in the street, she hurried off in the opposite direction, or slunk into a shop. Other friends mention her from time to time. Still married. Kids now. No friends... Looks guilty.

SAVAGE

Andy had the blade. Always taking it oot and showin' off wi' it, he was. And Sammy punched his heid and bust his nose. Andy did the stabbin'. The guy was asking for it! Shoutin' abuse at us from across the street! No one calls me a fucking cock sucker! Right! *No one*! I landed one right in his fucking eye! For the cock sucker remark. That's all. Wee Davy was kickin' him when he went doon. I just got a couple in when he tried tae get up. I couldnae get near him for Mick and Wee Davy, and Fast Freddy. Fast Freddy stamped on his face. I didnae touch him. It's no my fault he's deid. It's the stabbin' that done it. It's Andy's fault. And the guy shouldnae have said Sammy was a stand in for Shrek. Nothin' tae dae wi' me. Nothin' tae dae wi' me if Sammy does look like Shrek. And he fuckin' does!

BAD NEIGHBOURHOOD

I should've gave them my trainers. That's all they wanted. It would've been over in a second. But they was brand new. I still had the box and the tissue paper back hame. I SHOULD HAVE GAVE THEM MA FUCKIN' TRAINERS! I knew they was gonnae take them onyways. They wasnnae gonnae hurt me, if I handed them over. If I'd did it as soon as they asked, I'd have been okay. But I looked doon and seen how white they was. I hesitated. Their perfect white was holdin' me spellbound. Then Blam! A punch to the side of my jaw, knocked me right off ma feet. I was doon and ma trainers was ripped right aff! Then the guy was leggin' it up the lane. I seen the heels of ma trainers stickin' out, under the crook of the guy's arm. Trapped like two wee white doves strugglin' to fly hame.

POSSIBILITIES

I hate being alone. When I'm alone I get bored. I have these thoughts to do bad things. So, I go to bars to meet people. They talk like tabloid headlines. Just rubbish. Listening to them, I have these notions to do bad things. That's why I became a politician. So that I could act responsibly. So that I could be held to account. But when I spoke at rallies, I had these impulses to say bad things. To rouse the crowd to fever pitch—to make them want bad things. To provoke the mob to wickedness. I hoped they would shout me down or have me arrested. But they elected me President. Now when I address the nation, I get these urges to demand... bad... very bad... things...

GOLDEN YEARS

I thought I had an idyllic childhood. Long summers placing steppingstones across streams. Endless days constructing little piecemeal dams, and then fatally weakening them to watch the result—the flood. Playing in the woods and the meadows. Building dens and forts against imaginary enemies. Catching minnows with a net and a jar. Exploring. Climbing trees. Quickly turning over rocks to see what was underneath. Lying on my back and staring up at the high thin clouds. A childhood like a long satisfying sigh... I see now that I was abandoned. My wonderful golden childhood was, in fact, just parental neglect.

DEDICATION

I keep looking at the relics of saints. It's the discrepancy I notice—the gap between the withered toenail and the beauty of the Mother of Pearl and filigree setting. The disparity between what the faithful want the body-part to be, and the thing itself. That's where the real miracle lies— in that breach between actuality and wish. The remains of the saint are so obviously going the way of all flesh, and yet they encrust it with precious stones, polish it with belief. The power of delusion. The elevation of decay and rot to the level of immutable and changeless incorruptible matter. Conviction in the face of damning evidence. That's the real miracle.

GURU

I served the light in you, hoping to find it in myself. Your purity was beyond doubt. You were my master. I followed your teaching. I submitted to your rule. I practiced your austere regime. You tried to fondle my private parts. I didn't understand. I dismissed reality. Then you entered my bed when I was sleeping and tried to have sex with me. I wanted to kill you. I brought a rope to tie you with and a knife to gut you. You were praying, that didn't bother me. I crept up behind you and... held the blade in the air... The truth of your teaching rose up inside me. It was the message, not the messenger. It was the truth from the lips of a liar. I lowered the knife slowly. I threw the knife in the river. I will continue with your teaching... and phone the police.

FEAR ITSELF

I'm frightened. But I'm frightened by no one. I'm frightened. But I am frightened by no sea, or cliff, or night. I'm frightened. But I'm frightened by no creature. I'm frightened. But I'm frightened by no avalanche, or hurricane, or tornado, or earthquake, or tidal wave. I am frightened. But I am frightened by no punishment. I am frightened. But I am frightened by no lawlessness, or violence, or hatred. I am frightened. But I am frightened by no thought, or action. I am frightened. But I am frightened by no dying or death. I am frightened. For no reason... Sometimes, I am frightened of myself.

PLAY IT SAFE

I was watching this TV show about a dog that couldn't get home. Maybe it had got lost. I don't know. I never saw the start. But at the end, when it finally made it home—I was a wet rag. Tears streaming down my face. I didn't cry like that when my brother died. When my parents died, I wasn't that heartbroken. So, what kind of person does that make me? Who the hell am I, with no feelings about real things, and a jelly when it comes to sentimental slop? If that's an imagination, if that's what an imagination does, it should be locked in a vault with an impenetrable steel door, and dropped into the deepest trench, in the middle of the darkest ocean, to never trouble anyone again.

COSTUME PARADE

On St. Patrick's Day people wear foam hats that look like pints of Guinness. Sometimes the froth of the Guinness is green instead of white. Some wear red beards and dress up like leprechauns. They get on buses and trains with cardboard harps, sing Irish songs badly and without knowing all the words. I have lived in Ireland and people are not like that there at all. When I dressed up like that in Dublin people swore at me under their breath in the street and spat across my path. I felt like a phoney. A total tosser! When I see people dressed on the subway with green wigs and paper shamrocks now, I feel a great desire to stone them until they bleed!

TACTICS

I hate my family. I hate my friends. I hate the rain. I hate the heat. I hate sport. I hate the food I eat. I hate this city. I hate politics. I hate my clothes. I hate my job. I hate my car. I hate my furniture. I hate everything. I hate me. My hatred defines me. It makes people afraid of me. It makes people think I'm cool. It makes me a role model. It makes me superior. Hating everything means I win. I love winning.

TREATMENT

Waiting is the worst thing. Just hanging about the hospital. Can't concentrate. Waiting in the *Waiting* Room. Can't read. Can't think straight. The parade of human misery going by. Walking the corridors. Looking at the worst-case scenarios coming in. The living corpses in wheelchairs. Collapsed faces. Mouths shrunk without their teeth. Bruised purple arms punctured by tubes. Skin like tissue-paper. Yellowy hopeless eyes. And the only sentence I have against it all... against the possibility—what keeps repeating in my head, is —this can't happen to you. This can't happen to you. This can't happen to you. This can't, can't happen to you. Not you. This can't happen to you.

PERSONAL ATTACK

I've always had hay-fever and been allergic to pollen. But I'm allergic to wheat now. I didn't used to be. It just happened. I'm allergic to dust now too. My body is changing. Becoming more sensitive. Last month they told me I was allergic to three different emulsifiers. Last week I got the result that I was allergic to chlorine and alcohol. Yesterday I found out I was allergic to eggs, tomatoes and citrus fruit. Today I discovered that I'm allergic to direct sunlight. My partner is leaving me. Going tomorrow. Says I'm allergic to life. That can't be right. How can you be allergic to life? That cannot be right. Can that be right? Am I allergic to life? What does that mean? Oh fuck! I'm allergic to *me*!

STICKS & STONES

You can't reason with bullies. Logic just makes them angrier. You can try to joke them out of it. Make yourself into a clown. They enjoy that. They get a laugh, you prove that you're a fool. You can run away—but they have scouts and trackers who will bring you in. The retribution is worse. You can tell an adult and see the contempt on the adult's face. You can pretend to have a nasty big brother, or a gangster father, or a gang of your own. Some little traitor will always prove the lie. You can give up, give in quickly—try and spoil the torture. Do that and you will certainly be hurt. You are just gambling on the magnitude of the abuse. You can join the bully's side. Do to others what would've been done to you. Enjoy the terror in your friend's eyes! You can believe everything a bully shouts. You can hate yourself. But whatever anybody says, there is no defence against aggression—no solution to violence. Not even growing up.

SKIN DEEP

This guy I worked alongside had a purple birthmark, right down the side of his face. Every morning when I first saw him—boof! there it was. Disfigured. What a shame. I felt really sorry for him. He was such a nice guy too. Couldn't do enough for you. Sunny disposition, no matter what crap was coming down from management. Had a lovely good-looking wife and two kids. A close family. He was open hearted. Generous. A deep big laugh. Did he forget he looked like that? Or did looking like that—the mark on his face—make him try harder to get people to like him? Did that horrible blemish make him into the sweet guy I knew? If he had been born without it, would he have been a bastard? What a price to pay! If you had to choose—ugly and being a nice guy, or handsome and being a nasty shit—what would you be?

HOW TO EAT SOUP

I can't stand the way he slurps his soup. His lips barely touch the spoon. He creates a kind of vacuum in his mouth, and it sucks the surface of the soup into his big gob. SHLEEULP! I used to try to set him an example by eating opposite him and gracefully placing the spoon in my mouth, then soundlessly draining each dainty drop. I was like a hummingbird sipping nectar. Made no difference. SHHLEEULP! So... I tried imitating him after each of his slurps. Him—SHLEUURLP! Me—SHLEUURLP! Him—SHLEUURLP! Just the same! I stopped making him soup. But he loved my soup. His favourite, he said. His all-time favourite! So, I let my manners go. I let all those self-imposed petty bourgeois attitudes go... When I eat now, I express my pleasure. When we eat our soup now, he goes SHLEEULP, like he always did. And I go SSSUUURPP! He goes—SHLEEEUULP! And I go—SSSSUUURRPP! with pleasure.

SUPERNOVA

It's time to come clean, to admit how I really feel. To throw off the self-deprecation and false modesty I have been conditioned to express about myself and, to confess the obvious. I am exceptional. I am unique. I am amazing. I am wonderful. I am marvellous. I am fabulous! I am fantastically brilliant! It's just a question of what to do with it. What to do with all that gloriousness?... What?

THE UNIFORM

I always wanted to be a policeman. I always wanted to serve the law. The law makes civilisation possible. Without the law this city, with millions living together, would not be possible. Whatever you want to do, you must obey the law. That's a big idea! Out on the beat it's different. On the street you compromise. You turn a blind eye. Otherwise you would be arresting the same deadbeats and alkies every day. Out in the real world, the law in my head, is not the same, as the law that comes out my mouth. I am the law. But I'm flexible. I'm open to negotiation. I'm swayed by circumstances and personality and inclination and fatigue. I thought the law was one thing, but I am many things. With one law for everyone—with one rigid law for everyone— the weakest break… Let the poorest cheat. My law is forgiving.

A SPELL TO BIND

Now I have come to make the charm.
Now I have come to make the charm.
I know your clan. I know your name.
Now I have come to make you love me.
Now I have come to make you love me.
I cover your eyes with a black cloth.
I cover your mouth with a black rock.
I cover your memory with hemlock.
You would disappear forever if I was not here.
Now I have come to take your heart.
Now I have come to take your heart.
I cover your heart with my heart.
I cover your eyes with my eyes.
I cover your mouth with my mouth.

I cover your memories with my memory.
Open your eyes.
Open your mouth.
Open your heart.
You are mine.

HOLIDAY ROMANCE

We had adjacent caravans. The minute we met it was love at first sight. We just started talking—have you been here before? That kind of thing. It was like we had known each other all our lives. No, it was like we had spent all our lives getting ready to find each other. It was wonderful. We got our deckchairs out and sat chatting into the night, waving the midges away. Romantic under the summer stars. Butterflies in the pit of my stomach hour after hour. We told our life stories and finished just as the dawn came up. We were ready to start our lives together. New. Shining. And the dawn arrived… Grey. Then—more grey! It makes everything look wasted and sad. The sea looks like it died a long time ago. The dawn is shit! It isn't at all full of promise, like you'd think it would be. It's just flat and drab and fucking boring. A big disappointment. We kept in our caravans after that or sneaked out when the other one wasn't looking. We pretended not to know each other. I blame the dawn.

BLESS THE CHILD

The greatest pleasure, in my whole life, was playing football with my son when he was small. Just kickin' about really. Watching him swerve and run at me and strike. The sound his trainer made when it hit the ball. A good solid well-placed thump. There was no interruption between his impulse and his knee—ankle—foot. No doubt, no second guessing, got in the way. His body and mind merged. He was natural. Coordinated. Not brilliant. Not a football wizard, or anything! I didn't care about that. Just to watch him retrieve the ball, dribble, faint– shoot it between my legs. Free. Happy. That was my delight. Watching that... I knew he was well made. Made good. I made him good. We. Something to be proud of. He could take that into the future.

BULL IN A CHINA SHOP

I'm kind of clumsy. I'm always in a rush—that's why. Always behind trying to catch up. Always pushing through the trivial stuff to make room for the important stuff. Rushing the coffee and lunging at the biscuit tin, that's me! I'm in a lather doing the vacuuming, pounding down the stairs to empty the bin—so that I can create a space in my schedule for... concentrate on... my family—or—or—something—? But I rush from brother to sister, to other brother, to father, to biological father, to best cousin—to…? Then I leave abruptly, and pull the handle off the door, and I knock over the Peace Lily. I have to leave immediately—immediately—to get the unimportant things over with. So that I can... return... get back to... Perhaps—maybe—it's possible—oh! I'm clumsy. It's a pace I was born into. To avoid—because—to avoid—getting anything done.

LET'S DANCE

We were the only one's dancing. We danced slow to fast tracks. We danced tight. Everyone was watching. We danced fast to the romantic ballads. We made up our crazy little struts. I'm the shiest person in the world. But there I was on the dance floor. There I was shaking my toosh and pointing at the glitter ball. Because of you. Reckless inside the music. Showing off my love of you. I made a fool of myself. Everyone could see. But in your arms, I was no fool at all. In your arms I was free.

CHEATIN' HEART

When you told me you were having an affair, I burst out crying. It was a flood—couldn't hold it back. You thought it was because I loved you. It made you feel so sorry. So very very sorry. Such guilt! You instantly wanted to come back to me. You instantly decided to come back to me. But I wasn't crying for me. Idiot. I knew you were weak. I have always known. And I know how hard you've tried to—to—control it—overcome it. Sometimes I think you actually managed to give me your complete attention. But you gave in. Sex undermined your better nature. After all that effort. You lost your, your quality—the better self. I cried for pity. Pity for your loss of self-respect. Pity that you let sex, stupid sex, wreck your honour. Oh! you should have tried harder. You wanted to. But you didn't. That's why I cried. I cried for that big wide gap, between what you wanted for us —and what you actually did when my back was turned. Idiot!

THE JOKER

I laughed when you said you were having an affair. You!
You? That is not possible. You must be imagining it. It's
preposterous. Who would have an affair with you? I mean
—look at you! They would have to be desperate! Blind!
Then you told me who it was with, and that made it even
funnier. That made me start laughing all over again. You
really expect me to believe that? Claire would never look at
you sideways in a million years! She is way out of your
league. Then the big bombshell—you—leaving—me! I
couldn't keep the laughter in. YOU? It was hysterical. Just
magnificent... Now you've left. That's what your note says...
Where are you hiding? Come out, come out wherever you
are! Good joke. Never thought you were this funny. You are
cracking me up! You couldn't leave me. The very thought—
absurd... You, the waste of space. You!

ENTROPY

After a small lottery win, we put in a top of the range
kitchen. White marble worktops. Tiles direct from a
Cordoba factory. Smooth silent self-closing drawers. Then
three days after the sealant dried, I dropped a jar of rich
Italian roast from the cupboard and it shattered on the edge
of the draining board. When I cleared away the glass there
was a short deep scratch. Then, with the storms we had in
January, the rain got in. The white paintwork on the
cornicing went pale yellow and stayed yellow in every light.
Then when we had the Wellers to dinner, Marion scraped
her chair against the wall and left a—a—scrape! Last month
the neighbour's son dropped something pink and sticky on
the floor that has seeped into the seams between three
waxed ash floorboards. Now when I look around, I just see

the blemishes... The soiled raffia of the vegetable baskets. The grease smeared blind. I can see entropy happening. I see the direction of flow. Where everything in my new kitchen is going to go. Where everything goes.

DEM DRY BONES

I've always loved you. At school. At college. At university. Forever young and all that! Youth and love—us! Then I loved you when we worked apart and never really understood what the other one did. I loved you unemployed. I loved you telling lies about being the boss. I just loved the bones of you! I loved how those bones stood up. Defied gravity even when they lay down. But your bones grew old. Sorry, that's the best I can explain. Your bones moved you... different. You couldn't glide into a silence or reach into a hill. You moved like you were afraid. Didn't move you the way I could love. I don't love your bones anymore.

INSTRUMENTS OF TORTURE

I know by the way you strike the match and light your cigarette that you're in a good mood. How long you hold the tip of the cigarette to the flame is a sure indication of your attitude. The sound you make as you take the smoke into your lungs, indicates your anger. The length of time you keep the smoke hidden in your chest, tells me your disappointment, or your resignation. How you blow the smoke out, announces how sad you are. And I want to snatch your matches and your cigarettes away from you.

Grab them!... If I took your matches and cigarettes away, would you have any feelings? Would you be able to speak?

THE FIX

She checked the last number dialled on my phone, I know she did. She knows. She fucking knows! Oh, shit she knows now! Why did I leave my mobile in the kitchen? What a— what a total fucking idiot! What am I going to say? Come on—what are you going to say? Think! Think! Think! God! Saying *think* doesn't make you think! Why did you phone her? What earthly reason have you got for phoning your ex? Think! I can't think! She's going to leave you. She said she would if you ever went near her again! Meant it! I dialled it by accident! You arse! Think! I—I—she owes me money. You fucking fucking thicko! She—she—wanted me to—I phoned her to—to—she—Oh! Oh! OOHHH! I want to die! It wasn't me. Make it go away. THINK!... It was a pocket ring. The phone rang it by itself in my pocket... possibly. Unlikely. Hardly credible at all but—but —it is just—just possible. Yes, that's just maybe. You cunning bastard! That's what happened... That could happen again.

DISTANCE

Remember when you were in a terrible job in Somerset? And I was in a terrible job in Reykjavik? All that travelling. All that effort to see each other—three years. Hours in departure lounges and on railway platforms. All those tickets burning up our miniscule salaries. Misery. Misery when we met and couldn't match each other's mood, rhythm, melody. Jesus, that was unhappy! Through all of that, neither of us thought we were ending. Never thought we wouldn't find a way—to be together—to synchronise. So, why now, when we are earning loads, when we are with each other all the time. Together all the time. Why end it now? I don't understand.

I'M DOWN

Being a miner isn't as bad as you think. At least you know you're in a hole. A hole that's going to get deeper. That's where you are. Surrounded by black rocks. There's no pretending you're in paradise. No illusions. Your life is a big black pit. No metaphor. It is for real. As real as real gets. And it's as hot as hell! But your shift ends. The darkness ends... On the surface there's a blue sky. You hear birdsong. There's the sun. There's the stars. Cool rain falls on your face. There's the moon. There's everything you forgot to love about the world. You have it worse. You have these things all the time, and you see nothing!

NO MORE MISTER NICE GUY

Look at me when I'm talking. Look at me! Listen. Don't ever speak to my girlfriend again. She is not interested in you. Not—interested—in—you! Don't go near her. Don't touch her. Don't look at her. You hear me? You got it? Yeh? I catch you looking sideways in her direction, and it's lights out for you, buddy. Am I making myself clear? Crystal? You want to keep your teeth? Get out of here! Now! Why are you still staring at me? Now means now! Scram, or stay and take the damage. What's it to be?... NOW!...Or kiss me.

THE MIRROR OF LOVE

When you touch my face—you turn my head towards the mirror. You want me to see you touching my face in the mirror. When you stroke my hair, you stand behind me, so that we share it with the mirror. You kiss me in front of the mirror. When we make love, you are the man in the mirror, loving the woman reflected there. I don't understand. I want you to look at me. I want you to look at my face, my breasts, my body. I want you to be fully present with me. Being real with me. Loving the real me. I don't understand. Do you have to see me in a mirror to believe I am with you? Do you have to see me making love, to the man in the mirror, to convince yourself that you are loved? Does seeing yourself, performing as a man, as a lover—make you feel like a real man? I don't understand. Are you imagining that we are strangers? Are you the woman in the mirror? Are you...? I'm going to smash the mirror!

A LITTLE BIT ME, A LITTLE BIT YOU

Unrequited love, unreciprocated love, has a benefit that gets forgotten about in all the self-pity and misery it causes. I am hurting because I am in love. I am utterly miserable since, my love is not returned. And the thing is, the thing I realise now is—for the first time I feel—I feel *real*. You know—fully present. Up till now, until I fell in love I mean —I felt, kind of, half real—not fully. Like quite a large proportion of molecules was missing. Now I'm in a lot of pain. It's real pain. I'm totally here—suffering! Totally alive. This total me wants that total her... Oh God! I wish I was unreal again!

DOING IT

Why do you feel shit after sex? Even if the sex was good—terrific—out of this world... Your groin turns to ashes, your stomach wants to heave. You love her—you love him. Soon as it's over, you can't stand the sight of those knobbly nipples, or that seeping veiny cock. No guilt, no ancient religious squeamishness, but the body and the soul react. Someone else's moles and staring blue skin, makes you want to throw yourself off a bridge. The married coupling. The stranger fuck. Everything in between, from iron bedsteads, to up against a church door. After the orgasm—the disgust. The stink. The gunk. The sag. The blotches. The pubes in your mouth. The memory of that ridiculous sex face. The memory of two people failing to become one.

SELF KNOWLEDGE

I thought I was patient. When my mother talks over me, I stop talking and wait for her to finish. She doesn't notice. My accepting that she doesn't notice is patience. When my work colleagues contradict me, I accept their vehemence and heat, convert it into a mild face and a cool steady breath. What is that but patience? Definitely. When my sisters deny that they promised me, or arranged with me, or borrowed from me, I pretend that I must have misunderstood. That is a whole lot of patience! But in our row last night, Nigel said that I was weak. Not patient. The path of least fuckin' resistance, he said. I thought I was patient. I'll make him something tasty tonight. Bubble an' Squeak. His favourite. He'll come round. Loves his Bubble an' Squeak. I'll be patient.

HOW TO PLAY THE PIANO

Sit on the stool provided. If there is no stool, you cannot play. Open the lid of the keyboard. Press some of the white keys with your right hand. Simultaneously press different white keys with your left hand. Occasionally, depress some black keys. Vary which keys you touch. Sometimes hit the keys very rapidly but follow this with pressing the keys more slowly. Similarly, stroke the keys softly and then contrast this with striking the keys with force. Move your hands up and down the keyboard. When bored cross your hands over each other. Look down at your hands but do not see your hands. Look up at the audience but do not see the audience. Push down either of the two pedals under the piano with a foot and then release. Shut your eyes when playing the most sublime passages. Stand and smile during the applause but in your head, start practising for the next performance.

PLAY IT FORWARD BLUES

I'm going to sing you a traditional song that my father taught to me. His father used to sing it to him when my daddy was a boy. And he said that his granddaddy taught it to him on a banjo. So, this is a song that has survived the test of time. Each generation has found something meaningful in it. Something to relate to. You might want to teach it to your children. It's called, 'Fuck You!'

THE LION KING

Grow a wild mane that burns all summer. Grow a golden tail with a black ash brush to swipe away the shadows on the hills. Grow claws until they dig into the earth and rip off its hide. Grow gleaming white fangs to grip the neck of leaping dreams and bring them down to serve. Be the master of the grassland. Be the master of the sunrise. Be the master. Be the lion. ROAR!

I NEED YOU

I depend on you. I am dependant on you. It's funny how things turn out. I used to feed you. I used to bath you, and soothe you, and put you to bed. You were dependant on me. And now—switch! We've switched! I'm the child! In a while I'll be the baby. But before my mind goes, I want you to know that I never liked you. I still don't like you. Even when I need to take your hand. Even when you feed me my dinner and clean my mouth. Even when you clean my arse! I don't care for you, even though you care for me. And I have to say thank you, despite how I feel. Imagine that! Imagine how that makes me really feel! I have to say thank you. For every kindness, a thank you. Thank you. Thank you. Thank you. Thank you. THANK YOU!... Thank you.

FAMILY ALBUM

In the photo you've got your arm around my shoulders. I remember the shock of you putting it there. I was so used to not having it. I was used to being alone. And then your firm grip for the camera. A moment of warmth through our shirts. It felt too sudden, too intimate. I didn't trust myself to return the right pressure, I didn't trust my instincts. I felt inadequate, unworthy of your hug. I was embarrassed by its strength, ease, and public affirmation. I resisted an involuntary shudder. Perhaps you felt my shoulders tense. Just as the camera clicked. Perhaps you felt me about to reciprocate with a—a—clasp! Because a second after the click you swung your arm away. That was the second shock. Just as I was about to commit—the offer was withdrawn.

WHAT'S LOVE GOT TO DO WITH IT?

I am a sexual athlete. I stroke. I rub. I massage. I pump. I grind. I bang. I dig. I drill. I thrust. I penetrate. I gouge. I dive. I tongue. I slurp. I suck. I master. I surrender. I withhold. I divert. I return. I scream. I whisper. My climax rises with your orgasm. I flood. But I don't make love. I told you what I was. I don't make love. I'm an athlete— constantly training.

THE EYE OF THE BEHOLDER

You're so beautiful. You shine. Light comes out of your eyes. You're so graceful. Oh! The way you move—it's so fluid—well put together—poised. Rhythmical. I can't describe it. It does things to me! And your face! Just perfect. A perfect peach. You are immaculate. Devastating. When you look at me my stomach drops, my knees shake. You destroy me. I can't think straight. I'm dizzy. My head pounds. Then you look away, and I feel... I feel—lost. Bereft. All alone in the world. I feel like killing myself.

That's why I broke the date. That's why I never turned up. That's why I can never see you again. I am trying to save my life.

THE GREAT OUTDOORS

My advice *was* always to take the path less travelled. Don't follow the herd. Choose for yourself. At the crossroads put your foot on the dirt—not the bitumen. Make your journey interesting. Let your journey in, rather than focus on the destination. You might see things, hear things, smell things that the crowd will never experience. Let the journey change you. I took my own advice. Always took the byways, the rambling track—never the highway. I meandered. I wondered. I saw... bugger all! Now I realise that the road less trodden, is less trodden for a reason. It's boring! It's too long. There's nothing there! Go the way everyone else is going. They are going that way because it is the best way. I've wasted years! Years!

PUSHING THE ENVELOPE

I was sick of people complaining about all the junk-mail I shoved through their letterboxes. I was standing at the entrance to a tenement, facing a flight of worn stairs. I just turned around and went home. I couldn't face it. Free offers, loans, bargains, circulars, vouchers, coupons, 2 for 1, 10% off, 0% interest, buy now pay later. I made a fire out the back and threw them all on. Watched the trash burn. There were some real letters. Just a few. But I had to get rid of them too. When people didn't hear back, they'd try again. They'd try again if it was someone they truly cared about. They'd reach out. 'Why didn't you answer? Why haven't you been in touch?' Maybe they'd meet each other face to face. Embrace. Kiss... Next time I'm going to read them all before I light the fire.

INDIVIDUALISM

I'm going to join the army, because if I stay in this shithole, I'm going to hurt someone.

I'm going to join the army because I want to be tougher than my father.

I'm going to join the army because I have never worn a uniform.

I'm going to join the army to surrender to orders and to have no responsibility.

I'm going to join the army to defend liberty, fraternity and the other one.

I'm going to join the army because I'm frightened of intimacy.

I'm going to join the army to risk losing everything.

I'm going to join the army to kill the killer in me.

I'm going to join the army to kill people I do not know.

I'm going to join the army because I am way too big a coward to commit suicide.

I'm going to join the army, to see the world and not enjoy any of it, until I weep to come home.

SOMEWHERE IN BRITTANY

The town was all drifting banners. The town was blue sky flutter. The town was hoisted flag. The town was waving red ribbons. The town was hanging with streamers from balconies and open windows. The town was dazzle white awnings. The town was celebration... The bunting was nothing to me. I had nothing to celebrate. I had a stern appointment in a bigger town. The town was a parade of prettified horses in my way. Rosettes in my way. Fireworks and smiles in my way... I abandoned my hired car. I abandoned my ETA. I abandoned my angry face. I stepped into the festival. I heard my voice cheering with the crowd then becoming indistinguishable.

THE WINNER TAKES IT ALL

I love a bet. I love gambling. A horse called 'Backward'. A greyhound called 'Loser'. Irresistible! You have to take a punt. When you're bored—when the day unravels and doesn't make sense—when you don't have a reason to put one foot in front of the other—place a bet! Then you've got a stake in the future—a reason to look forward—you could win. Suddenly a structure to your day. Expectation and possible reward. An action, and an obvious consequence, within a timespan you can understand. And when you lose (and you know you're going to lose, you're not an idiot), you know exactly what is making you lose. It has a name. It's the Derby favourite, it's the Grand National outside chance. A nag! A mongrel dog! It isn't a creeping dread, a complex unidentifiable anxiety, a rising slow-motion panic, a disintegration of the self and what used to be its values... It's just a fucking pony! You can cope with that.

DANCING IN THE DARK

Remember that time we slept in the same bed? Slept next to each other fully clothed. Both of us frozen. Not daring to move. Frozen with desire. Wanting to reach out. Trapped in fear. Muscles aching. Awake all night to each other's breath. Pretending to sleep breath. Wanting all night. Imagining your move on me all night. The slightest indication, the slightest accident of proximity, and I would have given you my love. All night longing. How good we were to resist temptation. Not to touch. Not a single touch. That's all it would have taken. Why didn't you touch me? I still want you. The night goes on. So long... so long. The years go by, and I'm still wide awake... expecting.

THE FAILED BARNET

When Brandy took off her coat and sat at her workstation, I could see that she had been to the hairdressers. She'd gone for a new look. But, not a complete new look, just something touched briefly by scissors and spray. At the back her bob curved into her neck. The fringe at the front seemed a little shorter, stiffer. I should've said something the minute I noticed. But I didn't. Because I didn't react instantly and positively, I couldn't comment later. She would know I was being patronising. Brandy is not good looking. She would need—you know—something radical to make her look better. Because she didn't look any prettier, I let her hair go unremarked. And because I did not react— tell a little lie... Brandy knew she was an ugly woman. I felt ugly for her. We both felt ugly the whole week. She was ugly on her own after that.

DESIGN FOR LIVING

I clean this flat in the West End. It's got nothing in it. I mean, it might be in the trendy, up market, West End (and that's an arm and both legs in anybody's money!) but there's barely a stick of furniture in it. And what there is, is all steel and scrawny bits of leather. Awful drab, the colours. And not a single wee memento from holiday. Nothing somebody's brought back from Lanzarote, or somewhere they've been *wishing you were here!* It's empty. The mortgage must be so dear they can't afford to have friends. Can't afford family, that's for sure! No mess. Easy to clean. I'm always a half an hour early away. No reason to linger. Can't nestle down and get comfortable in that house. I'm happy to get back to my shambles. My kid's big loud multicoloured shambles, and crayon scribble on the walls. Home!

ENTITLEMENT

You owe me. Because I was born. Because I was born wanting. Thirst. Hunger. Because I have hopes. Longings. Because I expect more. Excitement. Completion. Fulfilment. You owe me a chance. You owe me an opportunity. For my energy there must be a reward. Yearning must end in satisfaction. For my fantasy there has to be a fuck! You owe me attention, time, wealth, enjoyment... happiness. Otherwise you are no good to me. Otherwise I will seek your ruin. Otherwise I will become your destruction. I owe you that!

NOBODY LOVES YOU WHEN YOU'RE DOWN AND OUT

When I had no money, I asked you for money. How could I ask you for money? you said. You said, how could I have no money? What did I do with my money? You said, I must have 'mismanaged' my money. That's the word you used. You said, if you gave me money, I would only 'squander' it. That's what you said. Now you have come to ask *me* for money. You say you will pay it back. I had to borrow money from an enemy of yours, when you turned me down. Because of your enemy, I survived. Not because of you. After that I managed what money I had. I was careful. Prudent. I have money now. I have kindness, I have affection, but I also have memory. If I only had money, kindness and affection, I would give you the money. But because I also have memory, I will not give you the money. Go begging to your enemy. Be kind. Become his friend. Perhaps he will help you.

SKIN OF MY TEETH

My parents gave me nothing. I clawed my way out. Out of thieving, drunkenness and hitting—hitting—hitting... Hitting everything—everyone. Determined to find a bit of stability. It's not much of a job but it is stability. It's getting out of bed at 7. It's regular. It's catching the bus at 8.15. It's arriving at 8.30. It's putting in a full day. No pub at lunch time. Leave at 5.10. No distractions. Head down. Straight home. No flaming out. No falling in gutters. No sleeping in back lanes. Keeping the wilderness at bay. Perfect timing at the bus stop. Don't look out the window. Home. Lock the door. Thank you lock. Thank you, routine. Thank you bus schedule. Thank you repetition. Thank you habit. Thank you, meagre little job. Thank you for keeping the great big howling wildness away.

FUNNY MEN

I hate party chitchat. Some people are good at it and can break the ice with jokes. But the conversation never moves on with those kinds of people. You're trapped into providing the right response, at the right time. Blah blah blah blah blah—laugh! That's how it goes. In the end you discover that they are the people you should avoid. They are inadequate creeps who have armed themselves with jokes to keep you ha-ha-ha responding. I like a conversation. Trouble is, I can't start one out of the blue with a stranger. I can't be instantly witty, or amusing. It has to arise out of the interchange. The cut and thrust. The craic. The banter. The badinage. There's no conversation at parties. There's only weirdos with one-liners. Or freaks who can't talk at all—like me… Like you.

RUN FOR YOUR LIFE

I don't kill people—well I try not to. I stab them to warn them. To stop being stupid, they need to be terrified out of their minds. Nobody changes if you just give them advice. They need an experience they will never forget—right up close and internal! Then they'll understand that they shouldn't be walking home alone and drunk from a party. Then they'll remember that it's a dumb idea to walk the dog in the park at night. Don't take the shortcut along the bridleway. Don't enter the concrete underpass. There are bad people out there who wish you harm. The city is dangerous. How else can I make people realise the risks? I'm the big scare that changes the habits of a lifetime. I'm the psycho that might just save the life of a dumb blond. I am a public service. I deserve a medal!

DREAM GIRLS

I was sleeping on the beach on Mykonos. It was early, really early in the morning. I heard this splashing and then girly squealing. So, I turned over on my side—and there they were. In their early 20s. Three golden Venuses. A tall redhead and two tall brunettes. They were dancing in the waves naked. They knew I was watching but they acted like I wasn't there. Sexy as fuck! But they were more than that —they were... complete. Then the redhead turned to me. I could see her amber pubes. She waved at me to join them. Her smile, was like I felt the sun on my body, for the first time. I took off my clothes. Let them look at me as I walked to them. The water was cold. My cock was tiny. Cold—cold! I was such a coward. They grabbed me and pushed me under. We laughed and played, and shouted, and horsed around until a family arrived. It was the most innocent time of my life. The most complete.

PYROMANIAC

I like starting fires. I like striking the match. Watching the tiny sulphur crystals crack into flame. I like to see the shape of the flame. Like a cathedral arch. I love the colours inside. Crimson. Sometimes purple and blue. I love the smell of burning—everything from pine and peat, to singed feather and melting plastic. I love the sound it makes. Crack! Woosh! The faintest fizz and cru-mm-p. The best moment though is when the flame leaps onto something else. Transfers to the newspaper. Catches the edge of the cloth. Bites into dry grass. The moment flame accepts new fuel and gets excited. The flame becomes fire. Lives. Takes over. Beautiful. Playful. Powerful. Uncontrollable. Unstoppable... I am fire. Secret fire. In the pit of my stomach I have a tiny little flame. All it needs is to meet someone dry and thin that it can catch hold of.

I'M NOT LIKE EVERYBODY ELSE

I made a silly decision about my life. If everyone was mad about reading Harry Potter—I read The Lion, The Witch and The Wardrobe. If all my friends grew their hair long, I cut mine all off. I decided to be the odd one out. The odd ball—the weirdo with no friends... I was miserable. Truly fucking miserable! Now I want to do what everybody else does, no one believes me. So, I watch the most popular stuff on TV. I read whatever is on the bestseller list. I wear the same clothes as everybody else. I say what everybody else says. But my reputation has been decided. Apparently, everybody thinks I'm living my life *ironically*. Which makes me even more of a freak. I wanted to be different. I wanted to be different, because I was empty and ordinary... I'm just as empty and ordinary but without any community. Be careful what you wish for. It might change your life. And life is a very very long time.

THE AMERICAN DREAM

I used to have morals. I used to have standards, principles. I used to have other stuff. But now all I want is to be popular. It doesn't like intellect. It doesn't want judgment. It celebrates enthusiasm. I choose enthusiasm. I'm going to cut out the enemies of enthusiasm. The drink, the late nights, the cake, the biscuits, the Coke, the burger fat, the couch. I'm going to cycle to work with wide eyes. I'm going to greet my emails with a grin. I'm going to listen to your office carping, and spin it back to you—with hope, with trust, with a belief in our remote bosses. I'm going to be popular, even if it makes no sense. I'm going to be popular, despite my brain. I'm going to be popular! Because all other rewards, like respect, or admiration, or concern, are not rewards at all. I'm going to be popular! In demand. Never by myself. Never under achieving. Never over striving. Never against the grain. Almost loved. Popular.

GOGGLE BOX

I watch TV every night after I come home from work. I've been watching TV, every day, for most of my life. If you added up all the time I've spent slumped in front of that glowing little screen, it would be shocking... far too long. And, well, that's what I've chosen to do with my life! And, I'm not saying I'm going to change. Too late. I can't regret all that time gazing at actors looking into each other's eyes. All the quizzes, cookery programmes, redecorating shows, bind dates, bush-tucker trials, singing and dancing, comedy —I enjoyed it all. What worries me is that I can't remember them. All those years of following the soaps, all the detective serials—and my mind's a blank. It's all gone. Not a single memory left behind. Just some of the titles. Blankety-blank... Terrifying...

HERO

He was the kind of brother who was always taking his top off and running around half naked. Broad shouldered. Good looking. A footballer. Cricketer. Swimmer. A pack of friends. Unselfconscious. And good at everything. Everything! School work. Exams. Puzzles. Pets. Girls. I was jealous. So—so—so jealous! I was only good at colouring in. Oh yeh! He was also good at art. I wanted to be good at art. So, I was fucked there too! Imagine how that felt. But the major fuck was that he loved me. Really loved me. There was no darkness in him. So, there was nowhere for my jealousy to go. Nothing for it to latch onto. It made me do everything the opposite to what he did. And what I did turned out wrong, of course. I became spiteful, vindictive. I went to the bad... I could have been good. I could have been very very good. If only he had been a bit more average. If only he had one tiny little flaw. I could've been excellent. I'm rotten to the core, I'm not disputing that. But it's all my brother's fault.

MISSING YOU

Right! Well—err, so—here it is! It's no big—don't think that—that—I... You're absolutely terrific, I'm not saying that—Terrific is great—it's terrific! Brilliant! If everyone was that motivated—! Yeh! Wow! What? Yeh! You are so focused. So, so focused—you get things done. Always on the go. I'm... I'm... Less... It's you that's got all the energy—

energy to spare! Not a moment to lose. Crack on—that's you. Isn't it—yeh? That works, that's fantastic for you. I— well, that's another story. That's it. Yeh? Where am I in all that—that—that—that—motivation? There's no—no time for—for no space for... I'm not really a part of, your—err, your busy—err, schedule. Your plan for life. Right! So! La! Sorry, sorry to keep you. Don't let me keep you.

MIRROR MAN

I knew you were using me. I knew you wanted to get to my friends through me. Did you think I was stupid? I knew it wasn't me you loved. It was Heather. And I let you. I could have stopped you. Don't think that I couldn't have stopped you. But I let you screw me and discard me. Why? Because you're beautiful. I did it for your beauty. I've seen you look in the mirror. Wondering how it could belong to you. Puzzled. Glad. Not really sure if it is you. I let beauty fuck me—not you! It's a stranger to you. But I had your beauty. I had your beauty in me—part of me. I had it more than you.

BODY MAP

Too much is concentrated in the face. The human body should be more evenly distributed. Think of it. There's a mouth, teeth to eat with—and lips to do other stuff with. There's a nose with two nostrils to smell with. There's two ears to hear with. Two eyes to see with. It's all going on in this tiny area. Eyebrows, eyelashes, cheeks, wrinkles, laughter lines. All focused in one place, the size of a single hand. Communication, expression—all the senses except one! Makes the face look too crowded and all the rest blank. Just unused empty white skin. A huge surface area doing nothing. Doing nothing but feeling once in a while. The face is busy! Messy! And then... just an envelope of flesh with a couple of holes punched in it lower down. Weird design! Ugly all that life churning on one side of the skull, while all the rest of the body waits, languishes—lies exposed, ready, for a single touch.

CONFESSIN' THE BLUES

I'd like to sing you an authentic old blues song. Unfortunately, all the real blues songs have been appropriated by advertising companies, and big multinational capitalist corporations who exploit the poor, the meek, and the very underclass that originated these painfully truthful songs in the first place. The wealthy, and the captains of the consumer market have stolen the voice of the blues. That's why the only song I can now sing is a silent protest. When I sing it, I will be singing it internally. You will only be able to hear it using your imagination. It is called, 'My Baby Done Took Up With a Short Order Cook and a Gold Toothed Sailor, Then Came Back in a Beat Up Red Caddy, With a Crate of Hooch, to Wreck My Shack and Wrestle, and All She Left Me With Was an Empty Bottle, a Blind Dog and a Weeping Rash.' Here we go. I'll count you in. One, two, three...

REBEL YELL

Don't conform. Don't give in. Don't knuckle under. Don't let them push you around. Don't let the bastards grind you down! Break the rules. Fight back! Every day do something against the law. One act of sabotage before your meek little noggin hits the pillow for bye-byes. One subversive counterblow on your weary way home from your zero-hours contract. Keep your soul free. Keep your dream alive. And never never never NEVER get caught!

ENVY

How does it all work, society? Social cohesion. Why do we cooperate? Why stop at a red light? Why pay for your packet of Maltesers at the checkout? Why play by the rules? Why obey the law? What keeps us in order? The rich against the poor. The poor against the poor. It's all falling apart. I'm afraid to go out the door. Dog dirt. Muggers. Spitting. Swearing. Benefit cheats. Scroungers. Police corruption. Litter. Hooliganism. Nepotism. Politicians lining their pockets. Thugs. Prostitutes. Drunk children. Anarchy. That's what it is—chaos. Tax evasion. Fornication. Drugs. Looting. Stabbing. Gangsters. Everyone's out for themselves! But do I care? Do I really care? Or, am I angry because I'm not getting any? The time has come to be honest with myself. The time has come to buy a gun and aim it.

TRUE LOVE

He's left me. Said he's met someone else. It's the real thing apparently. He met her on the train. She sat next to him and spilled her coffee—if you believe that! So, they got talking, and now after thirteen years, he's leaving me. He met her three days ago. Three days! Three days against thirteen years! He told me yesterday and then started moving his stuff out. I suppose I should be grateful it wasn't a text! Said it would be less painful for us both if he left immediately. How do you like that?! He's with her now, in her city centre flat. I said, think about it. He said, did I believe in love at first sight? He's gone. I loved him. I still love him. I love him still. Still, I love him. I believe in a love that lasts.

DISTORTION

There is something wrong with me. There is something wrong with each one of my five senses. There is something wrong with my eyes. I can see your face, but I don't see it smiling. There is something wrong with my skin. When you touch me, I should feel connected. I should feel pleasure. But I feel pain. Hurt. Pain. There is something wrong with my ears. I should hear you saying sorry. I should hear regret and promise but I hear blame. There is something wrong with my mouth. I should taste salt. Taste your tears. But I taste blood. My nose is wrong. I should smell fear. Your fear. I should smell something. You. I smell nothing. Where are you? There is no smell… You promised to stay. But maybe I misunderstood. Perhaps there's another sense, a hidden sense I don't know about, where I got your promise wrong.

TENEMENT GHOST

The neighbour above me walks the floor from two o'clock in the morning until dawn. Sometimes she tiptoes like a fairy, sometimes she scuttles like a troll, sometimes she pounds like an ogre. Never herself. Never at peace with herself. The neighbour through the wall is king of D.I.Y. I imagine his flat is on its way to being a palace, or a tongue-and-groove wooden chalet. The neighbour under me loves parties, loves screaming over the bass-line thump from Thursdays to Mondays. I don't know the music. It doesn't sound like music to me... My music is silence... No one knows I'm here. If no one knows I'm here, I can love my neighbour. Love my neighbour as I would love myself. Love them into silence.

MOUNTAIN GREENERY

I like the wilderness. I like being alone in the great outdoors —in a vast landscape with mountains completely unimpressed by my presence. My life and death, my thoughts and loves, my losses and strife—unimportant next to a rushing torrent. It scares me. It thrills me. I pitch my tent in front of a cliff-face and gaze at it in wonder. At its age. At its power and presence. It cancels out everything I know. My history cancelled. The rhythm of my pulse cancelled. My sense of scale, belonging, purpose, relevance cancelled. Time cancelled. Future cancelled. It produces a strange anxiety that builds the longer I stay, until... until... I almost... almost can't bear it! But I endure. I do bear it. That's what I conquer when I'm there—when I'm walking a ridge. Not height. Not danger. When I'm on the glacier, it's my insignificance—my aloneness—my nothingness. My final non-place in the non-scheme of things. I conquer the total indifference of eternity.

GUARDIAN

His faither legged it, as soon as he wiz telt he had a wean.
Waste a space. The wean wiz better aff wi'oot a Da. An'
she, the Ma, cannae handle 'im—the wean, I mean. She's
her ain worst enemy. Give's intae 'im one minute, an' then
changes the rules and sends him tae bed. Mixed signals an'
aw that! The poor wee mite doesnae ken whit's up, nor
doon, or whit the boundaries is. That's where I come in. I
think he's a wee smasher. Needs a Da. I'm good at it. I
didnae ken that till noo. I want tae be his Da. I want tae
sort him oot. Set him straight. Takes time. I wannae be
there fur 'im. A constant in his life, so tae speak. I want tae
make sure he grows up right. Love kin dae that. I can put
up wi' his mither! It's him I care aboot—love.

BLACK BLACK BIRD

I am the crow in the park. I'm a black hole with a beak. I
shadow down to your baby buggy. I perch on the handle.
What innocent blue eyes your baby has. I will take those
blue eyes for mine. I am the crow in your school
playground. I am a nightmare with claws. I am the crow at
the teacher's desk. What innocent blue eyes these children
have. I will take those blue eyes for mine. I am the crow at
the altar. I am a cancer with wings. I'm the crow on your
wedding day. What innocent blue eyes your beloved has. I
will take those blue eyes for mine.

SUCK IT UP

It's the kindness of friends you really need. Not strangers. Friends know you. You've got history. They remember... So, when you think your best friend is a jerk, or has fucked up their life—stop your mouth! Don't let it come out. Be wise. Don't be a smart-arse know it all. Be kind. You cut off their dream, their escape, their reason for going on—and then? Are you going to accept the responsibility? Are you going to take the backlash? Because we all know what goes around, comes around. And when you fuck up—guess what's going to happen! Guess what your friends are going to say about all your, oh so obvious, faults... Be kind. Be kind, and cross your fingers and toes, in the hope that kindness will be offered to you, even though you know you are a complete fucking tit and waste of space!

EEKSY-PEEKSY

We tried to share a flat together but—well, people cheat on you, don't they? They don't clean their dishes. They don't buy milk. They steal your biscuits. Somehow, if they leave their half-drunk coffee in a mug long enough—it becomes your responsibility! They actually think it is yours, even though you don't drink coffee. They've had the cheese scone—now the crumbs are yours! No memory. No connection between scone and crumb! So, you remind them. Then you become the bad guy. You become the nag, the torn-faced shit! And before you know it—you don't have a flatmate anymore, you have a child. You're the parent suddenly... Sharing is never equal. Well, that's how it was with Geoff and me. It was totally one sided. He loved me fit to burst and all I wanted was for him to take a cloth and clean the toilet.

BONDING

Just look around. What a great team! Aren't we lucky?! Let's give ourselves a round of applause! You too Gwen. And now we're a team, we need to behave like a team. Give each other support. Be open to each other's contribution, Fatima. Yes, I'm talking to you! Share the energy. Build together. Listen together. Act together. Isn't it great to feel that our responsibilities and cares are shared with each other, Gustav? I'm sharing my responsibility of leadership with you now. With even you Frieya I'm letting it go. I feel supported. I feel you care. I feel needed. I feel you want to hear my ideas. I feel you want to give me your commitment. Fatima? I feel you really want to be my team! Team Margaret! Come on! Team Margaret! Say my name! Team Margaret! Again! Team Margaret! Come on Freya! All together—Team Margaret! Group hug! Come to me! Come on! To me! Me everyone!

BACK TO SQUARE ONE

I came to drama school to change. To be something different from my parents. To reinvent myself. To be a new, popular, talented, exciting me. To get rid of the old lazy, fat, unpopular me. I came to drama school to lose my stupid accent. To get a seductive, juicy, powerful, yet vulnerable, new voice. To get myself a self-assured high-status walk. I came to drama school to transform myself into someone my old self would be intimidated by. But I'm still the fake unassertive little talent dodger I've always been. I haven't changed. Youse didn't do your jobs right! Youse are just the same as me—but old!

THE TEST

You said Stuart showed who he really was when the wasp landed on his polo shirt. A scared little girl. That's why you broke off your engagement with him... So, that's why I kept meeting Rory on benches in front of ponds in the park. I wanted to see what would happen when a wasp landed on him. He must have thought I was an outdoor fanatic! I arranged picnics and slapped jam on sandwiches and kept putting the plate in his lap. But over the months, years—I really began to love him. Just like you, we got engaged. Then last week it happened. A wasp buzzed his head. Rory sat up straight, really alert. The wasp looped around his head again. Rory's breath was... steady. The wasp plunged towards his mouth. His hand met it halfway and he crushed it in his fist. Then he threw the wasp on the paving slabs and stamped on it... I don't know what to make of it. I'm still trembling...

MINE!

I want to have a baby! I want to bring it up and teach it love and understanding and faith. I'm going to give it all the love I never had. I'm going to teach it trust, and forgiveness, and wonder and simplicity, and acceptance. I'm going to teach it independence of thought, and creativity. It's going to understand that it's all right to be hurt and cry, and express yourself, and find yourself psychologically and sexually, in any permutation. So that when it grows up and leaves, it'll be all right. It'll be able to look after itself in the world... And when it discovers that the world is cruel, and rough, and trivial, and stupid, and ugly and grubby, and indifferent, it'll discover loneliness. Then my baby will come back to me.

CUPBOARD LOVE

I confused my job with who I was. I thought I was respected and popular. But I was just *the boss*! I was the CEO, hiring and firing. That's why they wished me good morning and stayed to wish me goodnight. That's why they laughed at my bad jokes. No one laughs now. I genuinely thought... thought they liked me. So, they laughed because they felt threatened. They respected my position, not me. I wasn't popular... I've got it now. Power is popularity. That's for me.

TRIUMPH OF THE WILL

My body *is* the world! Every day I'm in the gym. Rain or shine. It doesn't want to be thin or do the things I want it to do. But I thump it, stretch it, push it, clench it, until it conforms to my will. It's a bad body—short, stocky. It's a sump of crap genetics. And really stubborn. It resists me. If I slacken off, if I call off the attack for a single day—it bulges and fattens and sags. Transforms back into the little piggy it wants to be. I will never let that happen. This is me —these abs—these biceps—these pecs! Look at the definition. These muscles are me. I control this body. I make it obey me... It's the only thing I control.

BAND OF BROTHERS

People want me to get angry about the war. People want me to get political. They think that because the bomb took my legs, up to my knees, I must be angry. I must think the war wastes young lives. A national scandal! They think because I got a medal, my voice on their side will carry some weight. I am not angry. I'm not political. All I know is that my mates fought right. When they were scared, they locked it down and fought... We did it right. I'm proud of them. I can't give that up. I will never give that up. We fought for each other. We knew who we were. If the army would take a man without legs back, I would go. There's always an enemy. You don't know who they are—you never know! But I know my mates. They know me. We're solid. Always.

SOME DAYS HAVE GOT AN O IN THEM

Some days have got an O in them. You are just walking to work in the morning and the sun comes out from behind a cloud and makes a prism from a Perspex bus shelter—O! Wind slithers through a field of dry grass—O! Golden coins between shifting green leaves—O! It's O for the moment. O for a time. O for a day. The broad brimmed yellow straw hat in the shop window—O! O as a bird opens you with song. O as you clear the hair from over your eyes and we look at each other. O! O! O!

MY FAVOURITE THINGS

I don't have a favourite colour. I want to have a favourite colour. Sometimes I really like red. I want to have a favourite song. One song that makes me remember one favourite moment. One favourite blissful moment shared with one other favourite person. Sometimes I prefer blue. I want to have one favourite place. A river-bend! A park-bench! A beach! I want to have a favourite animal. A dolphin. A Persian cat! I want to have a favourite flower. A favourite food. A favourite drink. A favourite film. A favourite flag. Fixed. Set. Defined. Permanent. Sometimes I love green. I want to have a favourite love. A favourite person. But I like yellow—purple—orange—magenta—pink—turquoise—beige, yes even beige!... There's not a colour I don't love, even when it's not really a colour. I still feel love.

BAD MOON RISING

I bled on your doorstep, but when I woke up I wandered away. Two weeks later, in bright sunshine, I wore a charcoal suit and knocked on your door. I stood on the first step, you answered on the top step. There was a brown stain on the concrete between us. Ah! I saw it. You didn't see it. You have never seen it. The old hurt. The old bad blood. Ah!

BEAUTIFUL BOY

My son has night terrors. Something deadly peers up at him from under the bed, with hungry yellow eyes. It unlocks itself from the shadows and stalks towards his pillows. It waits for the faintest breath, the slightest movement, a catch of the throat... pounces! Tears him apart! He's just an innocent little boy. He smiles and giggles all day long. He has only ever been given love from us. But he wakes up shrieking the house down. He cannot be comforted. A monster is ripping his head off. This is what he understands of the world he is coming into. He's too young to see the evening news or read. He's never been smacked, or heard a word raised in anger. But he expects to be attacked. He expects no mercy! Something ferocious, implacable and irrevocably opposed, devours him… He came out of the womb knowing there are monsters in the world.

OUT OF THE PAST

My experiments with time travel were completely successful, and a total failure. Being there, listening to Doc. Martin Luther King Jr. make his famous 'I have a dream' speech, was electrifying. I was ultra-cautious not to do anything that could affect the natural continuance of time. But in my repeated journeys into the past, I found that my nature became increasingly careless. When I returned to my own time, I spent weeks checking, and double checking, that nothing I had done back there in the past, had changed anything in the present day. No—nothing! Over the last eighteen months, I have done outrageous things all through previous centuries. Not a difference has appeared here and now. I should feel relieved… I feel despondent. I am destroying my time machine. There is no point in time travel. No matter what you do to make a difference, your actions are mitigated and lessened by the inertia and incompetence of others. Everything turns out the same.

THE PRICE

I know I've brought you trouble. Lots of trouble. You know I never meant to. But… I did. Time after time. We've been here before, with me apologising. A few times. What's the difference this time? There is a difference… Before, I wanted you to take me back. I wanted it to be like it was before. I wanted all my nonsense to be forgiven. Now, I've just come to tell you that I am really sorry. I don't want anything from you. If I could give you back all the time you've wasted on me... I want you to have a good life, that's all. You deserve it. I hope you meet someone who will be good to you. Someone who isn't a compulsive liar. I know you can't forgive me. I'm not asking you to do that. But if you could forget a little? Well, no—that's—I've no right to ask. Sorry. You'll be good. I've done my worst. You'll be all right now. Goodbye. Good luck.

EXTREMIST

When I was wee, I loved balloons. To me a balloon was *happiness*! I could be lost for hours floating it through space, bouncing it and playing. When it burst, I was gutted. All the magic gone in a bang. Reduced, in an instant, to an evil smelling wet rubber rag. I think the bawling and the screaming really pissed off my dad. Must have, because his solution was to buy me a room full of balloons—a hallway full of balloons—a garage full of balloons. What's one burst balloon when I had a hundred? I loved him for that. Endless balloons! Endless love and colour. I know what plenty is, what plenty feels like. Someone gives me a balloon now and I burst it immediately. Give me anything—I break it! I live my life with the belief that there's plenty more where that came from.

HOT RATS

I am a rat. You made me from greed. You made me from waste. I eat everything you leave behind. Without you there would be no rat. You made me from take-away throw-away!

103

I've got red eyes because when no one is looking, you have red eyes. You can't kill me. You want too much. You will always want too much. I will always feed. You will always have an appetite. I will always gorge. I am the rat in you!

BEBELPLATZ (Site in Berlin of the Nazi book burnings.)

I wanted to stand beside your bonfire. I wanted to watch you sing songs into the flames. I wanted my face to be too hot and my back to be too cold. I wanted to look up and see the sparks turn into stars. I wanted the sparks to fly at me and make me turn away. I thought I wanted to see the sparks in your eyes. I thought you were harmless. I never looked at what you threw into the blaze. It took too many bonfires for me to realise that whatever precious things you burn, the flames always look the same.

RECIPROCITY

After she came back out of hospital, I invited Jean over for coffee. We talked about how fat the nurses were. Jean's a great talker. She stayed longer than I thought she would. A fortnight later Jean invited me for coffee. (It was also a Thursday). We talked about Jean's knee and my high blood pressure. She made an orange zest sponge. I only had one piece, but I felt like having another. Two weeks on Thursday, Jean came to me and I made a carrot cake. I thought it was a bit dry. Jean talked about her daughter sailing up the west coast of Scotland. Then I was at hers the second Thursday after that. I made macaroons but Jean only had one. Then she came to me on the fortnight with some cherry scones. We talked about her second daughter's graduation. Then I went to hers. Then her to me. And so on, every fortnight for four years. I don't like baking. I don't really like Jean. She never stops talking. It's all about her and her family. But Jean looks forward to it. And I don't want to feel obliged. If someone invites you over, you have to invite them back. One good turn deserves another.

EXISTENCE

I feel; therefore I am.
But sometimes I don't feel anything.
Therefore; I am not.
I think; therefore I am.
But sometimes, I must admit, I'm pretty vacant.
Therefore; I am not.
Sometimes, I think that I'm feeling.
But I am not.
Sometimes, I feel that I'm thinking deep dark important thoughts that connect me to everyone else.
But I am not.
Sometimes I'm confused.
And I am!
I'm half thinking and half feeling.
And I don't know which half is which.
Or thinking one thing—then the opposite.
Or feeling one thing—then the opposite.
Therefore; I half am and I am half not.
Half here with you now, and half... beside myself.
Half waiting to be complete.

I AIN'T GOT YOU.

His wife was not his own. His children were not his own. His house was not his own. But in the morning as the sun warmed the dust of the half-decorated bedroom, he felt a promise light up his soul. And he owned that. It was coming. Perhaps today. Perhaps his wife would make herself his. Or perhaps he would find a lover. With that unlikelihood he turned himself out of bed to begin the real day. The real day was not his. But he worked at it hard. So hard, he deliberately banged his hip against the wall on the way to the bathroom. And hearing the noise, the wife (that was not his) swore under her breath and ached for her dream man.

THE MASTERS OF SONG

If I could sing, I would sing. Oh, you would hear something. Oh! If I could sing... I can't sing. Not really. Really. Can't. But occasionally, I hear my voice, the voice I should have. Harry Nilsson's pitch belongs to me. I sing, 'Can't Live if Living is Without You'. I'm alive through that ladder of notes. I soar with the truth. And the pain goes away with singing. It becomes faint imitation pain. I can't sing. But I sing. I sing through others. Masters... Who sings through me? No one.

HUMBLED AND DOWN

Because I am brave, I live in a bad neighbourhood and fight my way down the street, going out and coming home. Because I'm brave, I took the worst job in town and ruined my health with toxic fumes and the insults of the foreman and his favourites. Because I am brave, I married you and wasted all my love trying to warm your cold heart. Because I am brave, I hurt myself with a God who judged all my bravery as pride.

RANK STRANGERS

Everyone has got better friends than me. I've got friend-envy. My friends are okayish. I just thought that I would have moved on to a better, funnier, higher status bunch, by now. Classier, you know? I can't even remember how I became acquainted with any of them. I don't remember actually choosing Josh or Orla. I just drifted into spending time with them. Now we are all– invested in each other. So, we stay—friends! I wonder though, what would it be like to unfriend and start again? To unpick the stitches of mate-ship and familiarity? To unravel the friends from my life, like a piece of knitting. What would my life be like without my friends…? Seriously. Think about it. Bunny gone… Abbie gone. Aziz and Lorna and Taylar gone. Suzie Barton and Dickwad McAllister… None of them there… Lovely Billy gone… Unbearable… Unbearable… I wouldn't be me… There we are… Impossible.

BYE BYE LOVE

I got rid of it. I didn't want it. I was way too young and irresponsible. I was busy busy busy busy busy! I had a choice and I made it. The person I was then was right to do it. I would have been a terrible mother. It would have ruined my education, ruined my life. I wouldn't be where I am now if I had taken it to full term. But the person I am now would have the child. Is that a paradox? It's taken me a lifetime of struggle to fulfil my potential. The potential of that immature teenage girl I used to be. Even today I have so much I still want to achieve. But I know the value of potential today. It's the most valuable thing in the world. Here I am!... It hurts me when I think of the potential there was in that growing fist of cells. So, I don't—think about it. It's too much to think about! A whole potential person wanting to achieve potential stuff.

HAND IN HAND

You got lost in your children. You thought you could stay lost in them forever. Then, one by one, they lost themselves in alcohol, or pretending to study, or pretending to love, or pretending to wonder at the distant world. Then you were lost in your need. Then you were lost in blame. Lost to endeavour. Lost to everything but anger. Lost until anger was absurd. Lost until there was nowhere to go, no cover, no self to hide inside. Then you lost what lost is. Lost to reason. And after that you returned. You returned to stand in front of me. You held your original anger in a clenched fist. You opened your hand. I kissed your palm. There was no anger between us.

SOMETHING

I was married before. I think you should know that. And it was a loving marriage. A deep loving marriage. If we go forward, (you and me), I need you to know that. I have a past. I'm not pristine, not without memories. Strong happy memories. But I think it's possible to... I think that love, well... what I feel for you is love... But it doesn't feel the same as it did before. So, maybe, love isn't one thing, fixed —the same for all people, for all time. Perhaps each couple, each partnership, makes it their own. Unique to them. In their own image. Yes, that's what I think. I think we have our own love. That's what I want... I will never forget him. But I would like to marry you, have a future with you now. Now there's a different love. Our love.

THE SOLDIERS OF LOVE

I didn't know anything about girls. But I must have blustered something plausible because there I was alone in her bedroom. Sandalwood candles, scarves over the B & Q lamps and her trebly music. There were teddy bears and dolls on her bed. There were half-naked boyband posters. We were nothing similar. We were nothing to each other. But we had lips and deep red mouths, and that was dangerous and safe enough. Despite her green paisley patterned poncho. Despite her brown lipstick. Despite her black patent leather shoes, her eyes offered satisfaction to my much worse clothes, and my schoolboy hairstyle. Offered love to my eyes that only wanted approval.

ROCK-A-BYE BABY

I wanted kids. That's the sum total. Get married, have kids. Mrs. Conventional, that's me! Watch them grow up. Smile at them. Smile at their kids. Get old. Pass something on. Be remembered. For most people it's the most natural thing in the world. I've had three miscarriages. I've finished all the tests and the results are in. I can't have kids. I feel I was born to be a mother and I can't have a child. What use is a mother without a child? I ache. I ache... I ache!

A SURVIVOR'S GUIDE TO SUICIDE

I first tried to kill myself by being a good little boy. Consistently good. Good sustained. It made me lean out of trees, lean out until there was nothing there. It nearly made me fall. But I stretched away from good and I did not die. I adapted to being *not* good. I found a thin branch and balanced there. I tried to kill myself with partying. Partying hard. Partying indiscriminately. Partying on booze and chemicals, with no conscience, or memory, or tomorrow. Constantly dancing. It nearly made me burn from the inside out. Made me breathe flame. It nearly made me sacrifice. But I spun, shuffled and strutted, until the fire was a song. I made the music cold and I did not die. I adapted to obscurity. I kept my dance completely still. And I made my song a blast of silence. I tried to kill myself with love. Love without judgment. In love with only you. Constantly in love. It nearly stopped my heart. It made me not love myself. It made me want to abandon my body and find myself in you. But I could not become you. I could not change... and I did not die. I adapted to myself. I adapted to almost loving you.

RECIDIVIST

My first arrest was for shoplifting. A Pot Noodle out of Tesco's. Criminal vandalism after that. Drunk at a party, jumped on a car on the way home. The next three, or four convictions, were thieving motorbikes. I was used to the Nick by then. Home from home, almost. Arson—tried, tried I said, to burn down the school! I carried a blade when I went out. I was dealing—so you had to! Done for that. Then Grievous Bodily Harm. Better his bodily harm than mine, I think! Now I'm facing murder. Looks like it's all connected, doesn't it? Seems like it was inevitable. One thing leads automatically to another. But it just seems that way, when you make a list and read it out. No, each one of my crimes was different. Started different. Was in its own wee different world. The only thing they have in common is how I felt. Even though they were months and months, years apart, between arrests. I felt boredom. Boredom is the only link. Boredom caused it all! Boredom forced me to be interesting!

GUILTY

If prison gave you the absolute certainty that you could, in no way, be held culpable for what you're in for—you could find rage. If you believed that not a single action, or trait of personality, had led to you taking a little tiny step towards life behind bars—you could be outraged! A force to be reckoned with... But be honest, how many of us have had no part whatsoever to play in what befalls us? Never said 'befalls' in a sentence before now. You spend your time wondering about what you did, didn't do, should've done, could've done differently. In your chest, the part of you that should feel innocent, has—has just gone. It just isn't there. You begin to think, okay, so—I didn't do it, but I get why I'm here. I belong here somehow. I belong here because I was born bad. They know I'm bad. The world somehow knows I'm bad, and I have never been innocent.

INWARD INVESTMENT

I concentrated on the future. I put a line under history. I wanted to raise myself up. The only difficulty was *now*. *Now* kept talking to the past. Kept sighing. Kept being bored, while the future stayed mysterious and demanding. The future was all preparation. Hope deferred. Scrimping. Denying. The future used up *now*. I was exhausted. I decided that *now* needed pleasure. Pleasure would make *now* fun. I had pleasure. I had laughter. I had singing. I had novelty. I had drunkenness. I lived in the moment. All my savings went on company. When my savings ran out, so did my young beautiful companions. I was left with nothing but a worn out present—one continuous endless undifferentiated present without a future.

MOTIVELESS CRIME

Because I stabbed him and couldn't give a reason, they wouldn't leave me alone. They kept going at me. Kept suggesting things. Jealousy. Revenge. Rage. That kind of stuff. And I was kind of sorry for them. I wanted to give them what they wanted. But in the end, I found the strength. I discovered that I really did care about the truth. And the truth was that I didn't know why I stabbed him. Without a 'why' people go mad. The system can't cope. There must be a *why*. Without a why there is only chaos—insanity. Therefore, the person without a why is insane, by definition! And that explains everything, to everyone's satisfaction—except mine. Me. The sane person! Inside all this insanity, there's me, who knows... not everything has a reason.

SARTORIAL EVIDENCE

I've got a lot of green shirts. At school I had a lot of grey shirts. Then my shirts turned white. When I went to college and university, I was mainly T-shirts. At work I chose striped and checked button-down collars. My colours were blue and brown and soft yellow. Not green... I've got a lot of green shirts. I've got a first marriage and a second marriage. I've got a semi-detached house with a Virginia Creeper climbing the gable-end. I've got three children. I've got a Skoda Fabia. I've got a lot of green shirts I don't remember buying. I've got a corner garden. I've got a final salary pension scheme. I've got an exercise-bike parked in the corner of my bedroom with a green shirt across the handlebars. I've got a lot of green shirts. I don't like green. When I open my wardrobe, I don't know how they got there.

ABANDONED MIRRORS

The first mirror I recognised myself in, was hung over the living room fireplace. I couldn't get close for long, or I would burn my shins. The mirror I grew up in, had three sides and sat on my bedroom chest-of-drawers. One side was handsome, one side was plain. The front was all uncertainty. The first mirror that welcomed was in Auntie Jess's council house. In it I smiled all the time, but it had a double bevelled edge that blurred and made a part of me obscure. There was the cracked mirror I lived with when I rented. That mirror made me a stranger. My girlfriend used a hand-mirror in front of another mirror, to show me the back of my head. The back of my head had a Velcro strip running up the middle. And now this final mirror. You! You are my true mirror. In you I see myself. The truth at last.

Should I thank you...? Thank you for your honesty. You are my last mirror... I reflect nothing back.

WHOLE LOTTA SHAKIN' GOING ON

I used to love dancing. Shaking! Stomping! Kicking! Thrusting! Pumping! Never been taught a step. Don't know what I'm doing. I just feel it. Thought that was what you were supposed to do. Didn't care what anyone else was doing. I felt free. I felt like I was going to live forever. I felt good looking. I felt desirable. Sexy. Sexy! Sexy as fuck! Then I caught myself in a full-length mirror. Just a flash—an accidental glimpse. Reality. There I was. Dad dancing. Sweating white puffy face. Flab. Uncoordinated flailing. Limbs in every direction. Dad dancing! An object of ridicule. Not what I thought I was doing. DAD DANCING! I'll never dance again.

RUNAWAY JURY

So, the truth is that when we got to the jury room, at the end of the trial, nobody wanted to speak. None of us felt like discussing the evidence, or weighing up the probability of guilt, or innocence. While we were listening to proceedings, we were secretly scrutinising each other. Secretly coming to conclusions about our own little group. On our breaks, when we talked, we silently confirmed our original verdicts. Tasteless shirt, bad moustache, B.O., too much big jewellery, over done fake-tan, ugly mole, weird eyebrows, dandruff. And that's how it happened. None of us wanted to stay in that room a second longer than we absolutely had to. The quickest route home was to vote guilty. That's the real story. I knew the lad was innocent. That's the truth. Honestly... I'm sorry. I feel so guilty.

CONGRATULATIONS

I got the job! Whooee! Double whoooeee! I don't believe it! I got it! I bloody got it! I never thought—I never thought I had a chance. It's amazing! AMAZING! I stand amazed. I did it. Incredible! They offered it to me there and then— right after the interview. I'm staggered! I never never ever thought I'd—seven hundred applicants they said. And it's me! Me! How can it be me? Whooooeee! WHOOOOEEEEE!... Me.

RELATIVE VALUES

Aunt Megan looked down on us. She thought her sister, (my mother), had married beneath her. We thought she was stuck up, with her telephone voice and her fine kid gloves. She lived in a bought house. When she came to visit, she always had on a different hat. When she was sipping tea, with her little finger out, she would say things like, how can you manage to live without an eyelevel grill!? My brothers and I laughed behind her back. Mum said don't. But Da said bloody right! And we all laughed together. And I thought that our laughing was better than anything in the world. I thought we were all safe inside it, and smarter than anything outside it. Better than anything Auntie Megan had. But now I don't laugh so much. And when I laugh it passes quickly. Now I think that Auntie Megan had things that we didn't have... and I want them.

BLESSING

I've decided to be an angel. I've made myself some wings. A wire outline, scrim stretched over, then white feathers, and Copydex. I wear a white tabard top under white robes. Over my hair I have a wig of long golden curls. On top of that is a silver paper circlet of stars—my halo. I stand in front of the mirror. I look at myself. I am an angel! I feel good. I can do good things. I will do good things. All good. Everything good while I'm an angel. It can all be good. For the whole world.

INVISIBLE HIERARCHY

I'm not a leader. I get self-conscious. I'm better being an advisor. Chief advisor. In Council I whisper in the leader's ear and he listens. I narrow my eyes—the leader hesitates. I tilt up my chin—the leader agrees. I stroke my nose—the leader disagrees. I pull down my earlobe—the leader acts! When he wants to strike—I signal caution. When he wants to back off, to let go—I counsel attack. He is mine to confuse. He is mine to bend, twist and stretch out of shape. When he loves a loyal friend, I convince him that the friend is a secret enemy. When he is certain of an enemy, I advise trust and a partnership of allies. I have the power. I have power without risk, without responsibility. The power is hidden behind my gaze. I rule.

MELANCHOLY

I was alone, expecting my mother to keep me company.
My mother was alone.
I was alone, expecting my brother to keep me guided.
My brother was alone.
I was alone, expecting my best friend to keep me laughing.
My best friend was alone.
I was alone, expecting my lover to keep me happy.
My lover was alone.
I was alone, expecting the mirror to keep me contented
The mirror was alone.

DO THE RIGHT THING

I'm sorry I said no. And in front of all those people too.
On national TV. I know you were mortified. I'm so sorry I
embarrassed—embarrassed isn't the word! All those
viewers and the hockey teams looking on, expecting me to
—yeh! I fucked up. It's on the internet. Nine million, six
hundred and eighty-eight hits. Shit I'm sorry! I wasn't
thinking straight. It was the pressure. Everyone waiting for
me to say yes. Willing me. Saying it for me. I couldn't! I was
confused by the lights. Then the message flashed up on the
scoreboard. The pressure! The commentator saying those
things. The occasion was way too big. I wanted to run away.
It was panic. I felt dizzy. Can you ever forgive me? If you
still love me, you will give me another chance. Let me put
my mistake right. Please... Ask me again. Ask me. Will I
marry you?

YOUR PLACE

I want to stay. I'll fetch your peppermint tea. When you're hungry I'll fix something tasty in the kitchen. I will leave the kitchen spotless. I'll be useful if you want me to be useful. I'll be company if you want to speak to me. I can listen and agree. I can listen to all the instalments of your life story. I'll even smile at your singing. You can keep the TV Doofer, and I'll watch whatever you want. I'll pour you a drink when you come home from work. I'll clean the glass and put it back. You can lay your head in my lap. I will stroke your hair. Let me stay! That's all I want. Let me stay. I just want to be here with you. You won't even notice I'm here. I'll be whatever you want me to be. Let me stay. Let me be with you. I'll sit silent in a corner. I'll sit where you can't see me. You won't even notice.

WHATEVER'S WRITTEN IN YOUR HEART

When I was a child, I spoke comic books, supervillains and heroes, marbles, Lego, bragging. Endless let's pretend, let's pretend, let's pretend! I saw bullies, ugly teachers, graffiti covered desks, equations. I saw the X in everyone and the Y in myself. Then when I was working, I spoke spreadsheets, power-point, target-setting, scoping, framing, widening access, acronyms. I saw the profit in everyone and the cost in myself... Now I'm in love I speak summer new green, kiss, hug, squeeze, oooohhh! I see something real where there used to be an icon on a screen. I see something real where there used to be an outcome. And love hears me. And love sees me. What am I? I am LOVE!

ALL RIGHT NOW

I kept waiting for a turning point. A direct intervention. A stroke of luck. The Lotto Rollover big prize. I kept waiting for my life to change fundamentally, profoundly—completely. I waited for pleasure, and happiness, and physical perfection, and something more... to be envied! I wasted half my life away. None of these things are coming down the track any time soon. The age of miracles has passed. I'm stuck in this life. I'm stuck with a useless belief in divine intervention. I'm stuck with who I am now... Now what? Now what? Now what? Change? Change myself? I don't want to work that hard. Every song I listen to says that—'it's okay'—'it's going to be all right'. 'Everything's going to be all right'. Someone must win the lottery—right? Why not me? It could be me. An infinitesimal chance is still a chance, isn't it? That's all you need—a turning point. It can happen... Even to me!

FOGHEAD

I can't see the hills, can't see the sky, can't see the bends in the river. Everything is vapour. Can't see the signposts. Can't see the steeples. Can't see Sunday. Today everything is vapour. Can't see the city streets. Can't see the concrete. Can't see the glass. The people have disappeared in vapour. Can't see my house. Can't see my family. I'm walking into vapour. Can't see danger. Can't see hope. Every breath I take comes out as vapour. Can't see your face. Can't see your smile. Can't see your tears. All the words I gave to you just swallowed us in vapour. Can't see your hand. Can't see your wave. Are you waving? It's vapour.

TEMPORARY SURRENDER

I serve you to have a roof over my head. I serve you to keep you rewarding me. I serve you to remain invisible, while I steal from your larder. Steal from your wardrobe. Steal from your loose change. Steal from your breakages. Steal from your time. I serve you to serve myself. I serve to outlast you. I serve you to be free of your patronage. I serve you so that you can serve me. You only steal my patience. My honour was never part of the service. I keep it removed, under lock and key—in the service of someone else.

CRUSADE

As soon as my undeveloped testicle was diagnosed, I received pity on all sides. But I immediately refused to be defined by pity. I refused to be defined by my withered testicle. I decided to excel—at sport—at business—at love! On the squash court, on the factory floor, in the boudoir— I refused to be sorry about my shrunken bollock. And now... I am struck by the blinding revelation that I've defined my whole life by fighting to overcome my abnormal scrap of biology. Everything I've done—the trophies—the ribbons—the medals—the gongs—has been because of a fucking deformed testicle! I have been defined by it. In a good way. Not in a good way. A whole life spent trying to ignore it... Ironic.

BLUES FROM SOMEWHERE ELSE

This wonderfully evocative blues song comes from Alabama. And you can really tell. It's just steeped in that Tuscaloosa atmosphere. I sing it because—well, it really connects—you know. Even though I'm from Buckie in Moray, in the North East. Unfortunately, I've never been to Tusaloosa. Sounds great though, eh? Tusaloosa. Tu-sa-looo-sah! You can really hear the space. If it's got lots of space? Maybe it's a big industrial town with choking factory chimneys. I don't know. TUU-SAAAH-LOOO-SAAAAH. I can see oil bubbling up from the ground and Nodding Donkeys, can't you? Or maybe that's New Mexico? Actually, I don't know anything about Tuscaloosa. Not even really sure where it is, to be honest. But you can feel it, you know. That's why I sing it, because it takes you right there.

SKIN TONE

All my bruises are forgiven. Everything that has scratched, grazed, punctured, blistered, cut, torn and stabbed—my skin is forgiven. The circumstances did it. You did it. I did it. The world did it. All are forgiven. The skin makes itself again. The damage you did catches the light, and the damage I did flexes towards the light. The traces are slight ridges. The dermis is a little higher. A slightly darker tone. It looks like I have a history. It looks like pain is meaningful. You and I know there is no truth to that. And although your blemishes are similar, we would have been closer friends without the scars.

EXISTENTIAL MULTIPLICATION TABLE

Imagine a man made of popcorn.
Imagine a room made of eyelashes.
Imagine a house made of bad luck.
Imagine a village made of envelopes.
Imagine a country made of mothers.
Imagine a planet made of nettles.
Imagine a solar system made of cold hands.
Imagine a galaxy made of Barbie dolls.
Imagine another galaxy made of crucifixes.

And between these galaxies are light years of darkness
and the carcasses of rotting gods.

We are galaxies of closed doors. Galaxies of pleasantries.
Galaxies of viruses. Galaxies of I. Galaxies of you.

We have no idea how to combine.
We have no idea how to compromise

Alone we expand and multiply
until the crunch, until the bang.
Imagine.

YOUNG, GIFTED AND BLACK

But it is because I'm black! ...You think I'm a cliché. You
think my attitude is comedy. You think every black
grievance has been legislated into history. The injustices are
things of the past. Yeh right! But I'm still here with tears in
my eyes. I'm still here without an education, without a
father, without a job, without child support, without a
country that loves me! I'm worse off since you positively

discriminated against my anger. You think you've given me my fair share of chances and my bad black attitude wore out all your offers and good intensions. Anything I've got to say now is a lie, special pleading, poor me, wrong values, just ingratitude. The white backlash is gathering across every social platform. I'm being sneered back into the underclass. Soon I'll be your piccaninny, I'll be your nignog. Your prejudice justified if you call me by a funny name on Saturday night TV. Then I'll be the N word! And you will laugh.

YOUNG AT HEART

Old people getting into cars. Old people being helped, getting into cars. The world is full of old people being helped out of cars. Cars parked dangerously, for the ease of old people. Cars double-parked selfishly, out of concern for the fragility of old people. All this anxiety about old people ages us. We wither while we wait for decrepit old fossils to be grappled, supported, manhandled, lifted, bundled, onto cushions in the backs of cars. I hate old people! They hold up everything. They never die. They are so busy clinging on, they have no fucking idea that anybody else wants to *live*. All they think about is getting everyone to run after them. Old people should stay where they are. They don't need to go in your car! Leave them alone. Let them die at home! I'm alive!

REPOSITIONING

I used to think that I was against Exploitation, and Fascism, and Colonialism, and Sectarianism, and Imperialism, and Deforestation, and Pollution, and Genetic Engineering. But I realise now that I went on marches only because marches were fashionable. I picketed factories to boost my working-class credibility. I demonstrated outside the embassies of military dictatorships to show off to a girl I fancied. I painted slogans on the boss's walls to belong to the clever, the committed, the angry, the altruistic good-looking tribe. I went to prison to appear exciting and completely certain, and full of revolutionary vitality. But now fashion has moved on, with not even a backward glance in my direction. I am no longer fanciable, so I no longer need to pretend to care. Now I don't have to have any opinions, I can tell you how I really feel. DANGEROUS!

THE ESCAPE ARTIST

Once I've wrecked everything I move on. That's how I survive. After abusing everyone and using them up—I move on... I find new institutions. I select new committees. I groom new associates. I embrace new friends. I attract new believers. I present myself without a memory, with no trace of history. The only thing I take with me is confidence. Then I start the process all over again. New colleagues, steering groups and working parties put their trust in me. They elevate me and give me responsibility. I swell. I preen. I puff. I overreach, I over commit, and it all comes crashing down... But I saw it coming and I have already moved on!

I'M THERE FOR YOU

I'm a family man. I live for my family. My children are everything to me. My wife is beyond words. And my brothers and sisters are—well, they extend me, enhance me, develop me. And my cousins and my nieces and nephews, they keep me young. And my grandchildren are a gift, a real delight. You can see the whole cycle, can't you? You see yourself in them—living on, as you get older. Different versions of yourself in them. Variations of the path you chose. Alternatives to the arrangement of your features— eyes—nose—lips—likes—dislikes—interests. The better future I could have had, if I hadn't saddled myself with a bunch of thoughtless, selfish, messy, egotistical, bloody rug-rats!

COUNTER INTUITIVE

When it rains, look up. Lift your head. You will feel better. When it is cold, drop your shoulders. Think summer! Release the tension in your neck. You will feel warm. When you are down. Defeated. When you've surrendered. Given up the ghost. Raise your arms and put two fists in the sky. You will feel like a champion!

I'VE JUST SEEN A FACE

This is kind of weird. I don't know where this is going. As a joke at Higgy's stag-do we decided—well it was my idea. Anyway, Higgy had drunk the entire carryout and was snoring the trophies off the mantelpiece. I said, let's shave off his massive eyebrows! So we did. Easy! He stirred not a jot, through the foam and the razor. And when he woke up and looked in the mirror, he was fine about it—took it in good spirits. Higgy could always laugh at himself. But without eyebrows he looked kind of—broken. Like seeing him upside down. He looked ugly. A look you could never forget. He was my best mate… But… Sure the eye-bows grew back, just as huge—huger—hugerer! But I kind of dropped him after that. I could never forget what I saw underneath.

THE HERON'S GOSPEL

I'm a grey heron. I hunch all day by the side of the river. I do not move my legs. I do not move my feathers. I only move my head. I watch a highway of silver fish go by. Hundreds of flashing easy pickings. I could spear one at any moment. I let thousands of tadpoles glide into the safety of the tree roots and shadows. I resist the little trout as they rest, wavering over the oxygen rich gravel. I'm hungry but I resist my hunger. I resist the temptation to be satisfied. I resist the temptation to fly away from temptation. I can resist every temptation, except the temptation to be still. To be still and empty. Because what passes me by, is better. What passes me by, thinks it is free.

COMPROMISE

I want to disappear. To be nothing. To not care. To relax and float way. To open the exit door and fall down dark stairs. Have you any idea how hard that is? Just when the drink and drugs are kicking in—there's a phone call! When oblivion is just a breath away—some Mormon knocks on the door. I was hoping to get to zero by accident, but now I realise that I must put some effort in. I have to get organised. Dedicate my time, energy, intelligence and resources. Apply and sustain the elbow grease. Prepare the ground, plan, plot, scheme. Make getting out of here a professional fulltime campaign... It might take years... Easier, less effort, to stay around.

SHELTER FROM THE STORM

The only thing that matters is that you love me. I don't care about the war. I'm going to stay here with you. Let them fight! Let them kill each other. I'm not going back. And if the war comes here—if it comes for us, we'll die together. After tonight they can drop all their bombs on us. This time together—these few hours are ours, only ours. We can make them last forever. We can make this lamp, this curtain, this bed, our own little world. Nothing else matters. For the little time we have left, we will live it in love... Let's pretend there is no war. Let's pretend our love will bless us and make us lucky—so lucky that the war will pass us by and not turn its head this way.

LOVER MAN

It was time to do the birds and bees talk with my son. I was dreading it. I started kinda casual. Kept a natural tone—sneaked up to it. I got the male and female equipment bit done okay. He didn't know anything. I thought—what the hell has he been doing on the computer?! That's what the bloody internet is for! I did the erection and the semen—very matter of fact. Nothing from Davy—not even embarrassment. So, I had to keep going. 'When a man loves a woman, they take their clothes off and make love—they have intimacy. That was the word I used. I chose the word —out of the air—*intimacy*. And in the middle of telling my son all about it—what it meant—I realised... I didn't really know intimacy. He was confused. I couldn't explain it. *Intimacy*? I hadn't really got a clue. I've had no experience of intimacy.

THE ROAD TO NOWHERE

I drive a lorry. Birmingham. Dover. Calais. Frankfurt. Whatever the country—concrete, bitumen, slip-roads, off-ramps, junctions, tollgates—are all the same. I cover the miles with fantasies of difference. Hitch-hiking blond girls with backpacks and pre-torn jeans are always different, always the same. After two days a kilometre and a mile are the same. After five years a fantasy, and a delivery, is the same. I see myself go whizzing by in a truck on the opposite side of the road. I see my other self, reflected in an HGV side window. Another self, sustained by a stupid fantasy, just to keep his mind moving forward. When I run out of blond fantasies, I'm going to switch lanes, cross the central reservation. Crash into reality!... Get real.

CHECK LIST

I've got to be 'passionate' about acting—
or everyone will think I don't care.
I've got to 'connect' to the character—
or the director will think I'm stupid.
I've got to 'be in the moment'—

or I will be distracted by Sarah's tits.
I've got to 'react' to my scene partner—
or I will just be a blank walking plank.
I've got to 'activate my objectives'—
or everyone will be better than me.
I've got to switch off the 'cop in my head'—
or they'll see the prison I put myself in.
I've got to remain 'truthful', at-all-times—
or I will have to have an imagination!

I PITY THE POOR IMMIGRANT

I do not come from here. I'm not like you. I have no history. I have nothing in common with anyone here. I don't speak my original language anymore. So, I'm not that person now. And I have no witnesses to explain that person. Or entertain you with who that woman was. And anyway, you're not interested. So, I'll imitate you instead. I will go on imitating you until you accept me. I'm getting better and better at it. Soon I will be passable. Neither one of us will know who I am. I'll be your mirror. Watched and smiled upon. All previous experience cancelled. A woman without a tribe, whose conversation is an echo. An imitation of the echo you are.

THE INVITATION

You want what I've got! You want my money. You want my friends. You want my social ease. My popularity. My big sparkling eyes. My perfect teeth. You want my contented family. You want my intelligence. You want my terrific sense of humour. You want my business acumen. You want my capacity for hard work. You want my vitality and youth. You want my potential. My potential for infinite growth and achievement. You want my beliefs. You want my sexual confidence. You want my certainties. You want to be me. If you can take it, you can have it! Come on. Come and take it off me! Come and get me!

THE ORCHARD

I like women. I love women. The way they talk—like summer moving through trees. It's a picnic to be in their company. They make me feel that the time it takes to eat a sandwich is exactly the time it should take to eat a sandwich. Not a minute less. Don't worry about schedules, or being late, or being blamed. The excuse a woman comes up with, will sound like it was meant to be said, and that being on time would be pointless and rude. And the lie grows the day. The elegant lie grows the elegant day... Women are always forgiven. They can talk about the most intimate things. Every little nagging worry about sex, they can describe and admit to, like it was the most natural easy dream. Being with women is an expansion. It's a full fresh breath. It is civilisation. I am sure that's how civilisation began—three women talking on a pleasant uneventful afternoon, about... everything...!

SOUNDS OF SILENCE

You thought—words came out of silence. But only silence comes out of silence. Words come out of words. Silence comes when you give up. Silence comes when the words don't matter, or when the words can't make a difference.

These words come out of your words. These words touch your words. These words hold on to your words. These are joining words. Doing words. These words want new words. Responding words. Verbs. Your words. Don't be silent. Don't make silence. Don't make me silent. I will never make you silent. Let's TALK! Let's do doing words!

FOOL'S PARADISE

I like watching fish. The bigger the aquarium the better. I like to watch dogs running or playing. I like watching the waves come in. Mindless things that take me out of myself. It's better not to think. To question. It's better to practice vacancy. You need to keep working at it until you go stupid. It's possible to achieve it through exhaustion too. So tired you can't think. But I'm too lazy for that. The empty stare suits me better. Thinking is the enemy. Begin to think and you begin to want. You become discontented. Better to be stupid than unhappy, that's my motto... I watch the shoals of coloured carp circling the glass tank... I'm the most contented person in the world.

IF I WAS A CARPENTER...

I want to work with my hands. I want to serve metal and wood and marsh reeds. I want to be useful. I want to make fishing nets and tractors and unbreakable tools. I want to have a workbench where I can trust a chisel and an Alligator saw. I want to use plumb line. I want to centre the bubble—the bead—the bubble—in a spirit level. You can't trust people. People come apart in your hands. You use them once, then have to throw them away.

BURNING BRIGHT

I was coming back on the train past ripe yellow rape fields, from a big job interview in Newcastle. I felt really good coming out the interview. I had been confident. Even when the interview went on for much longer than I thought it would, I up-ed my game, I re-focused. OK the trick question at the end threw me a little. But I thought of something, just in the nick of time! When they asked me if I had any questions for them and I couldn't think of any, I made a joke of it and they laughed. They liked me... But as the train went by all the golden glorious flowers, my stomach started to sag. Everything in the sunshine outside the window seemed brighter than me. More natural... My hope started to fade. I had pushed too hard. That's for sure... I knew I hadn't got the job.

BLUES FOR FUN

Man, the blues is so negative. I wanted to get something positive going on, you know? The blues is so depressing. Just moaning and whining, bitchin' and complaining and feeling sorry for itself—you got me? I wanted to turn all that misery around and shout halleluiah! I wanted to make a joyful sound. So, I opened my heart and opened my mouth —! Nothin—. Nothin—! Nothin' doing! Nothin' doing— cause that ain't the blues.

ORPHAN HEART

Your mother didn't love you. Why? We will never know. She loved your sisters. But even when you were a baby and very lovable, she didn't love you. I'm so sorry. You have been deprived of what should have naturally been yours for all these years. I can't make it up to you. I love you. I love you very much, but I'm not your mother. I've loved you more than the others. You were a beautiful little girl. You were always my favourite. You were the best of them. But no matter how much I love you, it will never be enough. I can never compensate for what... or satisfy your need for... What I give you, you don't feel. You just don't feel it...We both lose.

THE GREAT PRETENDER

I knew it was over the day she was kind to me. The day she relaxed and gave in to me. Let me have my way in everything. No grit. No resistance. 'Whatever you want honey!' All her attention for once. Soft. Calm. Pleasant. Kind of low key—meek. Stroking my face. Caring. Meeting my gaze with a loving look... I knew it was over then. I knew she had already gone.

MR. RIGHT

He tries so hard to be interesting. A hint of a pause, or a lull in the conversation and he'll quote Spinoza or reveal some obscure but fascinating titbit. Has a controversial opinion, a colourful turn of phrase, on any subject. Politics, sporting legends, the technology of flight, the history of penal reform, Victorian gardens, Bauhaus fixtures and fittings. He makes my head spin! Any conversation—he does all the work for you. And he entertains and he pushes until I'm totally exhausted. I was interested in him at the start, when I first moved here, but now I'm looking for someone less significant. I'm looking for a very dull man who will let me show off.

THE BOGEYMAN

I think I've lived a kind of evil fairy tale where the wicked stepfather punished his children for not being his. I've read my life in a story book written to frighten children into being good. But I was already good. And my father was my real father. I grew up. Got away to university. Raised a family. The usual visits back home. Family Sunday dinners. Chitchat, political arguments, trying to keep a lid on it, trying to get along. Occasionally, an unguarded opinion from him on how to bring up a child. 'Show them who's *boss*!' On that he never softened, as he grew stooped and frail. He'd lift himself up to meet my eyes. We both remembered the blows. 'They have to know who's boss!', he'd say, voice completely even. Then the eyes went dead, and the stoop returned... My father taught me that wicked people don't learn. They don't feel remorse. There is no contrition. They don't long for forgiveness and absolution. They go on justifying what they have done all the days of their lives.

YOU HAVE PLACED A CHILL IN MY HEART

I was cruel to myself. All sorts of cruel. In all sorts of ways. Because I didn't feel good enough. Because I didn't feel good enough to feel good. I had to cut down my hope before you did it for me. Now I would describe myself as invulnerable... or worse.

CONFRONTATION

I'm going to rise up like summer, with no moss in my briefcase. I'm going to face the north with a smile that's all sheen and window glare. I'm going to be a wet footprint on a terracotta terrace—drying as you watch. I'm going to explode into the suspended dust in your bedroom shaft of light. I'm fire in the evening waves! Fire in the surge where you will not swim. I see the low grey sky you see. But I also see what's coming. I'm going to rise up like the month of May. I'm going to love you with soft velvety buds of hazel. I'm going to be summer! I'm going to give you summer! Then you will see what I see. Sunshine. I'm going to rise up like a lover! Love makes summer. Love me!

TURNING POINT

I was feeling sorry for myself. Ooh! nobody can do self-pity like I can. You are never on your own with self-pity. It's your friend. I was thinking about... love. Wanting, needing to be loved. I was wondering who had loved me in my life. I wasn't getting very far. A couple of names. The vague beginnings of a list. Then I went blank. And in that blank space I heard my voice saying aloud, 'and who have you loved? Where's your long list?' And then it hit me! AHH!

DIVIDED WE FALL

The enemy you are to my people, is no enemy to me. Your religion hates my religion, but you don't hate me. My tribe hates your tribe, but I don't hate you. We love each other. Despite the differences of race and nation and belief. Despite the consequences—we have belief in each other. Against the armies massing on both sides—our tender embrace... our single love. We will win!

HERE, THERE AND EVERYWHERE

When I was fifteen, I gave my life to Jesus. I was certain of his love. At seventeen I decided I was an atheist. Well actually more of an anarchist. But at nineteen I knew the lotus path was the path for me! Buddha and Zen, and never coming back as a maggot, had to be the way. It wasn't until I was a mature twenty-three that Allah called me to prayer five times a day. Wherever I was, whatever I was doing, I knew the direction of Mecca. Then at twenty-four I went a bit alternative. A bit Druid and Beltane and into the gods of Earth and Fire. At twenty-five I became obsessed with all the Hindu deities. Wow, those stories! No shit! Now I'm less interested in world religions. Still plenty to investigate. Still lots there to worship, if I wanted to worship anything but you... But I found you. And from now, to the end of my days, I will worship your being alive in the world.

TRAVELLING LIGHT

I sing about the highway! I sing about searching for the truth, the authentic. I sing about travelling the shining silver motorway. But the road is an escape route. The empty road is a fantasy. It's a song, it's not the truth. It's the concept, the idea of freedom, it's not the roar of truck traffic, the diesel fumes and the monotony of travelling. The boring concrete cladding on a motorway repair—that's all there is... the fatigue. Every time I come to an understanding, a knowledge of myself, a settlement—there's the distraction, the impulse to find a crossroads, stick out a thumb. There's the thrum of a song curving into the treeline. There's a song to be sung about what might be on the other side.

FRIENDSHIP HOKEY-COKEY

I like my friends, but I'm oppressed by the effort it takes to like my friends. I like my friends, but I'm depressed by the amount of time I feel I have to spend with them to keep them being my friends. Perhaps I could keep my friends as friends by just talking with them in emails and text messages. Perhaps I don't deserve friends? I'm in despair! I'm in despair at having to contact them. Are my friends in despair at having to contact me?

KNOWING ME, KNOWING YOU

When people die, and before they are burned, or lowered into the ground, their lives are summarised by priests, ministers and humanists—people that hardly knew them. Family members tiptoe around the edges of the more *challenging* aspects of a loved one's life. To know the inner character of someone you need to know their secret thoughts and fantasies. You need to know all those transgressive, random, free associations—immoral, irresponsible, visions and connections. Think of all the time you spend fantasising... If you added up the minutes spent on sex alone, it would be years. Never mind the time spent dreaming over revenge, power, success and glory. Think of all the nasty little thoughts and betrayals, that convince you that you are uniquely *guilty*. That's how much you don't know about the dead! If all the fantasies of our loved ones were read out at the end of the eulogy, we would know them and understand them so much better. That would really test our forgiveness!

LOSS

Why did I let you go? Why did I just stand there when you said goodbye? It was as if part of ourselves had already left. Why did I go along with the platitudes, when I knew perfectly well what was happening? Why didn't I shout, DON'T GO?! Why didn't I scream? Why didn't I hold on, cling to you? Why didn't I fall at your legs and grab them? Why hide what I felt? Why pretend that this was just another test? Why didn't I tear at your clothes? If I had let you see—see what you really meant to me—I could've kept you. I could've stopped you going. Why did I shy away from giving all of myself to you? You left because I kept something back for myself. I always kept something back. I always keep something back... Now I'm alone.

PLAN B

Starting work is rubbish. My Dad says—'welcome to the real world!' But if this is the real world, you can keep it. I have to get up at 7 a.m. 7 fucking a.m.! It's two buses to get near the industrial park—then a boring walk. And once I'm there, it's not like everyone's cracking jokes and friendly. Miserable shits! A bunch of grumpy fucks, making work even more crap by being nasty bastards to each other. If this is what it's going to be like for the rest of my life, you can fuck right off! I'm not gonna be a loser hating every minute. Not me. I'm not doing it! I'm going to start thieving. I'm going to start robbing houses. I'm going to start mugging old dames. Tomorrow I'm going to begin the easy life.

THE WEIGHT

What's going to happen to me?
Will each sense quietly, gradually, slip away day by day?
I know a lot of people, but will they remember me?
Will I compensate with booze and the normal addictions?
What's going to happen to my body?
Who is that person in the mirror?
Will I be the exception?
What's going to happen to my potential?
Will I pass into mediocrity without any discernible achievement?
What's going to happen to the promises I made?
Will I benefit anyone's life?
And if I did, how does that help me?

HAUNTED HEART

I am a ghost. I'm dead but returned. Here, but not quite here. The machinery to get me gone only half worked. Someone must have wished me to stay. Someone in the real world wanted me to remain real. Someone real still wants to love me. I can't think of anyone. Nope, no one springs to mind! Can't be that... What then? Maybe, someone real still wants me to love them. Oh, perhaps that's why I'm back. What if I have to stay until I love someone? Fuck! Who? I never loved anyone. This is no time to start—after I'm dead! Crazy. No one gets out of this world without some pain. But *love*? Christ, I might be here forever!

YOUR GHOST TOWN

I am a ghost town. As you walk next to me, I drain the colour out of the street. Take the next left. There's no blossom on the trees. Take the right past the office glass. There's nothing to reflect but grey sky. I take the perfume from your collar and leave you with the smell of chlorine. I turn birdsong into siren shrieks. When I touch your hand, you feel like running. When I whisper in your ear you want to surrender. My breath chills you to the bone. Everywhere you go, I take the pleasure from your lips. Everywhere you lie down, I take the rest out of your sleep. There's nothing you can touch that's real. Your fingers move through doors like memories. The food you eat tastes stale. The family you claim, cannot remember your name. There's nothing here that can love you. I am your ghost town. You are living inside what used to be. You are haunted by what used to be me.

EVERLASTING LOVE

When she was gone, I lived for six years totally without being able to conjure her face. Then, I must have said something to my sister-in-law, Cassie. Because she said, don't think of her frozen in a photo. Picture her moving, doing something ordinary. So, I thought of her cleaning the bread bin. Her face jumped instantly into my mind. I could see every changing expression, every thought moving across her eyes. I can see her now! The images keep coming —an avalanche made up of her living face doing a thousand little household tasks. It's destroying me! I can't make the avalanche stop. I love her but I need her to stop. I need to put her back inside a photo-frame, before I lose sight of my own life. Before I surrender my life to her ghost. Her ghost is taking me over. I need to see her face dead.

THE CONTRACT

I want to comfort you as much as Robert's Dad and no more. I want to care for you as much as Mr. Graham but not as much as Mr. Franklin. I want to spoil you 30% less than your uncle Frank. I want to control you a hell of a lot more than Jack's stepfather. I want to play with you for only as long as the other dads. I want to love you the same amount as your mother does (maybe a little bit more— secretly). And in return I want you to love me more than all the rest of them put together!

SIGN OF THE TIMES

Sometimes you just have to change the sheets. What's there is grey on white. Or yellowish on white. It could be urine. What's there is last night. Last night groaning, snorting. Last night with *guff*! Last night with the office joke. Someone you just have to change the sheets after. You came back from the party, out of control, and some stains were already there. Your victim did not notice. When you put out the light the only control was to fumble for the bed. That was passion. You were well at it. Naked. Fucking to burst that dam. Letting it flow... Stains on top of stains... Now change the sheets. Pretend to be decent.

MANIFESTO

I'm mad me. Bonkers! I'll do anything. It's just the way I am. Looney tunes! Full of crazy ideas! I'm excitable. I'm exciting! Nothing off limits. I'm a fun person. Laughing all day long. Well, if you can't laugh at yourself! Don't take yourself too seriously—that's the best way to be. Nobody wants a po-face. Nobody wants a dreary wet blanket. Party! Party! Party! That's my advice. If you want to be popular. If you want to be wanted—party! party! party! party! party! party! party! PARTY!

WHAT GOES AROUND...

I'm happy at work. I adore the people I work with. They are so nice, and they work so hard. But I gossip about them. (I can't help it!) I make up stuff about how idiotic they are. And deceitful. And hypocritical. Not like they really are. I don't know why I do it... Maybe I'm bored. Maybe I'm jealous. Maybe I should get a more frenetic job, where I don't have time to notice other people's faults. Where everybody is perfect. No, I'd just snipe about the perfect people! I'd make them flawed. I'd invent stuff. Maybe I should learn to control myself. Or accept people for what they are... They don't talk about me. Nothing to talk about. If I don't talk about them, how do I know I'm here?

LEARNED BEHAVIOUR

I am exhausted. I look after a big filthy hairy-backed man and two dirty boys. And I work full time! And cook when I come home! And clean! What is it with men? They can't fold, or clear, or dust, or hang, or fill, or gather, or sort, or wipe, or polish, or dry, or empty, or fill, or find, or brush, or replace, or vacuum, or plump, or love! They are useless. Any attempt they make only makes the mess they originally made worse. Leaving it to them only means I have to do it again later. Then I'm even more tired. They never get it right. (Not my right). It's easier in the long run to do it myself. Plump! Plump! Alone. Some things have to be right.

LOVE LIES BLEEDING

I think I love her. I really think I do. But then I think— would I give my life to save her? Isn't that the ultimate test of love? I imagine situations—all sorts of unlikely dangerous scenarios. She's being attacked by sharks, or Somali pirates, or the Taliban, or a gang of zombies... and I wonder if I would jump right in. Intervene in a heartbeat—

without thinking for a second of myself. And in my fantasy, (when she's at the centre of a house fire with the roof crashing in), I hesitate. I calibrate the threat. I freeze. I just freeze. Even in my fantasy life I can't respond. She dies! I fail to save her. So, it must mean I don't love her. Don't love her enough. I feel I do—but... She deserves a hero. Sad... I really thought she was the one. But I'm going to have to break it off. Otherwise, otherwise... one day something horrible might happen and then she'd find out.

HOUSE PROUD

I never invited friends back to my place. I wanted to. But I wanted to get new curtains and a new carpet first. Then I wanted to change the torn three-piece suite. And I couldn't have anyone see that ceiling—the paper peeling off. Friends wanted to come, but the toilet pan was an accident waiting to happen. The bath was old and stained. And you never have the time to get around to all the stuff you need to do, not when you're at work... So... by the time I got the new curtains—by the time I fixed the toilet... by the time my flat was just the way I wanted it—all my friends had gone to have fun in other people's old shabby rundown flats.

ROADRUNNER

I love driving. I love speed! Whizzing past all those houses and factories and shops and people—and not being part of any of it. All those junctions, possibilities, putting your foot down—zooming on! ON! I love the highway and the open road. I love the adrenaline rush. I love leaving everything behind. I love when the real world becomes a blur. Then

I'm the important one. Then I'm apart from all the mess and confusion. I'm the only thing in focus. I'm special! Special—with no destination. No death over the horizon. Just another road to travel. Forever forward! Moving ON!

PRIVATE LIVES

I love acting,
But I hate meeting new people.
I'm passionate about the theatre,
But I'm intimidated walking into a plush velvet red auditorium.
I open a text as if I'm going on an adventure,
But I'd rather be safe, at home, watching daytime TV.
I use the rehearsal room as my playground,
But I don't want to take risks or let my guard down.
I thrill every time I put on a costume,
But they always smell of Febreze and bum sweat.
I'm fascinated by rigging, sound, mark-ups and technical stuff,
But I'm really just a tart for a round of applause.
I'm a big fan of ensemble playing and being part of a creative team,
But I'm more relaxed in a follow spot.
I can totally transform myself into another character,
But that's all I've ever been.

POOR ME

I go through the bins. I find what is necessary. It has to be edible or wearable. Finding what is necessary, makes life simple. Makes my work simple. I am not repelled by what I see, or smell. I am not sickened by what I touch. Even when it gives way and leaks over my hand. If it is not necessary, I turn it aside, or throw it behind me. There is slime. There is stink. I am not insensible. But it is unimportant. I am focused on what will keep me going for a few hours—for the night—for tomorrow. I find it wherever you threw it away. You watch me searching. How did I fall so low? But there is no down or up, there is only need. I look at you... You need nothing but novelty. Novelty does not last. I contains no nourishment.

BACKGROUND ARTIST

People look at these tattoos and they see a freak. People look at these tattoos and they see danger. Do you think I'm doing it for attention? Do you think I'm a joke, an entertainment—a carnival attraction? Are you distracted by the roses and the thorns? Are you distracted by the skulls and the daggers? Good! That's why I carved them there. So that when you stare at me, you never see the obvious. The very very obvious.

MOUTH FULL OF NORMAL

It's not that we don't feel the same way about each other. It's a break down in communications. When she says she doesn't want anything to eat, it actually means—get off your lazy fat arse, make me something to eat for a change! When she says she doesn't feel like going out, what she really means is—you never suggest anything new, or exciting, or anything worth doing! When she says—let's go to bed, it means that she wants me to stop drinking and talking shit! When she says—I love you, it means—do what I want you to do... When I say, I love you honey, it means, I haven't yet found anyone better to spend my time with... Not yet.

PRIVILEGE

My work takes me across the world. My work takes me to yachts, film sets, catwalks and palaces. I'm enjoyed in those places. I'm not necessary. I am a luxury they could easily dispense with. But I've made myself wanted. When I get to those places I'm scintillating. I'm effortless. I'm pixie dust! On the way, I'm an empty waiting room in an airport. I'm a suitcase with a damaged wheel. I'm between weather fronts and cancellations. I'm missed connections. I'm passing the time with earnest strangers. I fly over droughts and war-torn villages. I fly over swimming pools with no one in them. I fly between limitless constellations... In my pocket all I have is my pixie dust.

ISOLATION.

Keep each debt in isolation. Then no debt is a lifestyle. It's just gas or electricity. It's not staying up all night with the lights on. Make each bill a unique surprise! Then it has nothing to do with satellite channels and the mobile phone. It's not the early morning hours, talking with your fingers to a tiny screen by the side of your pillow. It's not the price of vodka! It's not the price of petrol at the pumps for those long drives beyond the city lights and the city boundary—to nowhere... Make sure you disconnect the bill from the cause. So there is no connection between outlay and loneliness. Deny that any bill is the true cost of your loneliness... Loneliness is too expensive! Loneliness costs a fortune. That's why you can't pay. That's why you will never be able to pay.

LIVING DOLL

You used to play with dolls. Cherry was your favourite. Now your old dolls are a collection. When did the impulse to play change into the impulse to display? When did Cherry no longer need to be consoled? When did the bright gleam in her eye go cold? You can't collect playfulness. You can't collect 'let's pretend'. Your little plastic playmates are dead. Why keep them? Why prop up more dead bodies on the bed? How can you stand all those dead eyes looking at you? Waiting for you to pick them up. Waiting for you to tell them who they are. When did you want something to keep instead of something to share? Cherry's eyes are vacant. My eyes are alive! My eyes smile. I'm not for you to keep. But we can play. For a little while, we can share... Your eyes are the same as Cherry's!

PICK UP

If I were you, I'd have more sense. If I were you, I'd set the alarm early, get up and join a gym. If I were you, I'd have more confidence. If I were you, I wouldn't give it another thought. If I were you, I'd just go for it. If I were you, I'd see a doctor. If I were you, I'd ask for my money back. If I were you, I wouldn't let him get away with it. If I were you, I'd start looking for someone else. If I were you, I'd do what I do. If I were you, I would fancy me rotten! If I were you, I would think I was perfect. If I were you, I would do everything I tell you to do. If I were you, I'd give me a kiss. If I were you, I'd come back to my place. If I were you, I would take my clothes off slowly. If I were you, I would let myself make love to me.

LOVELESS LOVE

He wants to do it with me. He says it's time. He's running out of patience. He says he loves me, so he wants to make love to me. He says it's natural and what's wrong with me? He says I'm a prick teaser and that he could get someone else. He's done it with other girls. He knows what to do. He says he's a brilliant lover. He's a real good kisser, that's for sure! And sometimes, when he's kissing me, I feel like—I want it. I really want it. But—oh God! I don't love him. I don't love him at all. I don't love him. I don't love him. He doesn't love me... I'm going to do it with him tonight, do it and get it over with. Then he won't mind that I don't love him.

FIXED EXPRESSION

I have never frowned. My face has never worn a frown. My face has never known a frown. My life is happy. You have made me happy. Always. Anything else is impossible. I can smile easily—see! That's my natural state. That's the expression I am meant to have. I can't respond any other way. No matter what you say. I can't frown. I can't frown! You will need to tell me something else. Something pleasant. Because my face can't accept anything that sounds like a frown. It only responds to happiness.

HA-HA SAID THE CLOWN

I'm the funniest man who *never* made you laugh. I've tried double entendre, punchlines, accents. I've tried sly innuendo. And I even managed a pun from time to time. But nothing I do makes you chuckle. I hear you laugh at other people's gags. I love your laugh! I would love to make you laugh. Titter. Guffaw. Roar! Even a smirk would give me hope... Perhaps you have no sense of humour... You laugh to disguise your lack of, err, mirth... I couldn't love you if you had no sense of humour... You've never made me laugh. You've never told me a joke. Oh no! That's what we've got in common. That's the attraction. We're both terrified that we're as boring as fuck!

THE FINAL SECRET

I lit a match and held it under my secret, until the flame threatened to burn my thumb. I held my secret under water, but my secret did not need to breathe and after several minutes I lost interest. I folded my secret and pushed it through a letterbox, but it was returned—not at this address! I gave my secret another name, but I still heard the old name muttered at dinner parties—called in the street! I poisoned my secret. I dropped it from an office tower. I ran over it in a hired car, reversed over—then another go with my foot down! I gave my lover the secret, but she had plans of her own. I half told my wife the secret but before I could finish, she interrupted to confess her own secret. Fuck! I began a life of crime to distract myself with new secrets. Burglary. Mugging. Murder! So many secrets to remember now. Just one I can't forget. The secret that makes me different.

NATURAL HIGH

I am not a cockroach. Cockroaches hate themselves. I am not a bug. I'm not an insect. I'm not a locust. Locusts do not sing. I, my love, am an evening cricket. I'm the swamp opera. I'm the thrill of the dark! My song is falsetto. The pitch is all vibration. Clear star to clear star. So high your atoms shake loose. I'm shrill like a scalpel. I cut night into your waiting heart. I'm late harvest excitement. I'm full moon promise. I'm midnight fever!... I am the woman you love.

MR. MALCONTENT

When you thought the world was warped—so you were just as twisted. When you believed in hellfire—you made damn sure you deserved it! When the sun hurt your eyes, you put bullets in your gun and lifted the barrel high. When you wound up feeling lonely—you pulled down the blinds, locked the door and refused to answer calls. When you knew I loved you, you fucked the girl next door! When you knew that you loved me, you refused to love yourself. When you knew that you loved me—you packed your bags and left.

YOU CAN'T ALWAYS GET WHAT YOU WANT

I get through my lengthy conversations with you by fantasising that I'm about to have an affair with the neighbour two doors down.

I get through my lack of social success with two fantasies, both about becoming a chat show host, but only one that I can tell you.

I get through negotiating with the fixed positions of my family by destroying them with the fantasy of Armageddon and the End of Days.

I get through my inability to apply myself, or commit, because I'm distracted by the fantasy of having infinite time to do everything.

I get through my inability to feel sincere, on any occasion, by fantasising about becoming God.

I get through not receiving any positive re-enforcement, or positive feedback about my values and actions, with the fantasy of being ahead of my time, then being famous posthumously.

EXCUSE ME MISTER

I was obliged to go to a party, only the obligation made me go. I was putting a good face on it. I'd defy anyone to detect my real feelings. I was about to dilute my Chablis with a long dash of soda water, when this guy I knew from Uni days said hullo. It was great to meet him. We'd had a lot of laughs in halls and then sharing a flat. We hit it off like we were back in the Student's Union again. We still had the same old rapport. We even showed everyone a mad dance thing we used to do—like a Hakka parody. We still made each other laugh. We could have carried on. Cancelled out the intervening years of professions, and knock backs, and wives, and kids, and mortgages, and dinner parties with less exciting friends. But we hugged goodbye without exchanging numbers. A friend out of context is no longer a friend.

FOREVER YOUNG

I am always on the make. Was from as early as I can remember. The first thing kids do is lie. Growing up is learning to lie better. When I was little, if I had an idea, I would try it out. Good or bad. Result—disaster! Now I'm an adult, I still remember being caught out. Shame... It keeps me on the right side of the law. But lying is my habit. I tell everyone I'm a player. A lady's man. A real *player*, I say in a low voice and then smirk. I don't say that to my kids, of course. They tell me that they are innocent. Ha! I know better.

THE DAMAGE DONE

My advice was to stay, when you should have left. My advice was to leave, when you should have stayed. There was nothing uncertain about my advice. My advice was to invest, when you should have saved. My advice was to believe, when you should have asked the obvious question. My advice was to confess, when you should've lied—lied—lied! My advice was to hate, when you should have loved. I'm sorry I got everything so fucking wrong. How can I make it right? I'll do whatever it takes. Tell you what! I'll follow your advice. I owe you that. Your turn to instruct. My turn to obey. You can damage me. Do it if it helps you... Just speak to me. What do you want me to do? What should I do? What?

EYES WIDE OPEN

Nothing happened but everything changed. Our eyes met. That's all. You met my gaze. You returned my look. You didn't look away. You didn't smile it into a pleasantry. You didn't pretend it was something else. You didn't dismiss it. You didn't shrug it off. You didn't deliberately misunderstand. You didn't trivialise. You gave me my curiosity—my invitation—right back. Not hard. Not defiant. Not teasing. Cool. Interested. Mature. Taking the time to make it clear. The whole way into who you are. Everything you are... Soul mate. The rest of our life together. New for each other... How long was that look? I know the stop you get off at. I'll be ready tomorrow. Ready to touch you. Ready to speak. Everything is about to happen.

RELEASE

I'm so angry I could hit you. I could punch you. Really hurt you. I'm furious! I could stab you! I could kill you! I hate you. I despise you. I loathe you. I could torture you. Watch you suffer. Beg for mercy. I want to destroy your body, bit by bit. I'm frightened of my feelings. I'm frightened of the images in my head. The things you are making me think. This isn't me! This is *you*! This isn't who I really am. I'm a good guy. Nice, you know? You've made me into this raving lunatic... And I really like the power. I can do anything. I can really let go and express myself. Thanks. It's a new me!

WILD DOG DAYS

I'm the snarl not the bite. I'm the threat on your flank. I'm the bared teeth stand-off. I'm the snap at your tail. Then I slip back into the pack. I'm harrying kind. Harassing the weakest. Confusing the smartest. I'm the follow on. I'm the unfair advantage. I'm the wear you down. I'm the tire you out. I'm from the blind side. I'm at the same time as everybody else. I'm the anonymous terror. I'm the gang! I'm the mob! I'm the horde! I'm the mindless multitude. I kill! But never alone. Alone I have no power.

THE BOTTOM LINE

Well, this is it! Decision time. It's up to you. I'm not going on with you the same old way. You don't get it! You just don't get it! You don't make the connection between income—income generation—and expenditure! I am not subsidising your lifestyle any longer. I'm not your financier. I'm not a cash-cow! I'm not bailing you out—not a penny more! From now on you earn it, to spend it. That's it! If you can't promise me—here and now—then—then—we are over. I've had enough. You've got to want me for who I am, not what I can do for you. And if you promise to change, you've got to mean it. I must believe it, believe you'll change. Are you going to change? Are you? ... Are you going to try? Try just a little, for me?

OUT OF IT

Yesterday I found myself in the garden. I don't remember wanting to go there. It was a surprise. I looked around. My garden had decided it was autumn. How did that happen? Inside—when I was in the kitchen making sourdough—it was summer. Now there were piles of crimson, and scarlet and oxblood leaves. I didn't know what to do. What did I want to do? I didn't know what to feel. So... so... I lay down on the frost and I scraped the leaves over my body. I covered myself with beautiful burning leaves. Even my head. Even my mouth and eyes. I found I could breathe under them. Breathe through the smell of rot and earth musk. I lay there in the garden. Letting the cold and the wet seep in... Then I knew why I was there. Then I knew how to feel... I still feel that way. I think I will feel this way forever.

MAKING AN EFFORT

You thought I didn't try. I didn't get a job because I didn't try. I didn't find love—a lover—a partner—a husband—a soul-mate—because I didn't try. My trying didn't match your trying, you thought. Wasn't as sustained. Wasn't as bold. Was only half-hearted... My trying was within these walls. My trying was between my ears. Silent. You don't think getting up in the morning is trying. But it is! You don't think going to bed, instead of staying up all night playing computer games is trying, but it is. My little trying occupies me, as much as your big trying, occupies you. You try for subcommittee leverage. I try to find the energy to clean the kitchen surfaces. Futility is its own reward. I try to make myself wipe up crumbs. I *try* to make myself try.

SILENCE

Some people get chosen by aliens and then abducted. But no being from another planet ever singled me out—I am not what they are looking for! Some people get haunted by apparitions, or unquiet spirits. But nothing spooks me—I'm not sensitive enough. Some people survive terrible accidents, or disasters, because a Guardian Angel arrives and folds them in golden wings. But no angel has ever put itself out for me. Some people know they are loved because they hear God answering their prayers. But, I guess, He doesn't think I'm worth it. Some people win millions on the lottery and change everything about their lives. But I am spookily unlucky. For me tomorrow will be the same as today. And the day after... every day after—because I am uniquely sane and ordinary.

FIREWATER

I am an alcoholic. I drink to find connections. With other people and with memories. But mostly I drink to connect with old words that people don't use any more. Not for themselves anyway. Words like glory. Freedom. Beauty. Loyalty. Wonder. Exaltation. Exaltation. Exaltation! ... I'm drunk now.

ONE HANDED CATCH

When I was little, now and then, they'd be a day when I could do no wrong. Words would fly out of me and make friends laugh. I could climb a tree with the grace of a gibbon. I could leap from stone to stone, all the way to the head of a river, and never doubt where my feet would fall. And it still happens every so often. I feel... expansive. I parkour through conversations and parties and friendships. Hand, eye, thought—flying together! It wants to take me further—lead me on to something—amazing! What? ... And that question takes me out of it. Takes me out of feeling special. And then, I think, does everyone feel special like me? Does everyone have 'special' flicker on and off inside them? Do we all feel brimming—about to access an infinite capacity? The whole population of the earth? Eight billion people. Feeling special. Where does all that 'specialness' go? How disappointing. That I'm the same as everybody else.

BADLANDS

I thought all fathers were brutal.
I thought all mothers were slaves.
I thought all children were savage.
I thought all teachers were cruel.
I thought all wives were whores.
I thought all husbands were rapists
I thought all brothers were rivals.
I thought all sisters were idiots.
I thought all friends were losers.
And then I met you.
I thought I was an animal.
And then I met you.
I thought I was a monster.
And then I met you.

DISTANCE LEARNING

When I was little, I was small for my age. And I was timid —shy. No one seemed to notice me. To get to school I used to cross the motorway, over a big concrete and roughcast bridge. Although I was late this day, I stopped to watch the traffic zooming under my feet. I stood there, above it all, nobody seeing me. There was nothing special. The cars were as boring as I was. Insignificant... Then a red car catching the sun. Making it stand out. I threw the rock! The bang was... enormous. Like a... Like a close clap of thunder. After all these years I still hear it echoing every time I close my eyes.

DEAR SOMEONE

I'm not blaming you. I used to do it too. Say positive things to friends in desperate trouble. I used to think it was support. I was being up-beat for both of us. But... it's something else... It's minimising the problem. I'm blind. Everything else about me is the same as it was before I became blind. My hearing has not improved to compensate. Your wanting it to have improved isn't really being sympathetic. You saying the other senses sharpen—take over—is just—reducing my loss. Minimising your obligation to care. You want me to repair myself. Not for my benefit, but to excuse your lack of concern—empathy. You want my symptoms to contract, disappear. You want business as usual. I hear that loud and clear. I see right through you!

THE SUM TOTAL

They died within a year of each other. Both had been earning decent money all their lives. Climbed about halfway up the corporate ladder. I was in the house to start cleaning it out. Get it ready for sale. Standing there in the living room with Ikea boxes at my feet and a black bin bag in my hand, I saw mum and dad's place for the first time. Tiny glass ornaments everywhere. Lots of bright patterned cushions. Jokey nick-knacks—two ceramic fat ladies in bathing suits. A plastic fish in a hammock, slung between plastic palm trees. Nothing worth anything. Nothing worth keeping. Years of steady good money coming in and this tat is what they did with it… Tears came down my face. I just stood there in my childhood home… dripping. Then I thought, I need to find a new definition of value.

FAR AWAY MY WELL-LIT DOOR

I took him for a curry. A curry—that was a risk! But I wanted to offer him—flavour—something he wouldn't get out in the sticks. He ate too much to show he liked it. He drank too much to help him swallow down the foreign muck. We were leaving—he insisted on paying. He made it through the door to the pavement, then he slid down the wall. I thought he was dead! I phoned an ambulance, but he came to, and insisted he was fine. Insisted I cancel it. Under the purple neon of the Masala Twist sign, his face was ash grey. I felt responsible. I felt… that I wanted to make it up to him. So there, in the empty city streets, I said I would phone him, come home to see him, take him out, spend time with him. But Dad just wanted a taxi to take him home. He had had a fright. He didn't want me there with him. His home was somewhere else. His comfort was somewhere else. I hailed a cab… he insisted.

ON THE BEACH

We were determined to be ragged, with our tattered jeans and threadbare canvas tent. Our borrowed sleeping-bags had someone else's stains. We were careless. Ciggy lighters sheltered by cupped hands. Desperate to make music inspired by half wet boulders, rock-pools and dried out starfish. We wanted mermaids in the grey tide and the ghosts of sailors in the sand dune grass. We were experiments in waiting. Virgins posing as burned-out songwriters. Virgins lying to each other. Making our lies poetry. Half friends, almost friends. Conjuring futures from damp biscuits and improvising comedy routines. Playing with crab shells and seagull feathers. We were young. We invented everything and then didn't want it… Later, there was a song, but it wasn't mine.

BAD FOR YOU

I said that I was having fun. I said that I was happy. I was lying. I said that I was contented. I said that I was untroubled—satisfied. I said that I was enjoying myself. But I was lying to you. I said that I was healed. It's not true. I said that I loved you. But… but I was lying to myself.

THE FACTS OF LIFE

She wants to keep it. I don't know why. She was as drunk as me. It's amazing that we managed it at all. It was a complete accident. She admits that. But she's going to keep it. I don't think that's fair. I don't give my consent. I don't want to be a father. I'm too young. I'm not ready. I'm not a grown up! She's decided for me. She wants to be a mother. Selfish. Just selfish. Using that one night we can't even remember properly. She was sick on my neck, that's all I remember! It's going to change our whole lives. Why has she got the power to decide? Why doesn't my opinion count? She's just taken my sperm and made a baby out of it without my permission. Half that flesh and blood, and tiny, tiny teensy-weensy spot of tissue, is made of me. So, I should have half a say in what happens to it! Oh Fuck! Oh fuck! What am I going to do? WHAT AM I GOING TO DO?! My whole life is fucked!

CRY BABY CRY

My father cries. I've seen him when he thought there was no one in the house. I was looking out my bedroom window instead of studying. I saw him in the garden. There he was as usual, digging round his beetroot and radishes. We have to eat a lot of radishes in this family! He was working away as normal, but his face was somehow put together wrong. He was moving it strange and his cheeks were wet. He was crying but still turning up the weeds. I saw a tear fall straight out of his eye. I wanted him to stop blubbin'. I want him to stop... I don't know if I should tell mum. She never cries. I never cry. What's he got to cry about? I'm the one with the exams! I will tell mum, that'll give him something to cry about!... I won't tell mum.

KEEP YOUNG AND BEAUTIFUL

I am addicted to plastic surgery. I don't look like I am, right? That's how good it is. But without the flash of a scalpel—a nip here and a tuck there—I'd look a hundred years older. Baggy saggy eyes. Crow's feet. Lips like stretched worms. Double chin. Chicken neck. Laughter lines, like train tracks up and down my face. You can't imagine the sad, clapped out, old wreck I was. This new face is a miracle of cosmetic technology. I look so young, so bright, so carefree, so unscathed by life! But look real close. Closer. Closer... Can you see it? My age is in my eyes. No laser, no Botox, no blade, can cut deep enough to cut all those years of hurt away.

CLEAN UP TIME

When I was cleaning the sink, you were online. When I was cleaning the cooker, you were playing games. When I was cleaning the toothbrush cup, cleaning the bath, cleaning the toilet bowl, you became an avatar. While I was cleaning the shelves, cleaning the ornaments, cleaning the windows, cleaning the blinds, cleaning the sheets—you were...? While I preserved our home, you were scoring points and winning rewards. While I cleaned myself—my hair, my skin, my face, you were killing aliens. You said you were cleaning up the world. The whole world. I felt—I felt... irrelevant. All my work felt wasted!

WILD THING

I am the outrageous one. I'm the one that takes it too far. Steps over the boundary of good bad taste. Breaks the conventions—the moral code. You think it's because I want attention, or love, or validation—that kind of thing. But you're wrong. I try to stop myself. I see the opportunity, and I floor the brakes nine times out of ten. I could be a lot more scary... But I stop it. I don't want to be the centre of attention, despite what you think. I do it because you are so dull! Tame! Unimaginative! Boring! Frightened! Because you are just a fucking energy vampire! A leech! You need me to make a fucking tit of myself! Otherwise you would have nothing but fucking golf to talk about! Admit it. You want me to be shocking. You want me to live dangerously while you stay safely moribund. Admit it! Admit it! Tell the truth and take a risk. Tell the truth and surprise me for the first time in your life!

YOUR SONG

You played me all your favourite songs. Trying to reach me. Heart breaking songs. And I called them names. Clever insulting names. I made fun of the rhymes. Ridiculed the sentiment. Sent up the style. Ruined them for you... I didn't realise they were all you had. All you had to keep you attached. Just a bunch of silly sweet ballads to keep you hoping. To give your hurt some sense... some companionship. Those songs were little silk threads keeping you hanging on... I'd sing each one for you now, if it would keep you with me. I'd mean every word. I'm sorry I wasn't listening. Please keep singing. I am listening now.

MYSTERY MAN

I'm not a robber, right! I'm no burglar, like. So, explain this to me... I was on holiday with mates in Spain. Costa de Lux, I think they cry it. I was catching the rays on the beach, nobody there. Mates fucked off to an Irish pub. I was looking at the red inside my eyelids. I was looking at these apartments with their metal shutters down. No one in them to September, like. Then it turned overcast. Gloomy like, suddenly. Heavy air. I started walking back to the hotel. T-shirt soaked in sweat. One block away and I seen this shutter—this scuzzy peeling paint, kinda purply shutter... It wasn't secured. There was about four inches of window showing. I didn't want anything like. But—but... but—sounds ridiculous—but like the apartment needed cheering up. Needed a human being to step inside and make a human noise. Laugh. Sing! Like something human lived there. So that's what I done. Then the police came—the Policia. I couldn't explain. Can't explain. So... I'm asking you... Do you know why I done it? Can you explain it to me?

THE HOUSE THAT JACK BUILT

I'm a bricklayer. I'm an artist not a machine. I'm an artist who is always counting bricks. You have no idea of the repetition it takes—brick after brick to construct your house. There is discipline in repeating the same small skill. In the same time what did you do? What did you repeat? Did it make you an artist? Measure for measure, thought for thought, between us—what did you make that will last? My thoughts built a light filled atrium. My thoughts constructed an arch. When you go inside you count away the hours, count away the nights hoping to dream a masterpiece. But I divided the inside from the outside to provide you with a shelter. A refuge fit for more than you can imagine.

SLIP SLIDIN' AWAY

I keep a cage with nothing in it.
My dog has no lead or collar. It barks to invite intruders.
I have removed the locks and made the keys into a wind chime.
The suit in my wardrobe has never learned to tie a Windsor knot.
I read newspapers to savour the guilt of others.
My house is lined with books because I have never found my story.
I never look at the sky in case it has something to say.
I sleep looking at you in case you disappear.
I sleep looking at you in case you disappear.
I sleep looking at you in case you disappear.

OBJECT OF DESIRE

I'm so—so—sorry. I didn't mean to laugh at your thing. You must have felt like—like it was a disappointment to me, or pitiful, or something. I didn't mean to—I'm making it worse, aren't I? They do look funny though—willies. Dicks! Wangs! Shlongs! Cocks! Got lots of names for them, haven't you? But they all look comical, don't they? Not yours! No! Not—I don't mean yours—I mean in general. All of them. None of the bits seem to belong together. And they are always so over eager—bouuyyyiiinnnggg! Hullo! Big grinning shining silly face! So puffed up and self-

166

important and pleased with itself. No idea what they really look like. So bare and blotchy, waving about unsupported—and as for balls—well! Oh—I've gone too far... Poor you. And you were so excited, weren't you? Oh dear. We'll try again. Would you like that? Yes? I'll keep my eyes shut. OK? I promise. I won't peep. It's not you! It's not you! Sorry!

BLUES FOR BAD BOYS

This is a song about the wild days. The girls, the booze, the drugs, the touring. The penthouse orgies. The wilderness years. Crazy times. The fights! The endless mad party. Trashing the recording studio. Breaking my front teeth opening a beer bottle. Trying to string my guitar with dental floss. Trying to find that sound in your mind, you know? It's all there in the groove. Best song I ever wrote. Best song I ever sang. I just don't remember writing it or singing it. It's gone. All gone! This is the replacement song.

I PUT A SPELL ON YOU

I appear to be unconscious. I appear to be unaware. When I reveal the pale parts of my body, it seems to be accidental. But I want you to notice me. I want to arouse you. I want to overcome your reserve. I want your desire. I want you to make an unequivocal move on me. So that I can reject you. And make you feel ashamed. And make you doubt your judgement. So that you will never again mistake my power.

MIRROR WORK

I make my bed with care, but I rarely sleep.
I wash the dishes with scalding water, but I hardly eat.
I scrub the windows clear, but I never look out.
I collect wood for the fire but I seldom light it.
I sing a happy song, but I am not happy.
I breathe steadily but I am not completely conscious.
I say I love you, but it feels like an accusation.

BORN UNDER A BAD SIGN

Bad things happen to good people. Good things happen to bad people... Makes you think... What's the point of trying? No point working flat out, making sacrifices, if all you get is—a hurricane—a mudslide—a stroke—cancer—a virus! If input doesn't correlate with output? If there's no relationship between human effort and what you get back? If it's random... just luck? Just your Donald Duck! Then... I'm going to change. Why do good? Why restrain yourself? Why defer the pleasures of life? I want instant gratification! I'm going to get stuck in! Drink what I want, when I want it. Say what I want. Say what I mean. Fuck what I want! Because nothing matters... Nothing matters... Too late!... I can't change now... I'm—I'm—conditioned... I'm good. Oh!

PAPERBACK WRITER

I am not enough. I thought I was self-sufficient. I was content inside my own ideas. I was happy exploring my own imagination, my own world—my own bubble. I generated articles and short stories from my limited experience. Invented more from the same basic source material. Repeated myself with small variations. My recent work is all repetition. I have run out of experience to fictionalise. I have run out of conjecture, speculation, fantasy, introspection. I have run out of myself. So... I must turn my attention to what lies beyond me... You! All my work will come from you. Now, at last, I'll be free of myself. At last I will be able to call myself a writer.

ETERNAL YOUTH

I'm missing out on things. I can't see as far as I used to. The worst is not hearing. In company, in a pub, or a restaurant—I haven't a clue why people are laughing. Even over the phone I'm scared I'll give the wrong reaction. So I talk! I talk without a pause. I talk with no allowances for interruption. Then everyone listens to me. And there are no tell-tale signs of aging. No, 'sorry, could you say that again?' No, 'what!?' No, 'eh?' I'm frightened of running out of things to say. I've begun to repeat myself. But, so far, I think it's working.

EVERYBODY'S IN SHOWBIZ

It's a waste of time what you're doing. All that emoting. All that sincerity. The music was banal. The writing was clichéd and predictable. The other actors were not gifted. The direction was heavy handed. Everyone gave their all but their *all* was shite. And you—you—you were really pushing the boat out. You wore your heart on your sleeve. Real tears! No one could fault you for effort. Rehearsals must have been demanding—exhausting. But the play is not worth the paper it's written on. It's not worth your effort or investment. Don't prostitute yourself. Don't give it all away. Go home. Just go home—don't turn up for the hour call tomorrow. Do something useful!

INFLUENCES

All that summer I listened to Nina Simone. I needed something authentic to stop the blue sky lifting and taking my soul. All that autumn I listened to Lady Day—heard the fire on her tongue. The fire kept me warm in my shivering Stornoway flat. All that winter I listened to Bessie Smith to hear what sex was all about. Sex was all about losing. I knew what she meant. All that spring I listened to Ethel Waters, so that yearning could enter my open window! Yearning entered my open window. I wrote some notes. All the next summer I sang my own songs. I sounded like I had no history. I sounded like I did not know who I was. I sounded like nothing had happened to me. I never got a recording contract. I still listen to Nina Simone. I will always listen to Nina Simone.

TALENT SPOTTING

I thought I would paint a marvellous work of art. But it took years of struggle and dedication just to produce a couple of human looking squiggles. I thought that I would write the great story of our time, with unforgettable characters, and a heart-breaking dilemma. But after years of scribbling and ignoring my family, all I produced was a pastiche of Martin Amis. I thought that I would compose music. A tragic passion filled opera, or a deep reflective symphony. But after years of absenteeism, and sick leave, I only managed to strum a parody of 'Bohemian Rhapsody'. Now I'm alone and jobless, I realise that my talent lies in self-deception. My only hope of earning a living now, is to teach this talent to others for extortionate fees. But my fear is that deception is an innate ability everyone is born with. Something so natural it doesn't need taught, because everyone already takes pride in it.

I'M LOOKING THROUGH YOU

You loved bad causes, lost causes. If public opinion was against it, you were for it. Did you see yourself as a champion? An antihero? Did you believe you could change hearts, habits, ancient grudges? Did you think you could make the cruel kind? Did you expect the underdogs to lick your hand? Is that why you raised me up? Was I your pet rescue? I'm going to be your worst cause. I refuse to be saved! I cannot be saved by you. For that you would have to be humble. And you are so proud of your fight against every kind of oppression... I could make you humble. My pride against your pride. Your pride riding on a white charger to the rescue. My pride pulling tight the tripwire! You will be my first cause and my last cause.

EMOTIONAL RESCUE

Do you want to—err—come back to—I know it's late— you probably want to get home—it's cold—but my place is —it's just 5 minutes in a taxi, if we can find a taxi, there's probably not a taxi around here for miles—but if you wanted to—just for a coffee—or—or—a nightcap—I've got a good malt whisky—whisky makes you frisky—not that I'm—no—I'm not suggesting—you... Oh!

DEATH

At the start I spent all my time throwing a ball. Then it was music. Hip Hop. Had a bad street attitude. Stole some cars. Popped pills. Went gay, yeh, I tried that for a bit, then tried my boyfriend's sister. Prostitutes. On and off relationship with a mother of three. Got into boxing. Strange, I know! Then after that—I think it was drugs again. Smoking weed mostly, but then coke and heavy dealing. Merchant Navy. Call Centre. Threw myself into a big love affair. Met someone else. Management training. Got married. Had kids. Ran away. Odd jobs. Bars. Stayed in an Ashram. Plumber. Moved to Swansea. Bred dogs. Whippets. Shaved my head. Got tats. Roofer. Drank myself into a coma. Forestry Commission. Then I woke up to Jesus. And that's the answer. No more searching. I know myself now! I don't have to look for validation, or love, anymore. I can finally stand still. My head straight. No more confusion. No more questions. No more changes. Finally, I am what I should be. Yeh!

NE ME QUITTE PAS

Since you left, I can't get excited by anything. I can appreciate things. I can look forward to stuff. I can be impressed, but I can't be amazed. I can get anxious and nervous. I get alarmed and surprised, but never thrilled. When you were here there was a slow steady wonder. But now it's gone. That participation... it's gone. Now I'm just reacting later than I should.

HARD MAN

I like to break things. The sound of teeth cracking had me hooked from the get-go. I tried the usual tools—baseball bats, hammers, chisels, hunting knives, machetes, Samurai swords. Each had its own shiny kind of splendour, and its own limitations. Now, I don't use any equipment. It's a longer game, but I find out what makes people tick. What they take for granted. What they long for. What they think they love—and then I remove it. I do it piece by piece, if I'm in a bad mood. It keeps me interested. But if I like them, I might be merciful and do it all at once. When they fold and crumble, they make a peculiar noise from deep inside. Each person is different, but they all share the same hollow core of sound. It has a small grandeur that nothing else can match... I have become death.

THE BOY WHO PUNCHED FOUNTAINS

You ran into the fountain jets with both eyes shut. The fountain tricked you by dropping into the pavement and appearing somewhere else. You spun with both eyes wide. When they all came on, you shrieked towards the thickest spray with arms outstretched. The plumes disappeared as you snatched at a hug. Another trick. A stream surged up under you. You sat on it with legs apart. The water breached from an adjacent spout. Surprise! But you expected it. You thrust in your groin. The fountain was deformed but gurgled up behind you. You turned and

173

punched and laughed, tried to leave your impression. The water seemed to wilt and weaken. Your last punch was off balance and all air. You fell. Then all the fountains flew into the blue sky, taller than you could ever be... You left them there to sparkle all the rest of your life and never felt alone or separate again.

DON'T LET ME BE MISUNDERSTOOD

I want you back. I'll do whatever you want. I mean it. I can't pretend that I've changed completely—that would be unrealistic. But I've learned my lesson. And that has changed me. I think differently now. I react, I behave— differently. I'm different in here, in my head. My heart hasn't changed. I love you. I know you don't love me right now. But I believe you did at one time. I know that seems a long time ago. Let me try to get it back. Let me just try. You'll see. It'll be good. Better than it ever was. Because we're different people now. Older. More solid. Aware of how it can slide... My eyes are different. I wanted you to see that for yourself. Can you see?... Please come home with me. I need you! If I go now... if I leave alone... I'll be alone forever. Do you want that? It's time. Let me hear your answer. I need to hear your answer.

STRESS TEST

I don't understand you. Even when you've got nothing to hide, you lie to me. You weren't eating fries with mayonnaise. You don't. You don't eat fries, for fuck sake! You don't even eat mayonnaise. What is the point of that lie? When I catch you out, your next lie is so bizarre, it just makes you ridiculous. What are you doing? What are you doing with me? Am I in a game? I'm clearly losing if I am. Your lies are making you desperate. Is it worth it? That's what I'm asking. What are you getting out of trying to squeeze me into your complicated life? Why over complicate your life? If you don't want me, you could just tell me the truth. All the agitation would go. You could start it all over again with someone else. No? What? Am I some sort of catalyst for your powers of invention? You like improvising away from my attempt at pinning you down? Tell me! Tell me with a single word.

THE ICARUS FISH

I am a shark. Swimming is effortless. It doesn't interest me. I spend my time dreaming. I dream I can fly! I can almost fly. If I did not have to eat, I could fly. My senses are tuned to the clouds. The tiniest changes in air pressure register across my skin. I could ride the up drafts. I could glide into eternity. A flick of my tail and I could jet beyond the curve of the world. UP! I know if I'm soaring too high into the light! I know if I'm plummeting down towards the earth! But it's just dreaming. The only thing that keeps me a prisoner beneath these heavy waves, is my appetite. My pitiless appetite. My insatiable appetite. My hunger. Hunger!

POOR THINGS

I see myself as one of the small balancing forces in nature. I have a pet rat, not a pet rabbit. I'm drawn towards a tumbledown landscape and the neglected in life. I go to unfashionable pubs. I pick the down-at-heel hotels. I buy bargains that are not bargains, in the shops the smart people pass by. I like the rocky part of the beach. I respond to the unloved... orphans, immigrants, the disabled, the decrepit. I like to even things out. Redress the cosmic imbalance. Give a sucker an even break! That's why I started talking to you.

THROUGH A GLASS DARKLY

I people watch. I never mind waiting for transport, because there's the whole world going by to see. Every kind of foolishness—from the fat woman squeezed into Lycra thin clothes—to the pinstriped businessman, whose 18 carat gold cufflinks levitate him above the riffraff. A million kinds of narcissism! Dudes in black leather, too cool to smile. VANITY! Oversized belt-buckles. Padded swagger coats. Full price designer labels. Van-it-tee! Lip-gloss, spray tan, nail-extensions, patterned tights, pre-torn jeans, ponytails, moustaches, tottering shoes, fancy luggage. All saying—I am different, I'm the exception! Normal terms and conditions do not apply to me. I'm better than you. I have given myself the absolute right to make a twat of myself in public... Oh dear! Oh dear and fuck me! I have a far greater conceit. A much more exclusive bid for attention. To make myself invisible and then test your, your —detection.

FAR AWAY EYES

For a long time, I wouldn't touch anything. I was frightened of drugs. Frightened of losing control. But I wanted to lose control. So, I started with what my friends were doing. Es.

Half a tablet. Tab—sounds better! Good. I felt friendly, that's all. Whole tab. Better. I felt loving. Connected. No aftereffects. I've never looked back. It's all lies—everything you've ever heard about drugs. If you're an addict—you're an addict before you start. Whisky! Gambling! Chocolate! Anything! I go to work. I have a steady relationship. I pay for a car and a mortgage. I'm a regular person. The only thing different is that I experience the other half of my brain. I live in the other half of the world. The place where my friends think I'm worth loving.

PRIVATE DANCER

Music takes me out of myself. I spin and I'm beautiful. I kick left and right and nothing is impossible. I'm young. I will live forever. I am the backbeat. I am the soaring guitar. It's a fantasy of sequins and purple tights. It's miming to a hairbrush! But the dance is mine. It's core. It's my secret treasure. Without it I would have no soul. My hip-sway. My pirouette! My leap! Perfect in the moment of doing. Joy. Action. Joy in action! My private step-ball-change. No one can know. No one can see. I dance for myself. If anyone saw me—what a big fat fool with two left feet, and loser written on my forehead! I'd die! Fall flat.

LOSER

I mess up wherever I go. Let people down. Tell the first lie that comes into my head. Don't care enough about the people I care about. Reckless. Unreliable. I break people's good stuff. I drink. I cheat. Steal other guy's girls. Run away in the middle of the night. Do it all again. I pretend to myself that I'm going to fresh start. I cheat on that too! I'll always let myself off the hook. In the centre of my brain is one big EXCUSE! And I'm waiting... I'm waiting... for the one person who will say no. The one person who will not let me climb through a loophole—who will not accept my apology. I'm going a hundred miles an hour, so that I can slam into a brick wall. And STOP! Some people can't do it for themselves. I just can't. You've got to tell me no! A flat final no, with no exceptions. That would be a yes.

FIGURES IN THE DISTANCE

The fish below the mountain have no mountain above their lives. They live in another medium. The goats on the mountain tracks have no fish below their lives. They live high in the air. The goats have no sound for fish. The fish have no signals for goat. The man watching them both can describe what each species is doing. He lives between habitats but has no word for God. He has no name for God because here, (where the water meets the rock), his lover walked out of his life. His lover is in another place where new words are being made. His lover knows the name of God. But she does not know what the man she left behind is feeling. What the man she left behind is thinking. Thinking, because he can see a goat on a mountainside and a fish in shallow water. Then feeling... something in common

1066 AND ALL THAT!

History is the first six Goole listings. If the information isn't in that, you might as well forget it! Who's got the time and patience to look any further? Not the seventeen-year-old interns doing the research for TV and radio documentaries. So, reported history becomes this superficial thin layer of what has already been sanctioned, accepted and used as history before. Then the silly little potboiler, of all the wrong music, fashion, art, war clips, soundbites and events, is broadcast. A second later and it is filed and listed. And it authenticates and endorses all previous errors. The truth is what is repeatedly accepted. Only if you've lived through it can you separate fact from fiction. And even then... well... I've rewritten my youth. I've rewritten my history. It's when you start believing the lies that you should start worrying... Yes, I'm beginning to believe that I've always been a family man.

BESIDE MYSELF

When I play Desdemona, I feel pure and constant. No wrong can touch me because I am sure my innocence will turn away all anger. When I play Kate, I feel quick, alert, proud. I have a fire in my belly. Doused by the end of the play, of course. Completely extinguished! Just a cinder left. When I play Ophelia, I feel such yearning, such empathy. And then confusion. Senseless confusion. When I play Lady Macbeth, I feel fear. As simple as that. Every trespass makes it worse, until the final terror. When I play Juliet, I feel love. Passion! Infatuation. Release. It is beautiful. After the show, when I get home... I feel alone.

A PLACE OF ONE'S OWN

You've no idea what this means to me. Getting this flat. Getting a wee place of my own. To have my own space. To not be in shared accommodation. I can have my own things around me. You've no idea! To go out and come back, and everything's exactly the same as I left it. To put things I like in the fridge. And there they are when I want them. My Pepsi. My Toffee Crisps and Mars Bars. To have my own set of keys. My keys to my front door. That locks! That only lets *me* in. To not be in care. You've no idea what independence is. What it means to me. Thank you.

BARBARIANS

On the school bus there is no one near the driver except me. I'm at his back. The whole bus is full of little mouths making noise. There's a noise like the start of evolution. There's a noise like the excitement of lichen. There's a smell like barnacles. And there's everything standing up and oscillating between. Adolescents between hard plastic seats. The tight uniform and the open uniform. There's every kind of fear and fascination and skin condition. And not a single liar, not a single nutjob, not a single fatso, not a single nonentity, not a single freak, knows how beautiful they are. That's what makes young people exceptional.

ORDINARY MAGIC

There's a suntrap at my back door. I sit on the step. Sometimes I wear shorts. But when I put them on the sun goes in. So, I usually just sweat in my jeans. And sit on the concrete step. And look at nothing much. A bit of lawn. A hedge that needs cut. A garden shed needing creosote. There's nothing doing. Nothing in my head. Just sitting. Sometimes I hear the kids down the street, or a dog barking. But most of the time it's just the sun and me. Some ants maybe. Not a worry in the world. Just the sun and me, like I said. Then I go inside and forget what it was like to be happy.

BEAUTY AND THE BEAST

I'm famous for writing about prostitutes, heroin addiction and violent crime. It sells shitloads. The gorier the better! The more sordid, depressing, prurient and lurid, the more the international sales come in. What I really want to write about is a swan. The way it folds white into itself. But you are sappy if you write about swans. My reputation would crash. I'd go down in flames! I'm sick of decapitation and evisceration. I want to write about a butterfly. A butterfly? How twee. Quaint. Hardly cutting edge. Escapist mush. Sentimental Disney brain-rot. But have you ever looked at a butterfly and not been astonished? A butterfly is really something. I'd have to have an East End villain tear its wings off to fit it into my 'oeuvre.' It's impossible. I'm nasty. I'm not a child. Every word I write is worth crazy money. But I can't describe a butterfly. That's beyond me.

NO DIRECTION HOME

You've been very hospitable. You've tried your best. But I want my own things around me. I want to sleep in my own bed. I want my own scent on the pillow. You've really bent over backwards, but I want to talk with my own friends, even if they're not as clever as yours. I want to be a slob, or sing to myself, or pick my nose, or fart. I don't want to have to share or be on my best behaviour. My home isn't as nice as this. It's small. Lots of stuff doesn't work properly, or there's a knack to how it works that only I know. It's a bit shabby to tell you the truth! But I want to be there so much. So, please don't be offended. It's nothing to do with you—but I just want the freedom to fall asleep on my couch and drool. The freedom to be dull.

WAS IT WORTH IT BLUES

This song is about back breaking labour, starvation wages, layoffs, hunger, forced migration. It's a hard-faced song. In its time it was controversial, revolutionary even. When I sing it now, it sounds romantic. The melody is catchy. The rhythm is hypnotic. It sounds like a golden age of bravery and high principles, when people knew their worth and what they stood for. It sounds like authenticity and real values. Curse poetry! Curse the tunesmiths and the balladeers with sweet guitars! We make pain sound like entertainment. Curse the uselessness of words!

TRICK OF THE HEART

You can tell when someone falls in love with you. You can feel their eyes on you. You can feel their smile on you. Even if you're not interested, you begin to see yourself through their eyes. You begin to pose a little. You steal glances at them, to see if they are watching you—to gauge their adulation. Sometimes you catch their eyes. Sometimes you return a gaze. Now, you are flirting without realising it. Or maybe you do realise it! You're leading them on. You're enjoying yourself. You've got power! Then suddenly, like a sledgehammer, you realise that you've fallen in love! Fallen in love with flattery. Hooked. Damn!

OLD GLORY

When I was a flag, I loved windy days and the smoke of battle. I loved gold thread, bullet holes and promises. I loved absolutes and sacrifice. I was a child flag. I loved danger. I was the bloody flag of adolescence. I loved loyalty. I was the sky-blue flag of freedom. I loved my duty towards freedom. I loved the cause. I was the pure white flag of justice. I loved being a man. I loved honour. I loved the idea. I fluttered with torn edges. I rallied with a scorched corner. I was a rag. From the beginning. I was just a rag. Pull down the rags before you hurt someone!

A CHANGE IS GONNA COME

Because you changed before the times changed, you thought the times would change. You waited. You hoped. You persuaded others to hope. You persuaded others to march and raise their voices. You were a leader. But the times did not change. You stayed changed. The others you persuaded stayed changed. You waited. They waited. You changed back. You lost your hope. They said that you had lost your hope. You said the times were never going to change. Your lack of hope kept others hoping. Hoping that their hope was better than your ex-hope. Then the times did change! The others said that they had always been right.

They said that you were behind the times. They said that you were a danger to the times. You had to change again. You changed again, but not on your terms. Not in the way they wanted. You were history!

VICTIM

I had an enemy. His name was Jack Maddock. We were in the same class at Clevedon Secondary School. Then the same course at university. He just didn't like me. The instant he saw me—he made up his mind—the very first time he heard my voice—that was it! He decided to hate me. He looked right into my face and sneered. I felt like an idiot whenever he was around. I saw myself through his eyes. I was a prat, a twat, an arse, a muppet, a fanny, a wanker, a nob, a bell-end, a total fuckwit and chancer! Then, in my final year at Glasgow Uni, he died in a freak accident on his motorbike. I should've been relieved. My enemy dead. Me alive. Basically, I had won... But I felt terrible. I felt this hole where I had lost something invaluable. Something to measure myself against. I will never get over it... I will never forget that other person. That other person he saw in me.

TO BE OR NOT TO BE?

All my life has been an interruption. I feel I'm about to unblur, about to find a direction, a purpose. Then my brother phones about jump-leads. I'm about to know who I am, when my wife brings home a Garden Centre catalogue. I respond. That's my problem. No time for myself. Birthday friends to remember. Tax demands to challenge. Just when I'm about to bolt into action, an email arrives that requires an immediate humorous response. Humour takes time! Life is an interruption. This is the way it's going to be... Unless I interrupt life. Interrupt it with my direction and purpose. Oh God! Here we go again! Wait! Was that my phone?

THE BEREAVEMENT CARD

What? I can't think of anything... 'With my deepest sympathy'. Just a cliché... 'I'm very sad for your loss'. Sounds like my loss, not your loss. And I'm not sad. I'm heartbroken. 'I'm heartbroken for your loss'. No! That's all about me. 'With heartfelt condolences'... What is a condolence? I don't know what that is! 'I am thinking of you'. I am, but more than that. 'I'm agonising for you'. No. 'I'm distraught'. No. I'm torn apart! I'm destroyed! 'I'm destroyed by her loss'. How is that going to make him feel? Terrible. Can't write that. 'With caring thoughts'. Trite. 'Remember that people who love you are thinking of you'. And some aren't. And how is thinking about you going to help you? Oh shit! 'I will hold her in my memory'. It's a shame I never bothered much with her while she was alive. Hypocrite! What then? 'My heart goes out'— HYPOCRITE!... I'm—sorry? That will have to do... 'I'm sorry'.

THE COST OF LIVING

Stop! I don't resent you. It's not your fault. You are not a burden. Anyone can get ill—get a disease. You are no trouble. I still love you. I will always love you. You haven't ruined my life, that's nonsense. I'm grateful you're still with me—that I've still got you. Don't you know that? Anyone can get MS. It's genetics. You're the same really—inside.

This is where we are now. We've got to accept that... We are still in love... Ah! Why did you do this to me? I wish it had happened to me! I'd rather it happened to me! We are still in love.

THE HEART OF THE MATTER

The real things that don't help me are—polishing my shoes, fixing the dripping bathroom tap, switching to Camomile tea, making a dental appointment, throwing out the packet of mouldy bacon, getting the car in for its MOT, finally getting the white ring off the edge of the coffee table, repainting the nursery, going to the dental appointment. The world is unrelenting. Pressures mount. The unreal things that don't help are, drinking vodka all night, images of babies on a glowing screen, images of holidays and fantasy homes, daydreaming, dreaming, hoping, wishing, praying, taking pills, taking pills with vodka, promising, bargaining with God. The world is unrelenting. Time is unrelenting. Real time doesn't help. Unreal time doesn't help. The pressures mount!

MARVEL

I would love to be Superman. Or, The Mighty Atom! I think he's the one that can run around the world in—like—a split second. I would love it if I had a superpower. I stare out of the window, and dream about it, when the lecturers are droning on. The thing is, I can't think of one. Not a good one anyway. The powers I want are—like—already taken. There already is a Hulk and a Spiderman. The powers I think of are—like—lame! Ability-To-Chat-Up-

Girls-Man! Or, Never-Come-Too-Soon-Man! Not much of an imagination at work there. Maybe that's it, I need the superpower of imagination. If imagination was—like—my superpower—I could imagine anything. I wouldn't have to do anything, cos I could just imagine it… Cool!

THE HISTORY OF MY FINGERS

I served Tamburlaine. I charged the enemy beside Alexander. I raised a sword for Kublai Khan. I drove the chariot of Ramses. I told jokes to Stalin. I massaged the hairline of Hitler when his generals failed. But I came back to your bed. I came back to your face. I came back to the soft dimple on your thigh. My touch was the same to you from morning to evening, from century to century. My comfort was the same, from murder to murder. My fingers don't know names. Sensation is the same for everyone. Your skin is anonymous.

COWARD

Nothing changes I thought. Nothing in my humdrum life will ever change. At work, I dreamt of leaving my husband and kids and flying off to a beach, or a jostling souk, or a mysterious jungle covered temple. You get the idea! Years went by. I margarined my toast. Totalled up the monthly salaries. I said the usual chitchat to the usual people around the clapped-out photocopier. The alarm clock rang at the usual time… Then one day the phone rang. And the next day I woke up and I didn't have a husband, or a family anymore. They were gone. Everything had changed. But I was strong. I went on invoicing, photocopying, taking in traybakes and setting my alarm for seven. I was in that rut, deep, never ending. I couldn't change. I was brave, people said. Brave in the face of loss. I was that brave woman. But I wasn't brave…, I just couldn't change.

WORDS OF LOVE

He's not touchy-feely, lovey-dovey like me. I like to stroke and kiss and cuddle. He loves me but… he isn't a physical kind of person. He is more verbal. He says, I love you, to me. He says it a lot. So, he must mean it. Just doesn't show it. Doesn't show it in his hands, or lips, or body. I think I might prefer the lips and body of someone who didn't love me, but who was generous with his lips and body. Yeh, I'd like someone to share the spontaneous urge to touch with… Someone I didn't have to bother loving.

NOWHERE MAN

I have no opinions about anything. Okay—war is bad, peace is good, love is good, hate is bad, Etc. But when you drill down a bit—some wars seem worth it. Hating some people, like dictators and extremists, seems appropriate. I can see both sides. I'm swayed by opposing arguments. Bad employers—that's wrong. Bad unions—that's equally unacceptable. Charities (with really good intentions), can cause bad unforeseen consequences in poverty-stricken countries. It's messy stuff. Same in my personal life—bad decisions for good reasons. Good, positive decisions—with sad results. I won't go into that! I used to think that I understood every side of an argument because I was intelligent. I was open. I was balanced and reasonable. But my wife tells me that I'm weak and stupid and just don't care. She says, I agree with everyone only because I refuse to be responsible for the consequences of any decisive action... There is something in that.

DOOM

Please don't phone me, or text, or try to get in touch. I will not respond. I have a private grief that does not concern you. I will never get over it. I have finally accepted that there is no God. I have abandoned my faith. There is nothing but the black reaches of space. The Big Bang and the Big Crunch. Random events. Luck. Chaos. Bad luck. You. Me. Transient. The indifference of the cooling universe. A perpetual interface of matter and energy— that's all there is. The survival of the accidental. Our loves and labours futile. Chance. Reproduction. Catastrophe. Death... I believe it. But I don't feel it. I will close the blinds and keep myself indoors. I will express my sorrow quietly, with dignity. (Though dignity is pointless). Though meaning has no meaning. I will wear black and put ashes on my face. I will weep... Weep until the sky falls down. Somewhere else a sky is forming.

AWAKE AND SING!

Everyone you meet has got an interesting story to tell you. What's happened to them. People they met. Places they've been. Places you are never going to get to. And about the funny things that have happened to their family—my face is sore from laughing sometimes. The biggest kick I get in life is just walking down my home street. I always meet

someone I know. People from way back in primary school, or a mate from some job I used to have. People who are pleased to see me. 'Hi Bill, how are you?' Shared history. 'Good thanks, and yourself?'
'Good.'
'Good.'
People who smile when they see you. They smile *because* they see you... Good.

SOUNDBITE

I have an opinion about everything. Immigration. Housing. Taxation. The transportation infrastructure and the need for investment. Ask me and I will give it to you direct. No ifs, buts, or maybes. The EU? My answer is unequivocal. Labour or Conservative? I will tell you in two words. Coronavirus? How long have you got!? But if you ask me how I feel about you... If you ask me to feel... Well, let's just say that you will not get an answer. I can't answer. I'll never be able to answer. Because I feel. Because of the way you make me feel.

CLEAR-EYED BLUES

I switched to the blues after years of rock. Rock is pure raunch and sweaty sex. Rock is attitude! It's pumping, grinding and strutting your funk! A pair of dirty ripped blue jeans is all you've got in the world, but there's thunder in your adolescent heart. A lust for fuckin' life! Eyes wide with coke and glory. Rock 'n' Roll is a hard fantasy to sustain. It gets tougher as every mirror in your house gets older. When you don't see a stud looking back at you any longer, it feels wrong singing, 'hope I die before I get old!' So, I switched to the blues. It's a more realistic take on the world. You can look in the mirror any time and see the bum that you really are staring back. The blues is twelve bars where you sing the same truthful line twice before every chorus.

'Let me be your little dog, till your big dog comes.
Let me be your little dog, till your big dog comes.'

ALADDIN THE MAN

I found this old lamp in some waste ground. When I rubbed it a genie appeared, just like in fairy tales. The genie offered me three wishes. So far, so good! But I'd read a lot of books where that gift goes wrong. Faustus springs to mind. So, I hummed and hawed, trying to think wise and wily... I asked for an infinite number of more wishes! Clever, right?! So, the genie granted me an infinite number of more wishes. Yup! I got what I wished for. I had it. I did it. All of it! I made the genie make me rich, eternally young, gorgeous, of course! Popular and funny as fuck and, and thin, and... After a while, I was just taking the piss. All the things I thought of—they became—more—I don't know—crass—trivial—sordid... I debased myself, came back round for another go! My choices just got smaller, yeh smaller... I became irrelevant and facile. Irrelevant to life. Real life. I wish these wishes would end!

CLASS WAR

It's probably a power thing. Probably because none of P5 listen to me. I teach them all this, rich, fascinating, History —Science—Geography—and it doesn't make them... Their eyes just glaze over. So, in amongst the facts I place a big fat lie. Something that they will repeat with a smug superior look on their faces in later life. And BLAM! They'll be a laughingstock. They'll feel like total thickos! It's probably a revenge thing. 'Henry the 8th actually had a secret 7th wife'! 'Australia isn't technically a continent'. 'The Adams Family was based on a real family in Boston'. Stuff like that. It's probably boredom. 'Nobody has actually sailed around the world single-handed'. 'The Coronavirus came from outer space'! The young are greedy for surprise. They've only got themselves to blame!

WHAT A PIECE OF WORK IS MAN

I love Shakespeare. I love the electricity. The rhythm. The antithesis. The words that contradict and rush away from each other. They go in opposite directions but are held in the mind, in the heart, in the soul, by a single sentence. I love the sun and moon of Shakespeare. I love the promise and the waste of Shakespeare. I love the single ambition and the conflict of nations. I love that wisdom and stupidity speak out of the same mouth. I love that time expands and time contracts during a conversation. I love that time skips and time pounces according to the measures of hurt and love. I love Shakespeare. I love Shakespeare because he loves everyone no matter how wicked they are.

STRESS FRACTURE

It's impossible! I can't think straight! I can't keep running round to Granny May's. She's going to have to move in here. And I haven't got the space. God! I'm not putting her in a home. Nina's her daughter. That mother-in-law of mine, needs to shift herself up from London and her fancy man, and take a good look at the state of her own mother. My mother can't lift a finger with her MS. I've got her on my hands too! And my twins, with their autism and bad friends. Don't listen to a word I say. Now my Greg's being made redundant after twelve years. His face is tripping him. He's on pills and whisky. Great! Knock yourself out! Like that's going to help! I keep getting these migraines. It's stress, says Greg. It's not stress. It's— I'm fucked! That's what it is. My life is fucked! A total right-off. I'm not stressed. I have no future. I'm fucked! That's what stress is! Without my family I'd be fine. My family are killing me.

LOVE AND PHYSICS

I don't believe in love. Passion? Yes, I could make a fair stab at describing that. Longing, a bit of a favourite of mine. Yearning is even better. It hurts even more. But it is a little too poetic for today's taste. Union? I know what that is. Had that—briefly. I've had a lot of the love words actually. Not done too badly, all things considered. Desire, infatuation, delight, joy. Mad bonkers crazy delirium! Quiet trust and good conscience. Been there, done that. But love? Pure, untrammelled, unadulterated, unshakeable, undying love? There is no such thing! Love is a composite. It's a fusion of opposites. It's elation and hurt squished together. It's unstable. Can't stay that way for long before it collapses in on itself. Becomes a Singularity.

LET THE SUN SHINE

I don't want a big fancy expensive car. I don't want a mansion to rattle about in, with servants feeding me caviar, under crystal chandeliers. I just want the winter to end and the clouds to part. I want the sun to shine on me. I want the sun to shine on my face. So that when I close my eyes I can see it lighting my blood. The sun makes me happy. It costs nothing. It feels like a blessing. The sun is everything. A gift that wants nothing in return.

ONLY CONNECT

I want to blast off like a rocket! Roar! Zoom up into the vast black sky. Burst into a million blinding razor-sharp lights. Scarlet! Amber! Orange! BOOM! Because I'm young. Because I feel brilliant! I've got that special thing—the special-factor. It's pumping through my veins. It's got nowhere to go. It's keeping me awake all night. What am I going to do with it? Something must be done. Outside it's all grey, dull, drippy, ordinary and the total opposite of special. I can't live here. I've got to take off in a vapour trail. I've got to connect. I've got to connect with someone sunny like me. Now! Now before the drab world gets me. Now, before I get lazy and tired and sleepwalk through life. There must be someone with their bedroom light on, even in this timid little slipper shuffling town. I'm all *now*! It has to be now. Now, or I'll start to die. NOW!... Please... Now...

OUT OF IT

Throw both suitcases in the sea. Let wild things empty your coat pockets. Give the sun your watch to smash between rocks. The pine trees will be all you need of a memory. Now is not a part of time. Rip the mask from your body. Your skin is a track in the water and a spread of light. Let the mask sink out in the darkest water. Empty yourself. Purge. Those scars will always be unfinished. Shed what defined you. You can be the future without a mask. Turn your back on what you leave behind. I will be fine. I'll be all right eventually. You'll be different. Raw at first but you will have the rest of the world to love.

MIDNIGHT CHOIR

I get drunk because I'm not sociable and drink makes me talk.

I get drunk because I'm frightened of my lethargy and wine gives me energy.

I get drunk because I must fill every pause, hesitation, silence.

I get drunk because I have to pretend to be happy to spend time with you, and a double helps me twice as much.

I get drunk so that you don't feel threatened.

I get drunk to remove all pretence at beginnings, middles and endings.

I get drunk to give you a story to tell your friends.

I get drunk to undermine your control of the occasion.

I get drunk to remove you from my memory.

RIVALS

The thing about us is that I know I'm better than you, but you keep doing better than me. I should be doing better than you, because I am better than you. I'm smarter. I've got better taste. I've got more skills. I've got more interests. I know more stuff. I tell better jokes! I have better parties. But the better people go to yours. That's what I can't forgive. The injustice of it. The injustice of how you look. You look better than me. And that's just luck. Just a roll of the genetic dice. I've got imagination, energy, focus and you —you've got high cheek bones! I can't stand it! Life should be fair. I cannot cannot stand it! I will not stand it! I have to even up the balance. The only way it can be done is to kill you. You see my logic. It's entirely sensible. I must win. Even looking like this. I am determined, totally determined to win.

PLEASE MR. POSTMAN

Every year I get three valentine cards. One from my wife Claudia. One as a joke from my brother. He thinks it's hilarious. And a pity card from Aunt Isobel. But I have this secret fantasy that one day the postman will deliver another envelope. An envelope with unfamiliar handwriting and with a mysterious heady scent. Inside a pressed rose, and a confession of undying love. A tear stained pledge of insatiable yearning from a secret worshiper. Every year I give one card. And I wonder, as I open Claudia's card, and read my wife's endearments, if she is dreaming of receiving a card from someone, a friend perhaps, someone I might already know… Or… a total stranger.

CHARM OFFENSIVE

I'm sorry to ask, but I just want you to be with me when he comes. I don't want to be alone with him. The way he talks —he's so persuasive. When I listen to him, I feel, I can see, I... I can understand how he sees it. And I can tell how hurt he is. The more he speaks, he's so good with words, I find myself—I must do what he says. His voice just makes me do it. My brain stops working. I can't breathe! I can't argue with him. My legs just obey him and take me out the door, and I'm back home before I realise what's happening to me. I can't resist him. He won't stop talking until I am back under lock and key. He knows I will go. So, please, perhaps if you were here, when he—If you said something now and then—interrupted him. I'd hear your voice instead of his, and his spell would be broken.

FEAR

Last week I was walking alone in a forest. I was high up when suddenly there was an opening and a sheer drop. Below me the forest stretched for as far as I could see, spread into the distance. A cold fear ran up from the ground and entered my belly. It became panic. I turned and ran down the hill as fast as I could go... And I remember being on holiday, on one of the Greek islands—Zante. Lying on a beach and looking up at the sparking night sky. I expected to see frozen beauty. I expected to feel expansion and pleasure without boundaries. But the sky was too black, wide and there were too many stars without any rules. Multitudes of indifference. Volumes of silence, an infinity of energy moving without me. I felt horrified. I had to look away... It is not forests, or stars I am frightened of. It is immensity. Random uncontrolled immensity!

SELF IMAGE

She's beautiful! Simply that. From any angle. Beautiful. Stunning. I'm stunned. And she's chosen me. Wants to be with me. Forever! Loves me. She says she loves me. Sometimes I think someone's put her up to it. That it's some kind of a joke. I can't believe she'd fall for me. I keep looking into shop windows, mirrors, puddles—trying to see what she sees. What? Where is it? She calls me the loveliest man on Earth. She calls me her Mr. Universe! Her Prince Charming. I don't see it. She's in love with someone else. Who is he?

BOND

He said he had a skull ring and a Phantom costume. So, I walked home with him to his backyard. I climbed the tree he pointed to and waited. He came back pretending to be The Phantom. Standing with legs wide and fingers shoved into his little brother's black leather gloves. The same black school trousers but now he had a big plastic belt-buckle. He'd changed his white short sleeves for a black T-shirt. Climbed up to me trying to imitate the Phantom's super-stealth agility. One hand trying to hold his joke shop mask in place. He wasn't The Phantom. Nothing like him! But I was impressed by his dedication. He wasn't a hero, or a mate, but he had a skull ring. And I was impressed. Not by the fraud. But the effort he went to, for me—that was the best thing. That was something.

LITTLE ZEPPELIN

Just drums. Just rhythm and I can't soar. So, it's more drink and pounding authority. Pounding bass. Pounding bass explaining my history. Making it physical. Centuries of attitude. Centuries of sunglasses. And right now, on the 4/4 beat. That's how I feel. That's my signature. That's my spine. No high hat. No cowbell, no tambourine. Just the bass. Forever! Over the top, my falsetto explaining everything. My falsetto rising from the deep. Making it vibrate. And necessary. Boom! Bang! Bang! Bang! BOOM!

CUSTOMER SERVICES DEPARTMENT

They bring things back that have obviously been used. They wear a fancy dress to a wedding, dance about a bit, with big sweaty armpits, then return it the next day They don't even bother to wash it! And they expect their money back. Disgusting! I've seen ripped bras. I've seen jeans with a variety of unsavoury stains at the crotch. Underwear with skid marks! You wouldn't believe it. Then you get the craftier ones. Soap rubbed on a dirty hem, patches of white wine still drying on a red wine stain. The clothes are ruined! Low life scumbags the lot of them! Well, I tell you, it might say Customer Services Department above my head, but they are not customers. They are cheats. No one cheats me! I make sure that my loud refusal causes the maximum offense.

CONVERSATION STARTER

You don't ask me any questions. We don't have a conversation. You talk about yourself. You want me to listen to you? You have to do a little listening yourself. That's how interaction works. It goes like this. I say—'Hi, how are you?' And instead of telling me all the details, you say—'Fine. How are you?' Then I say something like, 'I had a rotten day at work'. And you say—'What happened to you?' And off we go—my turn, your turn. Turn and turnabout. It's called *manners*. There, you've learned something today! It's going to benefit you for the rest of your life. You're going to need it because I'm leaving you. I've met someone else. We fell in love through talking with each other at work. No—don't ask! No questions. This is not the time. You are way too late!

EXTINCTION

I like to shoot things. The best things to shoot are big things that move slowly. When they come down the earth shakes. You can feel the importance of what you've done through your boots. After I've travelled a long way it feels even better. I'm not interested in rare beasts. I don't want to kill the last of a species. I want to kill stuff that's easily replaced. Heavy creatures. Bang! A bellow, a cloud of dust, then a thunderclap in the ground. Makes me feel like I've achieved something when the earth answers... BANG!

TRANSLATIONS

I'm like Yeh! That's my personality. And I met this guy and he was like—Yeh! too. It was brilliant. I saw the Yeh! in him and he saw the Yeh! in me. So, we'd be like Yeh! together all the time. YEH! It was unbelievable. It was so fun. 'Yeh! honey'. 'Yeh! babe'. YEH! Then, we were in a club dancing, I noticed his Yeh! was like, well, it was well, Yeh! It had a different vibe. Can't really describe it. But I was like, Yeh! and he was like Yeh! And once I noticed the difference, it didn't feel like he was really a Yeh! person at all. He was pretending to be Yeh! but he was really—Yep!... Not really me. So... yeh.

WORKING GIRLS

I get in my Nissan on a Friday night and I drive past the prostitutes. My headlights make them two dimensional. Sexless, easy to reject. I go around the block and slide by them again. They want me. They don't want me. I drive on. I take the corner. I come back. They are rotting green, they are putrescent yellow. They lean into my side window and talk low. That's not the price. No way! I shift gears and go round another time. Not one I've seen before. They are purple under the concrete motorway supports. They're a hundred years old, they're fifteen! I drive. I loop round. They are livid crimson, laughing. There she is. She's the one! I accelerate, I circle. There she is again! Not yet. Another time. Another time. I fill the car with Super. I spend the whole night rejecting prostitutes. Rejecting what I want to be.

FEEDBACK

You need to change your attitude. You need to get on board, give something back. You need to read that famous Kipling poem, 'If'. You know the one—'if you can keep your head when all about you are losing theirs'—that one. It's not called, 'So What!' It's not called, 'Whatever!' Or, 'Who the Fuck Cares?!' Listen... 'If you can dream and not make dreams your master.' How good is that! Unfortunately, you dream about *being* the master. Everything you do is self-serving, lazy. You are at the mercy of Triumph and Disaster, not the other way around. If you wrote a poem, it would be called, 'What's in It for Me?' If you wrote a poem, it would be called, 'Wipe My Arse for Me'! Not that there is any chance of you writing a poem— that would be too much like hard work!

INTERIM REPORT

The opposite of freedom is not imprisonment. I'm not in prison. The opposite of freedom is not knowing what to do with freedom. The opposite of happiness is not grief. I am not grieving. The opposite of happiness is the constant struggle for happiness. The opposite of man is not woman. The opposite of woman is not man. The opposite of madness is not sanity. The opposite of kindness is not being mean, or selfish. It is not being able to accept other people's generosity. The opposite of loneliness is not company. The opposite of loneliness is becoming a friend to yourself. The opposite of love is not hate. The opposite of love is taking all the love and giving nothing back. I have come to understand these things, after not understanding these things. I have no opposite.

GOODNIGHT PILGRIM

You thought you were a pilgrim. You had to travel on your knees to distant churches. You circled sacred monuments in the direction of prayer. You carried torches up mountainsides to echoing caves. You hauled crosses across deserts towards half constructed arches. You thought you were on a spiritual journey. You thought you had to atone. It was important to suffer. You took your clothes off in rivers. You put on white robes under dusty domes... You thought you were a pilgrim. But you were just a traveller without a camera. You were just a tourist without a hotel. Pilgrims do not carry credit cards.

PLACES OF WORSHIP

Fear built the temple. Fear gave it an arch, or a dome, or a minaret. Fear put a prayer inside. Fear spoke in unison and in choirs, to sound less afraid. Fear made music to drown out the screams. Fear put on incense and perfume to offer itself as a balm, an antidote, a consolation prize. Fear became calligraphy to confuse and instruct confusion. Fear became a celebration, that's how sly fear grew. Fear became a parade, that's how bold fear swelled. Fear became a special day of gifts for family and friends, that's the pleasure fear gave. Fear became a ritual meal for loved ones, that's how fear slipped inside. Do not be afraid!

THE DECEIVERS COMPARE THEIR DECEPTIONS

I'm a spider. I make webs. I mend webs. I spin and wait. You admire the industry. The pattern makes you wonder.

You're amazed by my genius. How my arse makes something wonderful. Then you break it! Break it so easily. Just a wave of your hand. The lifting of a finger. Beauty ripped down. You do it because traps shouldn't be obvious. Shouldn't be hung out in public spaces. You like your traps hidden. Hidden in kitchens between the condiments. Hidden in phone calls. Hidden in bedrooms between super soft pillows. Hidden in jewellery boxes and between the clothes on their hangers. Your traps are more deadly. I eat my prey to survive. You kill the ones you love only because they dare to love you.

HIGHEST COMMON DENOMINATOR

I don't go to zoos anymore. I didn't feel particularly special being human when I watched the monkeys. And all the effort I put into being a homo-sapiens—the restraint, the co-operation, the acts of kindness—didn't seem like anything specifically unique to me. I stopped watching monkeys. To boost my self confidence, I tried animals further down the evolutionary ladder. The mammals were a no-go area. Every interaction was just like someone in my dysfunctional family. Same watching parrots, flamingos, and penguins. I was reduced to staring at lizards, newts, snakes and crocodiles. But even there, eventually... eventually... I saw that every individual had a personality. Everything they did—moving—eating—was an expression of who they were. Just like me. Zoos make me feel like just another genetic variation. I don't have children... no genes being passed on. I can't go to zoos anymore. I can't look out a window.

THE VOICE OF REASON

I'm an idiot. I can't learn anything. I'm a fool! A simpleton!
A nitwit! A dolt! A dork! A dumbo! A dumb ass! A
dickhead! Nothing goes in. I can't think. Nothing comes
out. I can't remember. I'm a div! I'm a moron! No one asks
me to do anything. No one expects anything of me.
Brilliant!

A MENACE TO SOCIETY

He had a chip on his shoulder, an axe to grind, a bee in his
bonnet, a bug up his ass! He was a very busy person. Loved
winding people up. Thin skinned. Quick to take offence.
Ugly. Nasty. Lash out with his fists soon as look at you,
then stamp on your face. A real mean rat. He picked a fight
with me. I tried to find a way out of it. But he was for it, no
matter what. My mates tried to push me back and usher me
out the bar. But something clicked in my head and I
decided—no! I'm going to teach you a lesson you will never
forget. So, I hit him with the snooker cue. He went straight
down and never got up. Turned out, he was fostering three
kids and had a wife who loved him. Who could've known?

USELESS GIFTS

I discovered I had a gift. A supernatural gift. I became
aware of it in primary school. The girl I sat next to. Mia,
well she was funny but she was fat. So, Zoe made her life a
misery. She was in it to torment. Mia cried and wished her
little bitch of an enemy dead. I wished her wish, and Zoe
was dead. I just needed to wish that same wish. Wish the

wish for Mia. And—woosh! Heart attack, I think they said it was. I did hundreds of other people's wishes after that. I cured some cancer cases. Won the lottery for people. Gave infertile women babies. Kept it subtle to avoid attention. I did it for people I loved. You'd think I would be happy, doing all these good things for good people. But right from the start, all my life—all I've wanted, was to make my own wishes come true. That's why I'm bitter, bad—fucked up! That's why I will not help you… I have finally realised, there is nothing in it for me.

MISTRESS PLEASURE

We do it my way, or buddy, you can hit the highway, understand? A hotel. Never in your place. Lights on the whole time. No kissing. You will shower for twelve minutes first. The water will be as hot as you can stand. I will supply you with the correct bodywash, shampoo, deodorant and cologne. If you have any hair, down there, I will shave you. I will provide the condoms. I will be on top the whole time. No appliances. No attachments. No gags. No masks. No manacles, or restraints. No rough stuff. No funny stuff with soft fruit, or food. No recording equipment, or photography. No moaning, no chitchat, dirty talk, screaming, or calling out of names. If I hear a sound out of you—it's over! Got it? No anal. No oral. No water-sports. Definitely no farting and no sweating. Start any of that and you are gone gone gone! After I come, and I will come— no conversation, no holding, no cuddling. You will shower immediately and then you will leave quickly and quietly. Agreed? Lovely. Right. Let's do it!

SMILEY FACE

I don't want to jinx it. I know we haven't been seeing each other—going together long... but do you think it's been going not too badly? I think it's been going well, quite well. Pretty well, don't you think? I mean, a couple of, err, minor, err, crossed wires, blips at the beginning. But the beginning's always the trickiest when two people are—don't you think? Not that I've had many—beginnings that is! So, what I'm saying is, this is fun—us. And I think we should just take a moment to—err—appreciate the moment, the situation. Not the situation, there's no situation. Because otherwise, I mean you never realise you're happy, do you? Not till afterwards—when you look back—when it's gone. Not that I think this'll disap—will go! I'm not saying—No, well, who knows what'll happen in the future—but not for me. I'm happy here and now—with you. I just wanted to tell you. Because, because it's rare, I think, to know you're happy when you're experiencing it. As you're actually experiencing the happiness. Know what I mean? I just wanted to acknowledge us being happy. Savour it. Live it—together. That okay? You're happy, aren't you?

DISCIPLINARY PROCEDURE

I need to have a word with, a discuss—a chat. We need to have a chat. Your work here—well, how are you feeling about your work? Would you regard your—rate your work —any part—aspect of your work as, err, satisfactory? Good even, or excellent, or poor—unsatis...? How do you think you're doing? Progressing? I mean, for instance, your communication skills? I've had, I've heard—there have been complaints. Well not exactly com—more concerns from people. Work colleagues, area reps—managers in

207

other departments. You must know—feel—be aware, that you are not pulling your—not exactly focused on your... Is there something in your home, in your personal life, circumstances perhaps, that you wish—need to tell me?

GRAMMAR

I can't take you seriously. It's not you, it's the way you speak. You say, 'I seen it.' You say, 'I seen her'. Makes you sound, well, it's incorrect. 'I done it', is just wrong. Is that what you read in newspapers, books and magazines? Don't you watch the news? Do the newsreaders say that the Prime Minister 'has came from Downing Street?' No! And neither do they say 'we wish youse goodnight'. So why aren't you picking it up? The rest of us are using a different code. A code that contains secret information about success. Your code is different. It contains secret information too, but about—. It tells me you don't know right from wrong. It tells me you're not listening. It tells me that you think the way I speak is the big mistake! ...Is this a fight?

WRONG SIGNALS

When we were splitting up there were times that I thought we might get back together. Just moments of, of—kindness, I suppose. Just little decisions we had to take about stuff, after being together for so long. We could've made it difficult for each other. And we chose not to... because... Moments when I felt we were moving closer again. Tender. That's when I asked her—I don't know what possessed me! I asked her what her favourite time was—when we were together. What her favourite moment was.

She seemed surprised. She looked me straight in the eye. Well, since you asked—I didn't like any of it, she said. Not a minute, not a second—not any of it. Nothing.

CHILLAX

I used to be energetic and run around like mad, doing six things all at once. God, did I get on everyone's tits! Then I broke my leg and had to lay it up for a couple of days. The pain killers made me catnap all afternoon. When I woke up, there was a cup of tea, a chocolate biscuit, or a piece of cake. That was the turning point. I got better quickly but hid it. Carpets got vacuumed. Meals got made, dishes got washed. When I went back to work, my work had been done. What's not to like? From then on, I did as little as possible. It takes no time at all before people don't expect you to be up to much. They tackle all the problems, the dilemmas, the family squabbles, the friends in crisis, by themselves. So, I end up blameless. A friend to all sides. I guarantee there would be less strife and misery in the country if everyone was lazy. Make the world a safer place. Try laziness. You'll enjoy it. It's a win-win situation

CURSE

The preschool teachers say nothing. He plays with the other kids. They seem to like James well enough. Nothing wrong with his brain. He eats. He sleeps. He's normal, but he's not! I thought his granny noticed it, but she looks away when I catch her eye. When I try to approach the subject, she suddenly finds she's got something urgent to do, has to hurry away. Today the way he looked at me and spoke to me! I immediately got it. Now I know what it is... In his heart there is a splinter of ice. Sharp and cruel. He knows it's there. He hides it. He thinks I don't know. But very soon, any day, he's going to realise that I know his secret. When he knows I know—then what will he do? What will he do to me?

ALMOST GROWN

Buy me toys! I'm an adult who struggles with wanting to be an adult. I'm an adult who wants to play with other adults. I'm an adult who can't yet whistle. I'm an adult body in a child's imagination. I'm an adult with no imaginary friend. Come and buy me toys! I'm an adult who doesn't want a bank account and a mortgage. I am an adult—that's the whole problem! I've never wanted to be. I've never wanted to be. I've never wanted to be me, here, now, with these debts, with this family... Buy me a toy! I never wanted to work. I never wanted to earn a living. I never wanted to be a parent.

SEIZE THE DAY!

My parents are waiting for me to get a real job.
My parents are waiting for me to find a real woman.
I'm waiting to find a real life, with real love, and real parents.
I'm waiting to stop believing that life is a rehearsal.
I'm waiting to hear from the real me.
Soon. Any day now... Soon... Sometime... Now!

EASY

This is the world... This moment of torpor when the soul falls into gratitude for blazing summer. There's pleasure in allotment wallflowers and in well painted eves on a smug little house. There's bliss in sun-struck windscreens. Lassitude on the High Street. Fatigue and sensuality in the bungalow crazy paving... Sweat merges the atoms of my body with the atoms of the sun-lounger. If only the material world was all there was, I could be happy. All it would want was my body. And my body would be everything. All of me... Easy.

THE ARC OF THE SUN

Sunlight on my swimming costume. Sunlight on my plastic picnic plate. Sunlight on my belly. Sunlight between my fingers. Sunlight on my birthmark. Sunlight on my tiny teeny hairs. Sunlight on my blue veins. Sunlight on my sex appeal. Sunlight on my legend! Sunlight moving down my crossed ankles. Summer shifting a trail of faint clouds away from the sun. Sunlight moving across sandcastles and children's legs. Summer moving the clouds back again. Summer stranded in the overcast grey north. Summer stuck with a used-up friendship. Summer slumped with an idle pair of expensive sunglasses.

REALITY CHECK

I can't get work. I really can't. I've been on courses. I've retrained and re-skilled. I've volunteered. I've begged. Yes, you heard! But I got zero. Nada. Zilch! So, I did it all again.

Brown nosed. Asked friends for favours. Re-begged. I know you don't believe me. There's just something about me that isn't credible, isn't there? People don't really see me, or hear me, or hold me in their thoughts. There's something lacking. I'm not fully present the way that other people are. I don't have status, or gravitas, or some mystery ingredient. I'm not really real to other people. I've learned to live with it. I've come to accept it... I am not really real to myself.

THINK TWICE TO MAKE IT RIGHT BLUES

This is a song about loving and leaving. About taking what you want and then never bothering to say goodbye. Careless fornication with a beautiful fox who falls in love with you at first kiss, but who you cast aside for the freedom of the highway. This is a song about a cheap hotel night of love making, that promises a future with a girl who will cherish you, heal you, and be your faithful soulmate. A girl you abandon without regret as the dawn arrives. And I want you to ask yourself, why do you want me to sing you this song? What does it say about you and your values?

MASKS

What do girls get ready for? All my teenage and adult life, I've waited for them to dress, or put on their makeup. I have the feeling that none of the preparation was done for me. I would be happier with a shabbier woman who was on time, if she was shabby for me. Is it for a tall dark stranger who will sweep her off her espadrilles, into a life of glamour modelling and danger? Are they planning on intimidating other women? Are they inventing another persona who enjoys life without family, or memory? Perhaps women don't really know what they are getting ready for. Perhaps it's a genetic code that makes them get ready as slowly as they can. Perhaps it's a secret ritual to defy age and ugliness. I don't have any more time to waste. I am ending my wait. I am going on my own!

RAGU

Cooking for your friends is one of life's great pleasures. The smell of garlic frying in extra virgin oil! The smell of chopped onions turning golden! A crimson chilli split in two on the chopping board. Then the sweet flesh so finely sliced it bleeds red juice. The *tizzz!* as you add it to the pan. Sauté. And a little glass of Shiraz to sauté you. Add the green and yellow peppers in their stripes of primary colours. Mix into a crazy flag of all nations. Have another little sip. Sauté! Add the peeled plum tomatoes. Mash them in until the whole broth shimmers and the surface globs and spurts, and crusts and clings. Take a slug. Sauté! Civilization in a pan. A lovely lumpy syrup. A meal for old friends who arrive in a roar. Hugs! Kisses! And then, well, it's kinda—kinda—downhill from then on.

ABUSE

I must be a terrible person. A horrible person. Vile. Making him want me. Making him aroused. Making him hit me. I must have something wrong with me. I'm depraved! He doesn't want to hurt me. I make him so angry. I make him lose control. Why do I do that to him? How can I love him, if I do that to him? He's so sorry after—I can see the pain in his face. He cries. It's terrible. How can I hurt him like that, if I love him? I must be cruel. Wicked! He's got to beat it out of me. So that I can love him with all of my heart. Totally. Give myself to him. With all my heart. With all my heart. That's what he wants. With all my heart! I don't think—I don't feel—I don't... have a heart. It was punched out of me... I can't give him what has gone... What will I do?

TIGHT AS

I am an octopus. I have eight strong arms to wrap around the world and everything in it. I will take the world apart until I find you. Until I find your secret place. Your secret cave. Your secret crevice. You cannot hide. I can slide into the smallest gap. There is no escape. Once inside I will embrace you with irresistible force. I will leave when I have taken eight things from you...

BACK STAGE BIG TOP

Backstage clowns are surly fuckers. Their mouths turn down. They curse their fate to have to earn their living under a big top by throwing buckets of confetti at each other. They clench their fists in anger. Their swearing turns the air blue. They throw punches at each other. How can they be funny in this world of cold-eyed atrocity? In this world of casual betrayal. How, when body parts are exploded over the marketplace and drip between the neat rows of sweet potatoes and aubergines, can they find a grin? That's my job! I'm the dressing room clown. I never go beyond the red velvet curtain. I'm the one that pokes fun at their long faces. I'm the one that offers a handshake of condolence and gives an electric shock. I'm the one that banishes hopeless lethargy with a dropped banana skin. You don't know my name. But I get the clowns ready to go on. For services to comedy, I'm the one you should applaud.

HIDDEN AGENDA

I thought I married her because she was so positive, so vital —a generous spirit, funny, hardworking and really really caring. I thought I married her to love her and support her and—celebrate her. But I realise now, that I married her to undermine her, to chip away at her confidence and to crush her love-of-life until she felt like me… I realise now that I have succeeded in everything I attempted. Succeeded way beyond what I could have hoped for… What the fuck have I done?!

LOVESICK

I love you but you make me feel uncomfortable. I love you but I feel threatened intellectually by you. I feel tense physically when I'm around you. I'm uneasy when you look at me. I love you so much, but when you come into the room, when you ask me a question, my heart pounds. When you touch me, I feel I'm going to pass out. So, for the good of my—for health reasons, I think we need to relax a little, to give me time to, to adjust to you. I'm not breaking it off. Don't think that! I just need to chill, to take some pills—see a doctor, or something, before we get too, err, you know—together. So, let's take some time out—to breathe. I can't believe I'm saying this. I feel like I'm going to faint—have a stroke! Oh God! I've got to go. Sorry! I'm going to be sick. Sorry!

RUNAWAY

If you don't come back, I'm going to kill myself. If you don't love me, I don't want to live. If I can't have you in my life, I don't want anything else. I'm going to park on the level crossing, wait for the coal train to come roaring through. Then you'll be sorry. I'll be dead and it'll be your fault! I'll be dead because you didn't love me. Couldn't even try to love me one little bit. My body will be mangled in the wreck and it will be all down to you. You did it, you killed me! Everyone will know. Everyone will blame you. How can you live with yourself, doing that? You can't! So, my life is in your hands. Only you can save me. You can save my life. You can. You can love me. You can do it... Murderer!

THE MAN WHO WASN'T THERE

I didn't see it coming. Chis hid his dirty doings perfectly. Which makes me wonder if I ever knew him properly. Did he have deceit and cunning in him when I married him? Or did I make Chris crafty like that? How can you live with a person for fifteen years and not really know him? I'm not unobservant. I'm not stupid! Who did I have two children with? Who did I comfort when his business went belly up? Who did I celebrate with when his mother paid for us to have a holiday in the Algarve? And, and then when his mum... I dried his tears in the hospital. Chris was sick himself—I dressed him and washed his shitty pyjamas. We laughed together... all the time. Was Christopher

216

pretending? I don't know who that was. Was he just hiding in his lair, waiting until the right woman wandered by? I can't sleep...The man I married was Christopher Mason. My husband still has the same name. But that can't be right. Where did the good Christopher Manson go? My husband has the same name but the man has gone.

THE BIG PICTURE

I can't sleep. I'm concerned about global warming, hair loss, another virus and economic meltdown. A possible lump in my groin. I'm all over the place. Wired! Blood pressure to the max. I stay up all night fretting about the damage to our atmosphere. I'm biting my nails. I'm shedding patches of skin. I'm twitching. Desertification. That's a threat. My allergy to wheat. That's more of a threat! Suicide bombers. I try to care. I have an eye infection. That's real! Child soldiers. I am shocked in theory. But my paper cut cancels out all wars—all the killing in my name. The seam in my lip tears—it's really sore! Armies collide. I don't care. My ankle twists. I do care! Nations divide. So what? What happens to other people is important, but my body comes first.

DR. FEELGOOD

When animals scratch an itch, they get relief, like you and me. But when you and I scratch an itch, we also get pleasure. Why not animals? What you see on the face of a bear, or a caribou, or a lion, is more than just the end of irritation. It is undiluted pleasure. And if animals can feel pleasure, it makes them more like us. Sentient. Aware of pleasure. Able to feel good about themselves. That's why

I'm not going to eat them. That's why I'm becoming vegetarian. Because I can see the chicken, the cow, and the pig, smiling when they scratch. They love themselves. How can you take that away? No one should kill the love for life.

CHILD PRODIGY

My three-year old is a genius. She comes out with some amazing, I mean amazing—stuff. 'Why aren't things mine?' was one of her earliest. I took more notice after that. 'Why is the sea there?' How can you answer that? I write them down in a book now. 'Why don't dogs purr?' Maybe she'll grow up to be a philosopher. But the best was last Tuesday morning. She was in her pushchair. It was a lovely day, remember? She looked up at me, with those piercing eyes of hers and, out the blue, she just came out with—'Why am I?' Not, why was I born, or, why am I here? Not why am I a girl? No! No, it was deeper. It's strange, isn't it? It's deep. 'Why am I?'... 'Why am I?' I've been thinking about it every day. Can't get it out of my mind. Why am I? How can a child ask that? Why am I, I? It makes me so sad. It breaks my heart... Why... am... I?

DIZZY

What made me behave like that? Giggling high with another voice. Dancing wild with vegetables and furniture. Falling. Saying things instantly, no hesitation. Staying up all night sitting on wet grass, with an empty bottle between us. Putting every star in place above the city park. Why did I tell the truth last night? Why no feelings of regret? Why no hangover? How did I manage to be funny, hysterical? I'm still smiling. Why do I remember every detail? When did I become observant? Sensitive? What is this? I can't stop smiling. I rang the number he gave me, and it rang. It was the real number. It was the actual number. What is this? What is happening? What is happening to me? It's happening to me. I will never stop smiling.

IT AIN'T ME BABE

I can't feel rain these days.
I can't feel good about holidays.
I can't find the beat on a dance floor.
I can't avoid dog shit on the pavement.
I can't buy new trousers.
I can't get money out of a cash machine.
I can't get drunk on red wine
I can't shave my pubes.
I can't tell my left from my right.
I can't make love lying down.
I can't recognise my signature.
I can't love the obvious.
I can't hate the hateful.
I can't return your gaze.
I can't give you what you want.
I can't love your love.
I can't remember your promise
I can't stay constant.
I can't stay here.

RAPE

I'm giving you a let out. You don't have to be the world's best boyfriend anymore. Top marks to you! But I'm not going to improve. I'm not going to get over it. It's not a thing you get over. What happened to me was—I can't even say the word. I can't even use its proper name... So, you and I? Yeh, what about that? It is not going to happen. I'm sorry. Damaged goods. You're a nice guy, of the normal variety. Time to let me go. Find a normal girl. This hurt isn't your hurt. This paranoia isn't your business. I'm busy! I've got an angry crowd in my head demanding attention. Blame, guilt, self-recriminations—they are all in there! But you are not included. I've got plenty of company! Grief and Fury are my lover boys now! You're too soft for me Michael. You're too far away, in the nice world.

STD

Well, it was, err... a kind of generalised uncomfortable kind of—aah, an itch, at first. Down there! I didn't pay it much attention. But then, when I looked, it looked a bit red. I was worried, not worried, just a bit uneasy. Well, it's been red before, quite frankly. But it played on my mind. So, I kept looking at it with my desk-lamp, right up close. It was a rash. Then, with the rash there were these spots. On the— you know where. And they joined up, got bigger. I thought I could detect a smell from—that area. Then the spots began to... err, kind of, err—leak. Sorry. Sorry. So, I went to the Doc. Girding my loins, so to speak! And, well, what I'm saying is that, I have probably given it to you.

DISAPPOINTMENT

No one has ever asked me to carve her initials on a tree. No one has wanted my name on their arm. No girl has wanted me inside her. Wanted me in her mouth. Best not to think about that! Turn on the television. It's more than a diversion. It's an alternative to disappointment. No woman has ever imagined me naked. There are some things that cannot be compensated for. Time makes it worse.

BABY LOVE

I wanted to be homeless. The landlord threw me out! I wanted to be an orphan. And then my parents committed suicide! I wanted to be tragic. An ambulance crashed into me at a roundabout! I wanted to be fucked. I was fucked by a total fucker! I wanted to be wasted. I wanted to bottom out. I wanted the clock to stop. I achieved everything except death. I achieved everything I wanted. When you've achieved everything you wanted, you would think wanting would stop. When you've achieved everything you wanted, you would think wanting would stop… Wanting does not stop. I am growing old. I want growing old to stop. Now I think wanting will keep me young. I keep wanting. Wanting… I feel like a baby.

FAMILY TRAITS

It's cheese he doesnae like. I love chedda but he cannae go it. Makes him retch. Makes you want to vomit yursel jist listenin' tae him. He loves pizza. The bigger the better. But I have tae take all the cheese off the tap. So, pizza tae him is jist the base an the tommaty paste. See that's jist like him. That's him all over. Loves playin' football, but doesnae like runnin' aboot in the rain an' mud and gettin' dirty. Loves the sea but only floatin' aboot on one o' those inflatable mattress thingys—no swimmin' like normal folk. He's clever and loves learnin', but canny go the school. I don't ken wit's gonnae happen tae 'im. I think he likes girls, but doesnae like their—you know—their ins and oots, shall we say. He's odd alright. Gets it from his faither. His faither likes cheese but he turns his nose up at pizza. He likes girls but he doesnae like me. He likes weans, but he doesnae like his ain son.

SAY WHAT?

I love debate, a knowledgeable conversation, a good argument. A Socrates / Plato, kind of thing. But imagine sitting quietly next to Sartre and De Beauvoir at a Paris café and getting an earful. Getting in on the lowdown! Or imagine being in the middle of it all between Gaugin and Van Gogh during those crazy art disputes! My favourite, (all-time favourite), would have been to hear Dyachenko and Stanislavsky talking for eighteen hours nonstop about how to change acting forever! But I've got so many clever, gift of the gab friends. When they get together, it's an education trying to follow their logic—their connections. All I can do is shut up, open my ears and LISTEN! Perhaps the next time I'll have learnt just enough to join in.

ART RAGE

Art is a leader on a rearing horse. Art is a guitar and a bottle of wine sliding up a table. Art is a bunch of saints slipping through each other's halos. There's no art of you staring at the telly. Art is a pagan god riding a rosy cloud. Art is a broken boat in the harbour. There's no art of me stacking the dishwasher. Art is a naked woman in rumpled sheets, or with her back turned. There's no you on your iPhone, or me taking out the garbage bags. Art is the puffy infant Jesus looking up to Mary, with a smirk on his face. Art is a pierced bull, or a skull next to an inkwell. There's no art of us. There's no us in art. We will have to make new art. We will make it out of ourselves.

WARRIOR

In the war I lost myself completely. My imagination gave me cruel ideas. I don't know where they came from, but they made me do wild things, worse than everybody else. I was wicked. Perhaps I was testing God. 'Please react. Save me from myself!' Perhaps I was just showing off! I think hell is having no barriers, no limits. It's worse now I'm home. The whole neighbourhood hugging me, happy to see me. Flowers in vases. The Persian rug vacuumed. The windows washed. Every object spick and span, ready for my use. When I shake hands, my friend's fingers should wither. When I kiss, my sister's lips should turn to pus and rot. Nothing happens! The hero has returned on the sunniest day of the year. There are no consequences. Do what you want!

CONTROL FREAK

This hand holds on to a white rock underwater and does not look like my hand. It looks like the hand of a real man —someone who could stop the tide slanting his soft body onto the pebbles. But the real man's hand is also my hand... and my body founders. I try two hands, neither of which belong to me. These are giant hands and giant arms. These mighty forearms are ghosts, yet clear and more defined than any limbs have ever been. These are supernatural parts of me, powerful enough to save me from the will of the tide. I can resist. The rocks give way, my elbows buckle and my flabby city body lurches sideways onto the beach again... Flotsam, that's me. Driftwood in the shape of a man.

A BRIEF HISTORY OF HAPPINESS

While we wait for confirmation, that this moment is happiness, the twin towers rise up out of rubble and dust. While we wait for confirmation, that this moment is happiness, Hiroshima unmelts and releases a shadow, that lifts into a blue sky, until it is only a speck against the sun. While we wait for confirmation, that this moment is happiness, the trains puff backwards along the rails from death camps, and golden stars unstitch and fall onto station platforms. While we wait for confirmation that this moment is happiness, a crowd gathers and chooses Jesus instead of Barabbas. While we wait for confirmation, that this moment is happiness, a brontosaurus raises its head at a rush of air and a meteor flaming towards him.

LET'S FACE THE MUSIC AND DANCE

I had a mentor. He was like—like on his own journey, and like—he was halfway going there, when he turned back around to look at me. So, we had a little, err—*dance*. Not a real dance. But, like, he led, I followed. He taught me stuff. He taught me the steps, he taught me the rhythm—of learning—of the dance. He came back from his relatives, and his property portfolio, and his one-night stands to—like—educate me. To dance! And instead of being grateful, despite my undiluted love, all I want to know is what was he doing spending time with me? I learned everything from him. He never... used me. But I wanted him to. That's why I danced with him. That's the only reason I learned. I don't know why he danced with me.

THE REDUNDANT WEATHERMAN

It's cloudy. It's overcast. Thick. But at least it's not raining. There's a bit of a breeze. It's cold. Really cold. That wet cold that gets into your bones. Raw. But it's not raining at least. Just a bit of drizzle. It came down hard all last week. Yesterday it was stair-rods. And this morning it was lashing across the fields. I think that's thunder in the distance. The wind's picking up. But at least it's not raining. Just drizzle.

RIGHT AND WRONG

I thought it was a workday, but you said it was an opportunity. I thought it was the east wind, but you said it was freedom. I thought it wasn't worth the journey, but you said that we were already there. I thought I was on the winning side, but you said the winning side had been betrayed by its leaders. I thought it was a fever, but you said it was a good idea. I thought you were speaking but you said I was reading your mind. I thought I loved you, but you said it was pity. I thought you loved me, but you said I didn't know the meaning of the word!

AIR ON A PREJUDICE

Because I play the cello, you think I'm a snob. You think I'm privileged. But I come from a sink estate. Because I was poor and now play the cello you think I've changed into a Tory. But I just turned out to like good music. Because I received a scholarship, you think I'm a sell-out. Because I'm from the underclass and bear no grudges, you think I'm a traitor. But there's no class war when the strings vibrate. There's no poverty, or privilege in Bach. You want to break my fingers. I want to break the rules. I want to break the rules in your head! Let's begin with a sound. Here's A minor.

CONSTRUCTIVE DISMISSAL

I was wasted in that job. My line manager hated me because he was bluffing his way to the top, telling the upstairs dunderheads what they wanted to hear. I told it the way it was. While he was ticking boxes, I was organising the schedules and briefing the men. He knew I could see right through him. When the grievance came in about me, that was his cue. Shit job anyway! Fucking numpties, the lot of them, working there. You should see the jokers they took on at the same time as me. All buying into the airhead mission statement and the five stars of excellence crap. Won't even joke about the company logo that looks like a steaming turd. Jesus, lighten up! Take a break. Don't break my balls! Get real. With what we're taking home, there's nothing left in your hand for a Saturday night belter. It's their loss. I'm better off spreading my wings and getting into management training somewhere. Aye, fuckin' management—that's where the livin' is easy. These bozos can kiss my spotty hairy arse bye-bye as I climb up the greasy pole!

THE MAGIC BUS

I always caught the last bus home. No matter how good the party was. No matter how much they shouted at me to stay. Once or twice I left it almost too late. Really last minute and had to run. Some nights I thought I'd missed it. Those nights when you were kissing me. But I always tore myself away. Despite the music and the dancing, there was a tick, tick tock in my head. What if the bus came early just this once? What if I couldn't find my shoe! Despite you wanting me. I always caught the last bus home. I still feel those hot kisses on my lips. I'm still running through the suburbs. Feet echoing past the sleeping houses. Why did I always catch the last bus home, while you stayed dancing? You never went home. I never really left home… I still hear the empty streets echoing.

GAME ON!

I'm the last to leave any party. Sometimes I don't leave. Sometimes everyone konks out, but I'm still there laughing and trying to get it started again. I love it. I love the spirit. I love the excitement. I love joining in. I love shining eyes. I love everyone's best clothes. Goodwill shared. Our lives open and available to each other. Everyone there to play. I love to play! The people who leave are the people who can't play. I fucking love parties! Every party's different. There is always a new game to start. There are always new rules to test and old rules to break. So, are you ready?!

PLEASED TO MEET YOU

I want the job because I'm a good guy really, and maybe with a new start I'll manage to tap into that, find that. Maybe you can find that goodness. I want the job because you look like believers, and I believe I'm good for something. My wayward energy needs to trust—trust something firm—you know? It just needs channelled and released. Connect with that little boy I really am, and you will have me always! I know this is wrong for a job interview. But you are meeting the real me. Hullo. Are we connecting? Are you real?

TRAVELLIN' LIGHT BLUES

This is a song about going home. Longing to go home. A journey so wandering and hard, that you disappear into the heat-haze one day. And when you reappear, in the dew of the morning, you are not the same man. This is a song about reaching back to where you belong. You arrive there finally, to find that everyone you once knew is changed. You've been gone so long that every street and every building is changed. And the changed man stands in his changed home, with what's left of his identity. He realises that he doesn't fit this place, or any place in the world anymore. So, he turns on his heels to find a wilderness, where everyone's a stranger and not pretending any different.

OB-LA-DI, OB-LA-DA

Wherever I am, I hear a motor running. I never get any peace. Deep in my dark bed, with my mind going deeper, suddenly behind my window, a motor starts turning. My eyelids flicker open until the car outside takes off. When I'm lazing on a beach under the shade of an old straw hat, about to tip into oblivion, above me on the road a motor starts running. I hear it everywhere—in the middle of a conversation, at a children's party, in the park, in cinemas, on ski-slopes and mountain ridges. A motor running outside my life. There is no peace and quiet! I hear a motor running inside my ear. I fear death but there is a greater dread. I fear that as I lie dying behind a worn cream blind, a man is idling the engine of his open top car. He revs now and then, prompting his date to fling herself down the steps towards him, one arm stuck into the sleeve of her summer coat. Both excited to be together.

NO PLACE LIKE HOME

When I came home from work my key didn't fit the lock. I tried all my keys. The door kept on not opening. A fear crept up the back of my neck. Autumn leaves blew up the back of my legs. I turned—the street looked the same. Lights in cosy windows. I knocked on the door, then stopped. The knock was too loud. I listened to the echo coming back from the canyon of the street. I smashed at the door with my fist… A light went on in the hall. The door opened. A woman I had never seen before stood there. 'What do you want?' she said. I stared at her—trying to place her. Why was she in my house? 'I live here,' I said. 'Where's Hannah? Who are you? Where's my wife? I live here! This is my house!' She backed away from me. She dropped her voice, 'I'm going to call the police.' The door closed. I don't know what to do. I live at number 8, Connaught Terrace. I live at number 8, Connaught Terrace. I live at number 8, Connaught Terrace.

FALLING OFF THE FACE OF THE EARTH

I've got something to tell you. It's nothing. It's fine. I'll be fine. But—well, I went to the doctor's, just to check, in case I was imagining—stuff, phantom pains in the middle of the night. You know how, things—your mind works, when, at night you're lying there? Well, yeh, it's not good but, all the results are not in. It's not conclusive. It's—there's a shadow. On the X-ray. I thought it was going to be—something else, my heart. But it's on the lung. Just a sight—shadow.

I'VE BEEN LOVING YOU TOO LONG

If you can divorce your wife, or husband, I don't see why you can't divorce your sister. So, for crimes against common sense, I'm divorcing you! You are the empty vessel trying to fill itself with the newest shiniest fantasy. A Land Rover when you live in the middle of the city! What's that about? A hot tub! Matching dune buggies! Where were you when mum was in hospital? Where were you when Alec lost his licence, then lost his job because he lost his licence? Were you around, or were you on a painting holiday? Were you around when Katie took to vodka and ran away? Were you a sister to me? What do you give me for Christmas? A phone call? What do I give you? The best! The best of everything! That's what. Year after year. Well, not anymore. Not from now on. We are not sisters. I divorce you! I divorce you! I divorce you!

YOU'RE NOT THE BOSS OF ME

I always wanted to be the boss. I wanted to boss people around.

So, I worked like buggery and now—I'm the boss! And do I boss people around? Do I fuck! All I do is deal with sick leave, and bogus sick leave, and the deaths of phony grannies, and self-diagnosed stress, and Friday absenteeism, and Monday absenteeism. Oh! and complaints about other members of staff. And complaints about working conditions, wrong chairs for bad backs, and management not following the proper procedure, or not implementing regulations, or not consulting, or not giving due notice, or not telling the truth. I'm management! It's me they are talking about. It's me they want to sack. I'm the boss of nothing but ingratitude and chaos. I want to fire them and can't. They want to fire me and can't. Stalemate! Or, as I call it in the boardroom—a professional working relationship!

DIVIDED WE FALL

When Sean and I took the big step and moved in together, we had a party and all the straight friends, on both sides, came. It was a great night. I felt strong. This is who I am. Can you see me now? This is the man I love. Can you see me with him? So, this is us, together, a same sex relationship—look!... It's never the big occasions, is it? That's not when you notice a change... a turning point... It's incremental. They drift away. The abandonment is in slow motion. Texts not returned. Parties you hear about later, after the event. Invitations friends just forgot to send. It's just no one's got any time—work! You know how it is! So, you don't notice the loss. The separation can take years. It's an art form. Years to make it clear that what you took for granted in the eyes of your mates, was never shared. Never for you. You're different. Separate. Not wanted.

STARTING OVER

I was in my new flat, without a stick of furniture, or a teapot, or a saucepan. Then all the boxes of my stuff arrived. I'd packed a lot of it away wrapped in newspaper, months before I finally moved. I only kept the essentials around me while I was trying to sell. So, I was picking out these shapes swaddled in old pages of The Herald and guessing what they were going to be. Excited as I ripped them free. Vases, ornaments, mementos, keepsakes, trophies. The person I used to be! ... I wrapped them back up again, as best I could. Put them back in the box. I'm never going to open those boxes again.

UNIQUE

When I went up to secondary school I couldn't settle. All my first reports were bad. I thought maybe I might be dyslexic. Eventually I had the test—normal. When I went to college everyone was crowding me. I was confused. They said I was crowding them. I thought it must be dyspraxia. That explains it! I had the test—normal. I went to a good university. It was weird. Just... a weird experience. I couldn't concentrate. It was Aspersers, pure and simple. They arranged the test. *Tests*—plural!... Normal. I've had a lot of tests. I've had a lot of tests because I've had a lot of anxiety. But I'm normal. Not autistic. Not even on the spectrum. I'm just bog standard anxious. Just a very average fucked up shy person! Not special, in any way!

SILENCE IS GOLDEN

I love you. I think of you every minute. I can't sleep for thinking about you! But there's a ring on your finger. You smile when you look at it. You smile when you talk about your children. I listen to your smiles. I listen to all your little domestic details. I listen for a frustration... Just once, I thought I heard disappointment. But I'm not sure. I might be wrong. You glow when you talk about your husband. He is my good friend. Someone to honour. Not hurt. You love your life. You like me well enough. You like what you see. You never think of me when I'm not there... My love would make you frown. I love you smiling. I love you every second... I can't say a thing while you stay in love. I can never say a thing... until...

THE OPERATOR

I fill up the glasses. I don't drink myself. Very little. But I bubble you up to the brim. I fizz until you spill, babe! I have the chilled pink replacement bottle uncorked before you know you want it. I have the extra dry. I have the Moet. Sweetie, I am the machinery. I am the servant that gives you what you want, that hears you tell all. I watch you prick all of the bubbles with a long steel pin as sharp as cynicism. I hear you roar at your own jokes. I watch the bubbles go to your head, darling. I serve your Ego, and report your despair to your enemies, to the tabloids and the rest of the world.

OSMOSIS

I steal because I can. I steal because you have got what looks like the answer. Looks like happiness and order. I keep on stealing because you haven't got it either! Maybe the guy next door to you has it? Maybe through a basement window I can get it? Maybe three in the morning is the best time? Maybe on the other side of a glossy black six panelled door it waits for me? There is satisfaction somewhere... It's been bought, annexed already by the cognoscenti, by the self-satisfied. The sensitive few. People like you! I don't mind it second hand. Third hand—heirlooms—that's absolutely fine. If you have it, give it to me! I feel bad. My life is shit! So give it to me! I've never caught a break. You owe me!

THE CLUB

I'm the Bouncer outside Fire Storm, on weekends. Everyone wants in. I've had offers of money, drugs, condoms, sex, tattoos, snakes, panties, falsies... I decide if you are in or out. And every so often, about once a month, I pick someone. Girl, boy—doesn't matter. Someone who *should* get in. Who expects to get in, but who I stop getting in. Good looking. Dressed sharp. Behaving decent. Clean. Lotioned. Perfumed. Expensive shoes. Clear eyes. 'You can't get in! Go away, we don't want you. I don't have to give you a reason. Leave, or I'll call the police!' They're astonished! Astonished abusive! Astonished wandering into the night! Why was I rejected? ... And you will wonder why your winning smile was rejected all your life. What didn't meet the requirements of the Fire Storm Club? All your life, you will try to figure out why you weren't good enough. My joke on you!

GRADUATION

The teachers of acting skills contradict themselves. They demand specificity and then they generalise. I'm too weak at the end of sentences. I start without a clue and then connect at the end of the phrase. Both can't be right! I need to find my giant. I need to find my dwarf. I'm in the land of make believe—sorry—acting! Nowhere else would they get away with it. I need to research. I need to create my character's history and hairline. I need to be spontaneous. I need to prepare. The young staff are right but have no authority. The old staff know what they are talking about but look totally done in. The facile want the authentic. The authentic want to be entertained. Make it young flesh. Make it half naked with the promise of what's coming next. That's the only thing all the members of the faculty agree on!

THE FINAL ADJUSTMENT

I was kind to you, but I did not feel kind. I listened to you, but I did not remember what you said. I felt for you and I felt generous, because I felt for you. I thought of myself as a good friend. We were both deceived! I helped you out of trouble twice, but I did not feel useful. I talked you into loyalty, but I did not feel loyal. I advised you to own up and be honest, but I was not honest with you. Finally, you called me your best friend, but I was not your friend. I did not do it all for friendship. I was curious. I was always speculating. Speculating on your judgement. Now you know my mind. Now you know why. Now you know me, you can judge. After judgment, I hope—hope we can be free of each other.

TV WILL EAT ITSELF

I used to make TV programmes about real people. Traffic Cops, Mountain Rescue, Hairdressers, Holiday Reps—that type of thing. I enjoyed it. Some of them became minor celebrities and made a few bob—squandered it on the way back down. I made a TV show about them screwing it up and bottoming out. That was called, 'I Used to be a Wannabe'. And there it ended... Couldn't get any work... After that I had to move back in with my osteoporosis ridden dad. Became his Carer. The only work I could get was washing the buses. Three years with a brush—suds and foam! Then, this tall guy interrupted my shift, introduced himself with a contract from Urban Fox Television. He wanted to make a programme about my downfall and humiliation. No, I wasn't really surprised. Full circle. Game on!

INVISIBLE ACCIDENT

I was on a building site, a student working the summer holidays. A dumper truck had its back end open, so that I could shovel the aggregate out of it. They are massive these things. Big heavy steel tailgate. The tray of the truck couldn't angle down far enough. So, I was sweating away—head in with the shovel—swinging and ducking back out. Shit grunt job! The seasoned men were watching how bad I was at it. Their watching made me awkward and uncoordinated. My rhythm was off. I missed getting most of it onto the shovel. The lack of weight kinda shallow threw me round quicker than I expected. WHACK! The gate slammed shut. I got the fright of my life. A split second earlier I would have been decapitated. No neck. No head. And the thing is, the thing about it is... that everyone on the site saw it and they never said a word. They put their eyes down, got on with their work. That's how quickly you can be gone from the world!

PRECIOUS

You never think you're going to die, do you? Never. You think you've got all the time in the world. Now I've been told my time's up, I still can't believe it. I spend half the time I've got left trying to remember, to realise—this is the end. Trying to make myself believe it. I don't believe it. I look fine. How can I finish, end, cease to exist? Not continue to think that I'm here—alive? I wish I could get myself to understand the situation, stop the denial and... and what? Use the remaining time to, to appreciate everything. Let everything in. Instead of stupidly doubting the prognosis and stupidly hoping for a stupid miracle... I've wasted my life. If I had another thirty years, I would waste that. I'm wasting these last six months. It's just waste! That's the truth.

TRAMPS LIKE US

I had expensive things once. Designer clothes. Flash car. Fancy friends. That kind of stuff. But... well... my mother said I was easily led. The hangers-on got it all. It trickled through my fingers. I've got nothing left. Not even my health. I'm on the streets. No pals now! Just this one bum I met in an alleyway. He's not very smart. He's irritating. He looks like shit. I'm ashamed to be seen with him. His breath smells like an arse! I'm mean to him. I keep leaving him, but he turns up. I don't know why he sticks around. I take the piss and he calls me buddy. He tries to tell me what to do, but I do the opposite. He's just a fucking piece of crap, like me! He's the most loyal friend I've ever had.

SELF-PRESERVATION

I love my friends, I really do. But I test them. I challenge them. It can be about anything. 'You don't seriously like that film?!' Or,' Blah is a better singer than blah blah'! I dispute opinions. Not in a nasty way. But just enough to— to... Just a knock against the foundations of friendship. To test friendship? Perhaps. To imply greater knowledge? Yeh possibly. But maybe not. Maybe not. It's more, more a kind of fear. Yes... a fear of being totally overwhelmed by friendship. Absolutely absorbed by love of friendship. Fear of losing my—my—personality! Yes. Losing who I am in you. Being absorbed by you. That's it! So, I put up my little defence. To stop myself disappearing altogether. Vanishing into the likes and dislikes, whims and attitudes of any friend who wants me. Now you know!

F-F-F-FUCK FASHION

A few years ago, young men started sporting big bushy beards. Where did that fashion come from? Why the desire for Mountain Man beards suddenly? Some of these same men scraped up their long hair into a kind of top knot, or bun, with a tassel of hair sticking out at an acute angle. Why? Who could have predicted this fashion? The fashion for lads wearing their trousers as low on their hips as possible, so that the crotch hangs down loose, finally disappeared. The wearing of odd socks arrived out of the blue. Students (both sexes) liked it a lot. Again why? To appear interesting? I wear odd socks, but not to be interesting. Ripped jeans and any clothing which suggests poverty, is still the choice of many. I am genuinely poor. I am not fashionable. I cannot afford rips at my shins and holes at my knees. I would freeze.

PROGNOSIS

I'm going to train as a nurse.
Because healing is possible.

And I've given up on myself.
I'm going to become a nurse.
Because you are curable.
It's just soap and starch and discipline.
I can give you that.
In curing you, I cure myself.
My disease needs your disease.
Without your disease to heal me
I am random and I wither.
Be my patient.
Be my antidote.

GORGEOUS

I like to dress up as a woman. You probably think that makes me gay, but you're wrong. I wear a long blond wig and a modest flowing long-sleeved evening dress. I like cool colours. I like satin, taffeta, tule. The only thing the least bit daring are my peep-toed shoes. I like to think that I've got good taste—guy or girl. You probably think I want to trans and have the surgery. Wrong again! I just want to sway my hips now and then. To flutter my false eyelashes occasionally. Be a different me. I just want to see myself with breasts—like any other guy!

SHIVER

When the wind winnows the grass and shocks patterns through it, I feel like the grass. Lifted. Tilted. Open to influence. Moved by breath in any direction. Waving goodbye. Lonely for no reason... When the great trees sigh, I don't mind losing. I don't mind surrender and the open road... When the barley blows, I feel there's something over the hill to find... When the breeze parts the rushes, I feel that there's a stranger, somewhere far away, who is walking towards me with a gift.

YOU REALLY GOT A HOLD ON ME

I miss you. It hurts me to see trees in bloom and dandelion seeds riding the breeze. Beautiful things shouldn't be beautiful when you're not with me. I want to lie in the park, with your head a little too heavy on my chest. My whole body thinks it's about to see you and hug you. The nerve ends are tingling and ready. My muscles expect to hold you and press into your scent. I miss you! What are you doing while I'm missing you? My longing is so strong, it is bending the air, clearing a path to you. You must know I'm thinking about you. You must feel it! You must be able to hear me. Just a tiny voice inside your ear, saying I miss you. Saying—there is no life beyond you. Can you hear me? Come and be here with me. Save me! Please. I miss you.

THE DUNCE

I got my exam results today. I failed everything, except the subjects I wasn't allowed to sit. I am officially stupid. I don't know where I go from here. I'm too stupid to know. I suppose I leave school. No loss there. Get a menial job, if I'm lucky! I suppose I have the life of a stupid person. That's a bit of a shock. Hard to get that into my head. I don't know how I feel about that. Maybe stupid people don't feel much. I never knew I was stupid. I just thought I took my time. That was stupid!... Maybe all the best people

241

take their time. Clever people are stuck up and nasty. I'm not nasty. I like stupid people. No one likes clever people. They always look unhappy. Always on their own. I'd rather be stupid, thanks! I'd rather belong. Wow! I really worked that out... Or was that all stupid? I guess I'll never know... No. It was stupid. What an idiot—thinking you must be stupid to be happy! Fuck—that proves it! I must be thick!

FLOURISH AND BE DAMNED

Youse need tae be in the world that suits ye. Youse need tae find the world where youse belong. Yur no in yur right world if ye want tae design a jet engine, and instead yur bringin' up weans and makin' yur man's tea! Yur no in yur right world, if yur gay and yur whole toon is straight! If ye want tae be a fitness instructor, get intae the world a gyms and exercise machines. Ya want tae be an astronaut? Don't work in a café! Find yur ain folk—that's yur job! Yur ain folk are no yur friends and family. They don't ken yur dreams. That's whits wrang wi' the world. It's no injustice that causes wars. People fight cos they're unhappy. And they're miserable cos they havenae found their proper world. The whole world wid be at peace, if everybody found the world that they belonged tae. My world is tellin' youse whit tae dae. I'm a personal motivator. I'm as happy as every happy person put together!

FAMILY ANTHROPOLOGY

I stopped taking the wallpaper off. I stood with the scraper in my hand staring. Next to the doorframe, on the wall, were tiny dashes—pencil marks. Like faint steps on a ladder. Heights marked each birthday. Our child growing. Our child gone. All that time. Inch by inch. The evidence of standing to be measured. Giggling and told to stop. Stand still. Feet flat. No cheating. Head back. Neck up. A moment held. Then released. Gone. Childhood gone. All recorded there. Faint HB lines. Less insistent the higher they climb. Some birthdays missed... Gaps in the pencil strokes... The redecoration isn't done. Sorry... Nothing's done.

MIND OVER MATTER

I used to enjoy swimming at the baths, until my breaststroke parted a drifting skein of tissue and menstrual blood. The sparkling clear water transformed itself into a sump of filth. No! Bacteria from unwashed teenage groins and old men's arses! No! Microbes sluiced from nostrils and verruca's, and open wounds and sores. Please God no! Flakes of eczema floating on the surface, about to be swallowed. AHH! I've never been back. I was teaching 2B, when one of the boys in the front row let out a stinking fart. I gasped and fled out the door. Someone sneezed in a seat behind me on the train, I saw the air filled with viruses! I don't travel on public transport now. I can't go to work. I can't leave my house. My imagination has restricted my movements to my bedroom and my toilet. I've lost my job! Imagination has ruined my life. My imagination has turned against me. I am TRAPPED!

OUTSIDER

I love the curve of your street. I love the shine on the curb outside your bedsit. I love the barking of the Alsatian in the flat above you. I love the cords from TV aerials looping and shuffling over your tenement building. I love the smell of Aspirin from your bedroom. I love the sound of your weeping. I think it's because of me. Power is delicious. I love the sound of myself forgiving you.

OBJECTIVES

I'm listening to your list of things to do. Feed the cat. Buy a 20-Watt bayonet light bulb. Buy a winter coat. Write a birthday card to Rosie. Take the empties to the recycling bin. Change energy suppliers. See Agnes in hospital. I'm listening to your list. Listening to your commitment, application, willpower, enthusiasm. I'm listening for my name. Finally, at the end. Me. The last thing for you to do.

GONE! GONE! GONE!

I had plenty of time to get the work done but I... just... I just... frittered it away... no that's not right. I deliberately wasted it. Deliberately! And I don't really know why. Fear of being functional, of having no other identity except the task. Completely subsumed by the task. Sounds improbable. Feels like I'm frittering away this attempt at understanding myself. Fritter! Fritter! Deliberate *fritter*. Until the word means nothing. Frit-ter. F-ritt-er. Sounds like nonsense. I make no sense. Maybe I'm not in real time! I'm in fritter time! Irrelevant to real time. Only functional in fritter time.

What if fritter time is real time? What if I'm nonsense in them both? Then I'm fucking well frittered!

JEALOUSY

I want to bring you down. I want to bring it all down. I can't tell you how much. I want to make an end of you. I hate you! I hate your tribe. I hate your offspring. I hate your world. I hate your false humility. I hate your praise for your friends, not mine, not me. I hate your claims of significance and legacy. I hate your hypocrisy and mediocrity. I hate myself for not being you, and better!

DUTY OF CARE

By the age of six my daughter was beautiful. Even her skin smiled! Each year I became more afraid. At puberty she turned heads. Crude men, low men would stare—the catcall stuck in their throats. Stunned. One more year, and her breasts rose up like two fresh fountains. It was early June. A new family with two brothers, a couple of years older than her, moved in next door. I saw their eyes go out on stalks. It was only a matter of time. And if not one of them, then another. How could I stop the world? So, I made a pledge to her beauty. I would never let it be degraded. I became its guardian. She would not be betrayed and brought down, by the grubby, the sordid. I would not allow her miracle to be made ordinary. I was beauty's protector. She was perfect at the end. Perfect when I held the pillow over her radiance.

HEAVEN KNOWS I'M MISERABLE NOW

If she had said it was my breath, or how I ate my cereal, or my looking at girl's legs in the street, I could have done something about it. I could've changed it. Stop wearing brown slip-ons. Buy different glasses. Beard on, or off? Stubble, or sideburns? Up to her! But she said it wasn't anything like that. Nothing she could put a finger on. Nothing she could explain. I was just me. It was just who I am... How can I change that? She doesn't love me. Me! The thing that is me. This me! The me inside... she couldn't love that... I will have to do it for her. I can change.

WHOLE LOTTA LOVE

I love you in bits and pieces. I don't love all of you. I love you when you walk. I love you when you move, when you lean, reach—stretch. It's so natural. You are so coordinated. I don't like you eating. You are greedy. It's too fast! I love your hair. It moves. Sways. I hate the way you pick at the spots on your nose. I love you sleeping. But not when you pretend to sleep. I don't like you pretending to listen. I like you shy. I like you unconfident. I don't like you arguing. But I like your opinions. I would love you all the time, if you kept moving. I want you to move on, so that I can miss you.

NO SURRENDER

If you are honourable you stick by your bad choice. Every day of your life you abide by your immature decision to start a family. You try to accommodate. Most people are honourable parents. They stand by their promises. But keeping a promise to a child can mean breaking a promise to yourself. Most people try to keep their promises, all their promises. Really try, until hypocrisy makes them despise themselves. But they go on behaving honourably and go on feeling dishonourable until they are exhausted—fucking worn out! Then... how they feel and what they do becomes the same. I have got to that place. Sorry family. Both my promise to you and my promise to myself are void. I have stepped beyond my moral signposts. The landscape is unfamiliar. I don't know where I am. I have run out of wisdom... We need to begin again.

THE ORACLE

Because Gloria is clever, I don't think she feels much.

Because Tony is always busy, I think he is running away from his true self.

Because Gwen is unemployed, I think she is really bone-fucking-idle.

Because Stacey has been promoted again, I think she's nothing but an arse licker.

Because Jack buys everything at auctions I think he is living off other people's misery.

Because Sofia is always praising God, I think she is trying to overcome her deep pessimistic nature.

Because Phil loves studying history, I think he is terrified of living now.

Because Zelda waxes her eyebrows and is called Zelda, I think she's a slut.

Because you have no opinions of your own, I know I can trust you.

Because I know everything about everyone no one dares to question me.

GOOD THINGS DON'T LAST FOREVER

I'm exhausted! I'm wearing myself out, trying not to let you down. Please let me let you down! Your good regard for me is flattering but... it's not... I'm not. I'm okay, I'm not a slob, I'm ordinary. An ordinary do-gooder. Not a professional. You know. I'm kind of kind and thoughtful and I like to lend a hand but... Well, I'm not—not—consistent! That's it! I can't sustain this effort to, to match your high opinion of, high opinion you hold of—I'm going to fall apart if I don't get a break. I suppose, I need to be good when I want. Sorry. I want it to be my choice. Not what you expect. Not obliged. Not when you expect me to be good. Is that bad?! I'll be good again. I'll be good soon. But I just don't want to be good now.

PERSONA

When I'm with my Granny Peanut, I'm the personification of patronisation, if there is such a word. Giving her that show of attention, because, I feel she needs it. When I'm with Granny Nettles, I'm the golden child. Butter wouldn't melt up my bum hole. When I'm with Uncle Charlie, I'm tough, and practical, and can-do, without anything grown up between my legs. When I'm stuck in the house with my mum—there's nothing I can do. Nothing I want to do but invent new swear words until she screams. When I'm with my best mate, Roddy, I am superman. When I'm with Auntie Sarah, I'm the joke teller. I can make her laugh till she pees her pants! When I'm with Cousin Jordan, I don't speak at all. I just have to listen. I don't really listen... I bet if you asked them all who I was, they wouldn't be able to agree. Am I lying to them all? Do I give them what they want?... Or are all these me's, *me*?

THE ROAD

When I left home, distances were longer, and buildings were bigger. There were no destinations on the signposts, or on the front of buses. When I left home scarves were compulsory. Back then clouds gave birth to pigeons, and whirlpools of starlings that fell upon municipal buildings and pecked out the eyes of heroic statues. When I left home, I had more memories than kisses. After I left home, I made other homes, and put people, and draught-excluders and animals in them. When I left home, I took home with me. But not the one you were in.

WHAT?

How do you listen? I don't know how. I try to listen to what you are saying, but instead I listen to how you are saying it. When I'm listening to your tone of voice, you suddenly expect an answer. I was listening for your expectations. I wasn't listening to your information. Or I was listening for your prompts. Listening to our similarities. I wasn't listening to our differences. Do you listen for yes? Do you listen for no?... How do you listen? ... Are you listening? Are you listening to me? What did I say? What did I say about you?

CAN YOU HEAR THE MUSIC?

I bought vinyl. Records! I loved them. Owning them. They changed me from old fashioned to now. I was dull, and dumb, and asleep, and waiting... I was suspended, in stasis... unformed—unfocused—un. I was *un*! Then I heard a song. A pop song. A basic beat. Urgent. It woke me up. It told me I was not incomprehensible. Not unformed, not loveless. It told me I was desperate but—! Emotional but —! But not alone. It told me I had a right to be dissatisfied. From that moment of drum beat thunder, of guitar distortion, of scream—I have never stopped arriving from *un*. Music makes me modern. *Un*-old. New. Transformed!

THE WHEELS ON THE BUS

I commute to work every weekday. Intercity bus. 40 minutes each way. Tedious. Tiring. For about three years I tried different strategies to make it more bearable and interesting. But phone calls, puzzles, music, reading, videos, computer games, listening to other people's conversations. All lose their magic eventually. The journey undermines the effort. This year I let it all go... I do nothing! I don't even look out the window. I don't even close my eyes. I don't even try to catch the direct bus anymore. The journey home is taking longer and longer. I miss buses and have to wait. I wait blank faced. Sometimes, I don't even board the next one. I'm impervious to delay and cancellation announcements. I've surrendered to the journey. A constant journey, without hope, but without fear. No destination.

SANCTUARY

It took a long time to get to the mountain and when I got there, the mountain was obscured, the mountain had better mountains behind it. I was disappointed... I gave up my savings and my comfort to go to the ocean. The ocean was grey like a mountain. The ocean was not being the ocean that day. The ocean was not an escape, or an answer... I found a lonely road and gave up friendship. All my friends back into childhood. But the road became treacherous and then turned back on itself… I found a quiet river and gave up love. But the river did not gurgle, or delight, or provide. It. It looked like engine oil. I came back to my house naked. It was emptied of possessions. Emptied of expectations. Emptied of you. Emptied of me… I stayed.

DARK SOLUTIONS

At night most of me knows that the noises my house makes, are the noises my house makes. But there's another part of me that has other ideas. I'm constantly being burgled, or crept up on by masked intruders, or peeped at from wardrobes by insane men with machetes. It's just the radiator cooling, I know that. It's just the electric motors in the kitchen switching on and off, of course. But the dark conjures phantoms, demons, outrages. I put in ear plugs. But if there really was a killer coming up the stairs? I wouldn't hear the third tread squeak. The knife would be at my throat! Ear plugs were no use. No. When I hear a noise now—I make a noise back. I growl! I snort! I snarl! I howl! I fight fear with fear. I terrorise the night. I'm so loud and mad and dangerous that the house doesn't dare answer back.

ANGEL WITH ONE WING

If it's not work, it's car repairs, roof repairs, netball practise, boiler trouble, wrong pay deductions, wrong gas bills, swimming lessons, buying the kids clothes, bins not emptied, and the broadband down. And—and—and… I'm too busy to be a good person. So, with what is left of me, I'm going to do one good thing a day. That's the plan! I'm going to do one altruistic act a day. The target is one. I should be able to achieve that. Then I would feel better about myself. There'd be a point to all this work, and endeavour, and commitment and stress. One kind act, amongst all these competing demands... Realistically, perhaps I could do one good thing a week... Hmm... Who am I kidding!? One good thing a month... You think?... One good thing a year... One truly good thing in a lifetime... Maybe. Difficult... I could try.

SELL OUT BLUES

This song is something I wrote myself. It's an imitation of a Robert Johnstone song. Robert had no success in his lifetime. My potboilers, pastiches and knockoffs, have all reached number one, and stayed in the charts for years. My conclusion is that no one wants the original and the authentic. Everyone wants pre-digested, signalled sentiment, gravel-voiced faux wisdom. And I'm the one to give it to you! What I have is a skill in-its-own-right. I was forged from a thousand nights trying to please in pubs and wedding marquees. But no one will remember me. I sold my soul at the crossroads outside Stoke Newington. The devil gave me a battered guitar and told me that to be successful, all I needed to do was transpose the blues onto the panpipes. The rest will never be history, but it is an easy living.

IF YOU MUST KNOW

I'm leaving you because you put Pepsi in a wine glass. I'm leaving you because you never buy roses. I'm leaving you because you smell of popcorn. I'm leaving you because all your victories were uncontested walkovers. Because you lied about writing your journal all night and watching the dawn come up on the dew-soaked grass. I'm leaving you because you have no modesty. Because you have too much modesty. Because you have modesty but at the wrong time, and in the wrong places. It was all just about getting attention. I'm leaving you because you lose the things I buy for you. Because you have started taking photographs of church bells. I'm leaving you because you say you have a negative address—and that's just meaningless! I'm leaving you because you say I am just making up silly reasons to leave you.

CAREER OPPORTUNITIES

What better to do than to look after people—get them back on their feet? Home to their loved ones. So, I became a nurse and looked after people—patients. I wasn't a good nurse. I was over involved, couldn't distance myself. Kept breaking into tears. And they ran me ragged when they realised I was a soft touch. 'Get this'! 'Fetch me that'! 'No, that's the wrong kind'! 'I need the blue ones'! No, please, or thank you. Really mean. Nasty. Scary. I found out that sickness makes people totally selfish. Really, really self-obsessed. Absolute bastards! So, I quit. I'm in Trading now. The Stock Market. I've learnt my lesson. Humanity isn't fit for purpose. Now I'm totally out for myself. A fucking Hedge Fund bastard! So far, it's better!

YOU

Thoughtful, that's what you are. Caring when I'm not expecting it. When I think I'm alone, you pop round and say hello. When I think I'm fighting a losing battle, you say something funny. And the fight is suddenly irrelevant and stupid. When I feel that I have no face, or character, or lines on the palms of my hands, you remind me of who I am. It's just a word or two, now and then. We don't see each other that much. But it's enough to make a smile possible. Enough to make a faint hope possible. And enough, is famously, of course, *enough!*

THE PROPOSAL

I came back here to love you. I've thought about all the vicious things you said, and I think they're fair enough. Some of it you made up a bit, but I did the same to you. So, I think we are quits on the revenge stuff. It's odd, I think, that all the horrible things you said, they didn't go in, they didn't touch me, or upset me. I thought about it all last night. It dawned on me—at dawn. Just a fact, sorry! It dawned on me—you swear at me because you love me. You're a bitch, that's your way. I swear at you, because I love you, I'm a bastard, and I don't want to be in love—that's my way. So, it works for the both of us. Agreed? Are we right, fuckface?!

FORMULA

I'm critical when I should be kind. I'm kind when I should be critical. I'm perceptive, when it pays to be dull and mediocre. I'm blunted when I should be perceptive. I'm candid, when I should be supportive. I'm vague and inclined to lie, when I should tell the truth. And I see a pattern here. It seems to me that I have the right attributes and abilities, but not the right timing. All the prompts come from you. I pick up my cues from you. I respond to you. So, it stands to reason, it must be you who's wrong!

MOTORMOUTH

I speak in long sentences, because I have complex variations of thought and contradictory mixed emotions that need direction and resolution. I speak in long sentences because I have a desire to reach you, and convince you of my sensitivity, my strength of character, and my sophistication of thought and my love of language. I speak in long sentences because my energy is young and my willpower sustains a constant effort to repress desire and control it with subtle shifts of friendship and camaraderie, and loyalty, and obligation, and trust, and the deadening familiarity of routine. I speak in long sentences, but nobody understands my ability to link ideas, concepts, conceits, references, while waiting moment to moment, for simple interruption and contact. I speak in long sentences, and will continue to speak in long sentences, until someone out there somewhere, understands how desperate I am for an answering no, or yes! Or a simple direct unequivocal very personal question.

SHRIEK!

My child was hurt. She was running on the beach and stood on a shard of glass. Her heel was cut deep but clean. What do you say to the tears, the wide-open throat, and the sound that slices at your heart? How do you say, it will be better, not now, but later? The pain is now! How do you explain to a child that reality is not in the moment of hurt, but in the later reality of healing? What you find yourself saying is, 'It's all right, don't cry. It's going to be all right. Be brave. You're fine. You're my darling angel. No tears. It's all right. It's just a little cut. You are going to be fine. Just fine.' That's all you have to offer, while your child screams, shudders, bleeds, and tries to flee from reality. Rejecting you and everything in the whole world. Being a parent is not enough.

BLACK ON BLOND

I'm a zebra. On the left side, I wear my stripes white then black then white. On the right side, I wear them black then white then black. When it's raining and I'm miserable, I switch them the other way. When I can feel spring coming, I keep moving them all the way around my body. When there's a growl in the air and lions are about, I wear my stripes upside down. When the herd is bored, when there's plenty of grass and nothing to do, we swap stripes with each other. When we are in love, we take our camouflage off. When we are pure white, or jet black, we climb inside each other. The union makes a baby with a unique new set of stripes.

CAUGHT

I thought the world was unlimited sparkling sunshine and open blue ocean as a child. I thought everything, from one horizon to the other, was given to me as a playground. Then I ran between two pine trees, straight into a spider web. It clung to my face. Like steel mesh. The shock reordered my senses. I grew up in that moment... The web is still across my face. I'm the man with the web over his eyes, over his mouth, over his breath. My soul is trapped in a net. I walk at a moderate pace. Careful.

PRESENT TENSE

You always think you're going to be happy. It's an idea. It's in the future. It's a year from now. It's next Saturday when the lottery numbers come up. It's a single moment away. It's a feeling. An expectation... Fulfilment. Balance. Achievement. Completeness. Connection. Happy... It's never now! Now, is always striving. Now, is always incomplete. I'm going to make *now* happy. As happy as now can be. Right *now*! I'm going to make now last a lifetime. *Now* with you.

CONTACT

I was with this girl on a bench in the park. She was my friend's friend, not really my friend. But my friend, she met this other friend, and had to go. Well, she left. They were decorating a bar for a surprise birthday party. And I was left with this—this unknown girl. The link between us had just up and gone. We were awkward and silent. But then the sun came out. It lit up a bank of tiny white flowers. Lily of the Valley, she said. They were the most beautiful and sad thing I had ever seen. And we were laughing. Just like that. Like the sun had come out in us too! Both laughing until the tears began to come. Then the sun switched off. We wiped our tears away. She said she had to leave. I will always remember.

A LITTLE LOCAL DIFFICULTY

I am the last person in the world... I used to laugh out loud for no reason, but I've stopped that now. For a long time, I couldn't accept it, I couldn't believe that I was the last. I searched. I hoped. I expected. But that has all gone. I am the last human being! But that's not the worst of it. The worst thing is that buds still form, and bluebells still flower on the slopes between the trees. All this beauty—who is it for? The hawthorn blooms white, radiates white. It breaks my heart. What is beauty for, when there's no one to see it but me? I'm almost an animal now, open sores, matted hair. I'm gnawing at bones! But it's the dog-rose and the honeysuckle—it's the flutter of tilting poppy heads, that's killing me.

SOLIDARITY

I went to a gay pride march to support my gay mates. On the march I felt gay. And on the march, I felt proud. Proud of something I wasn't. Gay, I mean. Funny that. I felt buoyant the whole way. Really noble. I had offered my sexual identity to another man's cause. How many Brownie points is that? Altruism, or what? Then Brendan, a straight mate, said to me—no one does anything for someone else without an ulterior motive. So that cast a doubt—see? It was an inference, a veiled accusation. It implied... He thought the worst. I've known Brendan all my life. How could he think that? I was on the next march. Brenden was never much fun. I know who makes me laugh. I know who I am.

TRUE LOVE WAYS

We argue all the time. He's a big spender, I'm a supersaver. I change down at junctions, he cruises the clutch. I keep switching the lights off, he whacks on everything we've got. The sparks fly! The time flies! I don't know what we would talk about if we really got on. If we agreed about everything. What a long day that would be! 'Yes love. You are so right, love. Oh, talking to you is just like talking to myself, love!' Yawn. We hate each other—that's how we love. Rows. Huffs. Slanging matches. Bust ups. Never a dull moment. Seven years gone in the blink of an eye. That's what I call happiness.

THE LOOK OF LOVE

I'm going to trust you again. I could give up. My head tells me to give up. You can't even look me in the eye. You can't even ask me to trust you. You can't trust yourself, that's why! You know that if you look at me, I'll see you haven't changed. You are still a liar. But I want you to look at me. It doesn't matter. It's your nature to deceive yourself. Maybe you never will change. Try to look at me. Look at me...

Look at me... LOOK AT ME!... Ah there you are! I will keep trusting you... That's what love is.

RESTRAINT

I notice everything. I say nothing. But I can't stand confrontation. I'm aware of your hypocrisy, of every lie you tell me. But I nod and agree with you—with an added smile, just to make you complacent. I say nothing. You are bigoted, and selfish, and vain, and cruel, and I am silent. Am I silent because I don't care? Am I silent because I'm frightened? Am I silent because I'm bigoted, and selfish, and cruel, and vain? No! I notice everything. You do not notice my love for you. My silence is my love for you. I love you but I say nothing. To find love, the one you love must notice you.

DREAM CATCHER

I am a bat. I sleep so far beneath the cliff that I do not dream. I hunt when there is no moon or starlight. I'm a shadow in the night. I'm a clot of malevolence floating against the wind. You cannot see me. I have cut out the night's skin for my wings. You cannot hear me. The sound I make has no defence. I can find you. The faintest rustle of a dream and I will know your safe place. Through the pitch black I come. Not for your flesh. Not for your blood. For something more precious than life. One swoop and my wings close on it. I lift it away from your resting body. Your dream is mine.

THE GAME

I think I'm addicted to boredom. I think I like it better than people—friends—family. You know where you are with solitaire, or just enough. You want another seven, you don't want a two. With family you don't want anything they say. With your friends you only want a face-card. Maybe I'm different. Maybe I'm strange. The strange is my strange. The strange belongs to me. I'm from a different pack. Strange is my ace.

NO TIME TO DIE

To save our marriage we invited another couple over. Tried a bit of swinging—swapsees! It was Vic's idea. It was Vic who said it would put the spark back into our relationship. But I think he just fancied Lesley. Lesley and Pete were up for it. They weren't even married. Hadn't been together more than three years, but they were—keen. Pete would've shagged a hole in the ground! But Vic only had eyes for Lesley. I thought, I am not having that! Share and share alike! So, I stuck my tongue in Lesley's mouth. Lesley squeezed my tits. It was the me and Lesley show after that! Vic sat in a chair in a huff and watched. Pete tried to wank him off, but Vic crossed his legs. No thanks. But Vic was right about relighting a flame. Me and Lesley are getting married as soon as my divorce comes through. I thought Vic might have worked it out with Pete—to keep things tidy. But not even Pete's offer of a BJ could bring Vic back to life!

PARTNERS

The best job I ever had was selling Christmas trees. It's usually mum and dad who roll up. Grumpy. Tired from work. Or harassed, badgered by the kids at the weekend. They just want to grab a tree that's half decent, and not deformed, and not going to be the laughingstock of the neighbourhood. They begin to rummage through the Nordmann Firs and then the Norway Spruces. And the bickering stops. It's the Lodgepole sap! The resin. The scent of pine! Then the missus picks one out and hubby hauls it free. He loves the feel of needles and the tug of resistance. He thinks he is macho again. She makes him turn it all the way through 360, so she can check it over, then back the other way. It's yes, from them both and a mutual smile. A fleeting smile, before they are back in Mr. & Mrs. Hassled and Responsible, mode. I love that fleeting smile. It is Christmas for me!

MEASURE FOR MEASURE

I don't like Shakespeare. Shock! Horror! The truisms in the speeches seem obvious to me. And the only way to make the comedy work these days is to pump, grind, and push the bawdiness and the cock gags. Shakespeare's genius is to state the bloody obvious. And his famous epic scale of king and pauper, God and Devil, conscience and loyalty, poetry and prose, is only the technique of contrast. Shadow and light—contrast! Action and doubt—contrast! Whim and resolve—contrast! Find what is constant in your own time if you really want the truth. The truth is subtle. Sometimes in life, being constant is barely perceptible. Contrasts catch all the attention.

BREAK UP

When I'm on my own, when no one is watching, I treat objects badly. I wrench the tops off bottles—squirt out the toothpaste, fling down the pot scrubber, throw off my shoes. Tiny rebellions I suppose. Tiny acts of revenge on things that don't do what I want them to. Just letting frustration out on things that have no feelings. Things that don't comply instantly. Tearing the corner off a milk carton! Snapping off a CD cover! Innocent enough. That's what I thought. But Maeve saw me knocking her miniscule cosmetic bottles off the bathroom shelf. I couldn't see myself in the shaving mirror. I couldn't even reach it because of the clutter. I would've picked them up later. But that was the end of Maeve and me. I still treat objects badly, even fucking worse now actually.

COINCIDENCE

They hired me to make rain. It took me three days to get to the village. As my lift roared away in a dust cloud, the first big drops started. They fed me. They made some kind of fermented alcohol from yams. They welcomed me into their homes. The rain fell non-stop for three weeks. They paid me again to make it stop. It stopped as the elders paid me the money in soggy American dollars. At first it was a cough. Then it was fever. It killed ten children. They paid me to make the evil go away. It left when I did.

ZEITGEIST BLUES

'My baby done left me', is fine, as far as it goes, but you have to admit, the blues has a very limited vocabulary. Things have changed a lot since slavery and cotton pickin' in a chain gang. I think it's time we had some new blues songs to reflect the modern urban experience of technology and multiculturalism, and the zeitgeist thingy. That's why I've written some stuff to move the genre forward into the world we live in. My titles are more embedded in current sensibilities and attitudes. Dust My Dyson. Got My Modem Working. Mannish Boy/Girl/ Transsexual. Smoke-Stack Liposuction! But to kick things off—let me give you my latest composition—Corina Coronavirus!

TIME PASSES

You said three o'clock. You said on the dot. You said 15.00 hours. I thought you might come early. Couldn't wait to see me. I prepared my lowkey surprise. I rehearsed neutrality. But you didn't come at two forty-five. I was alone for every second leading up to the stroke of three. I thought I heard your footsteps. I imagined you at the front door. I willed you to arrive. You promised... 15.01. I thought of phoning. But that would be a lack of trust... 15.02. If I phoned would you answer? 15.03. Perhaps all the clocks in the house were wrong? 15.04. Perhaps you were sick, or in an accident, or had to save a stranger's life while you were on your way? 15.05. Perhaps you were murdered! 15.06... 15.07... 15.08. You promised! You promised! Perhaps you just forgot... 15.09. How could you forget? ... 15.25. How could you promise?... 15.50. How could you not care?

SELFIE

If I was a tree
I would be a broad-leafed horse-chestnut
If I was a river
I would be the rumbling shallow Spey
If I was an insect
I would be a heavy bumblebee
If I was a mountain
I would be the crystal of Schiehallion
If I was a flower
I would be a perfect white Calla Lily
If I was an animal
it would be a ripple patterned tiger
If I was a herb
I would be sweet tarragon
If I was a city
I would be Renaissance Sienna
If I was a bird
I would be a simple song thrush
If I was a spice
I would be the dark itch of pepper
If I was another person
I would be you
You

BIPOLAR DIALECTIC

I must stop thinking about myself in terms of good and
bad. Of being intrinsically good or bad. I must stop
dividing my impulses into this false dichotomy. I must stop
using this one, or zero, binary code to map my true nature.
Ying and Yang are just imaginary abstract oppositions. Life
is not so simple. It doesn't separate into two clear divisions.

I must eradicate this script from my brain. I must scrub this blueprint from my DNA. I must start again from scratch. Start with this person and these circumstances. Start with this individual. This problem. This variation. This environment. This room. This woman. This time. This context. These feelings. This time! This time! This time! All different. All requiring different responses. Infinitely different. All requiring solutions. Unique solutions. Not a judgement.

THE THREE HUMPED CAMEL

We started off as horses but then the climate changed. In the new flinty dryness, we became goats. We ate everything and anything then. But over the millennia, we became choosy, and developed an appetite for eating secrets. The secrets were so succulent and nourishing that we stored them within our bodies as a swollen fatty hump on our backs. We became camels. But some camels were greedy. They were tempted by the pungent smell of guilt. Guilt usually grew close to the secrets, sometimes right in the middle of a patch. So, it was no trouble to switch. The camels who did this grew a second hump and were able to double the size of their territory. The climate is changing again, getting worse. I'm going to widen my diet to get me through. I'm going to try the taste of regret. Plenty of that around!

TALENT

I would be very good at stand up. Funny things just come into my head. I'm watching a comedy show, and I think of the punchline before the famous guy says it. I've got the knack. I mean Billy Connolly was a welder in the shipyards —so why not a Heating Engineer, like me? Stand up is open to anybody. I've got frustrations and pet-hates I can turn into comedy gold. I make my wife laugh. I'm a riot in the van with the lads. Okay, my daughter is not a fan, but that's her renegade teenage hormones. She'll come good when her neck stops blushing. I'll find a joke that makes her chuckle. I'll find a joke that makes her love life, even if it kills me!

MAGIC THINKING

I can read minds! You're a filthy lot! Stupid too! Trivial most of it, when it's not anger and lust. Ah! And envy. That was a big surprise to me. So much pride made nonsense by so much envy. Huh! Call yourselves friends! Oh, I can read minds, all right! Not much up there for the most part. Not much going on except hatred of what you most want. Not much going on until you speak. When you speak—that's where the hope is! Oh, when you speak, you're better. BETTER! Keep talking trying to think it out!

FAMILY MATTERS

I love you. But I really love your family. They are great. They are so open and full of life. There's so many of them and they all get on so well together. Your sisters are so funny. Your mum and dad are crazy and do crazy crazy stuff! All of them obviously love each other, even when they are saying the most outrageous things. They hug and kiss each other on the lips. They belch and fart in front of each other. Then laugh and laugh. And they don't pretend that they are anything they are not... My family is tiny. We never say what we really feel. Just as well, because we hate each other. We would never dream of touching, never mind hugging. Your whole family is a revelation to me. I love them. I want to marry them as much as I want to marry you. Without them—you are just you.

PERFORMANCE

I'm a sex worker, not a prostitute. Not a whore. During the day I'm studying law at university. Second year now. No makeup worn. No high heels. No jewellery. Just Ugg boots and a sweatshirt. Good grades, well not bad. I'm getting through it, just a bit tired. Difficult to concentrate. At night I have so many names, so many roles to play. They all put me at risk. But I'm in charge of my life! In charge of my *lives*! The two things—night/day—they're separate. They have to be separate. They are two different people. They don't know each other. They have different names. Oil and water! Once I've graduated, I will be one person again. Respectable in daytime and night-time. Inside and out—respectable. And I won't feel tired... That's the best thing. Not to always feel so tired. Tired for both people.

REGRESSION

What is the first thing you remember? Why do you remember it? Something focused the fug of childhood. Something seared the brain with its presence. For the first time, you noticed something other than yourself, and it began your memory. Was it love? Was it violence? Was it beauty? Was it pleasure, or pain? Ask yourself why, of all the things surrounding your toddler eyes and your toddler hands, you were stimulated into awareness by that first thing. If your first memory was something different, would you be different today? Trace your consciousness back to that first perception. You will recognise how your memory was formed, and who you really are.

GOODBYE TIME

It's just, I can't, I don't feel—don't you feel? You must feel it? It's been awhile, that I've been feeling it. Not that long but, long enough, to think... that we, we're not—well, it's not—is it? You must know that. And it's not going to change back now. I don't think anyway. There's someone else out there who'll—I'm sure. You'll meet someone, someone much nicer than me. I'm not nice. If I was nice I wouldn't be doing this to you, would I? Saying goodbye, I mean. No, not nice at all.

RUNNING ON EMPTY

Funny... all afternoon I've felt like there was something missing. I know what it is. It feels strange... I don't have a single promise to keep. There's no one to disappoint. Not a single person to try for. To be good for. To attempt something difficult, like trust, for. There's no vow that I will love someone. No oath to bind me to the future. No one to fulfil a wish for... Just things to do. Just the basic trivial business of living. Getting on with it. But no undertaking to please, to satisfy, to help. My promise—my pledge, has no partner. It hurts! It hurts me! This loneliness. That's a surprise.

PROGRESS REPORT

What are the illusions that keep me here?... The illusion that the opinions of other people matter. The illusion that I have something to achieve, and that my achievement will be significant. So significant that it will cancel death and the indifference of others. The illusion that I have not squandered my time and misused the time of my family. The illusion that my vanity is of a different nature, and quality, to the vanity of others. The illusion that for every action there is a consequence. The illusion that the consequences of my actions will overcome my illusions... Getting there. Working on it. Travelling. Oh, travelling... Getting closer.

CONFUSION

I hate spiders. I love parrots—they're very clever. I hate jellyfish. I love sharks—so beautiful. I hate scorpions and wasps. I love tulips. Such a simple shape. Love and hate—simple. A simple division. I'm a very direct, simple person, who knows their own mind... But... I love your eyes. I hate your nose! Yet, somehow the two things combine... I hate your chin! I love your lips. But, I don't know... together they seem nice... I hate you! I love you! I'm not as certain about anything as I was...

NEED

She was having affairs right, left and centre. It broke my heart, you know. She didn't even try to hide the evidence. Sometimes I would almost walk in on them. When I did walk in on them, she didn't react. Went right on getting fucked. Then looked me in the eye and said—'See something you like?' Sometimes some man would stick around for a couple of days, or a week or two. She acted like he was a member of the family. I didn't know how to act, but I answered when I was spoken to. Eventually she was cavorting with the real lowlife types. Rough and not too hygienic, know what I mean? Sometimes it was more than one at a time. She'd leave the door open, so I could hear her laughing. The other night she was screaming. Climax screaming—so loud I couldn't... I couldn't!... I walked out the door. Just walked quietly into the night. I don't know what she wanted from me.

MORE THAN THIS

You are making a big mistake chucking me. It's a big big massive mistake! I know you haven't got anyone else. No one else would have you. You're an idiot. You don't even know what you've got, and you are going to throw it away. I'm trying to save you from yourself, I don't know why. I love you, I suppose. And you love me. I know you do. You're just—just inert! And you don't want to be—ert!

There, made you laugh. Don't make the worst decision of your life. It's time you took responsibility. It's 'ert' time! We are together. What do you say?

CITY TO CITY

If you were a city, what city would you be? I think you are Barcelona, or maybe Rio. I'm more repressed, more Dundee. If you were an animal, what animal? Don't say dolphin, don't say Labrador, or any kind breed of cat. Disallowed. Too obvious. I think you are a jaguar. Elegant. Me? I'm probably a pigeon. A dove? No a good old pigeon. If you were a hobby, what would you be? Skydiving for you, no question. I'm more sedentary. I really like stamp collecting. So, what do you think? Can we make a connection? Any future for us? Will love build a bridge? ... If you were a bridge, what would you be? You'd be the Golden Gate, for sure. I'd be that Iron Bridge across the Severn in Shropshire. You know the one? Famous. Built by Telford or someone. Well...? Can we beat the game? Want to go on? Leave it up to love? Going to move in?

BUDDY CAN YOU SPARE A DIME?

I have no money... I have no money... I have no money. Nothing! Nothing in my pockets. No money somewhere else. No savings. I have no money. These are not my clothes. These were given to me. They smell of poverty. They had that smell when I got them. Damp. I am hungry. I am filthy. I need to wash. I'm hungry! I need food. Please. I have nothing. Please... I'm starving. Please! ... Did you hear me? I have no money. Help me.

PARDON ME!

Clean your windscreen?! Cheap! Quick! Let me clean your windscreen! Look at the dirt! Look at the dead bugs and flies! I'll get it gone. Lick and spit! Lick and spit! Look, I've started already. What's wrong? Don't you want to see good? You want to have an accident?! Look the suds! Look the froth! Let me clean your windscreen. What you shoutin' for? I won't break nothin'! Okay! Okay! Rev and off you go. Amber! You go on amber! Danger! Right! I can't help you if you don't want to see!

WORST CASE SCENARIO

We don't argue about the trivial stuff. We agree on most things, the day to day decisions. We keep our differences for big clashes, yeh? The major rights and wrongs. Our fundamental beliefs. Core values. Then we go for it, no holds barred, right? Shouts! Door slams! Smashed dishes! It's wounding. We're both battle scarred. Bloody but unbound. We certainly know what we stand for. I certainly know what you hold dear. What you define yourself by. Well—I did... Not anymore. I'm scared now. You don't react. You give in. You say 'whatever!', like it doesn't matter. As if nothing matters. You agree with me... And I've never been so frightened. It's a nightmare. I think I'm losing you... I am absolutely terrified.

DEFICIT

This town has no chefs.
This town has no artists.

This town has no inventors.
This town has no philosophers.
This town has no racing drivers.
This town has no ballet dancers.
This town has no savages.
This town has no saints.
This town has no poets.
This town has no pirates.
This town has no lovers.
This town has no lovers.
So—it is down to me!

IN THE NAME OF LOVE

You always brought a garden with you when you arrived on your Harley Davidson. It didn't matter where you drove me, I could always smell wildflowers. You always brought a waterfall with you when you took me out to dance. I could fall in spray and tumble in bubbles all night. You always brought a snow-capped mountain with you when you played games with my children. We took turns to sit in your lap and watch the snow fall onto the sideboard and the coffee table. You always brought a river with you when you came to make love. It took me out to the broad estuary and the deep breath of the sea. You always brought a rainbow with you when you came to dinner. I was one pot of gold and you were another. You always brought a clear blue sky when you came to say goodbye. So that I would feel better when you were gone.

SUN IN AN EMPTY ROOM

Towards the end of his life Edward Hopper painted an empty room. In it the late midsummer sun throws a double rectangle of brilliance through a window onto a scuffed wall. The light is hard, but it has life and energy. It has the warm colour of the outside world. Although you've never been there before, the room seems familiar. It is your room. And you have nothing left but a ribbon of cream skirting-board and a volume of exhausted air. There is only a high and a low slab of shine, giving dust its smell. You see things as they really are... The past was a distraction of furniture. The present is only a reflection. The future is the same flat light forever.

WAKE UP AND SMELL THE COFFEE

There was no such thing as coffee in our house. There was no smell of it. No aroma of frying onions, or garlic, or pungent spices. Just the sweet smell of Heinz tomato soup accompanied by burnt toast. We were rural. We had no class. I was twelve when I was taken into town to buy long grey trousers for high school. My mother and I were walking across the front of a big department store on our way to a cheaper shop. Suddenly the rich smell of real coffee smacked into me. I was dizzy with it. It gave me a headache. I was almost sick! I could smell South America and Africa. The blood left my face. My body went limp. I could hardly lift my feet. My bones buzzed with excitement. By the time we cleared the big brass framed doors of Myers, I knew what culture was. I knew I must drink it down scalding and black!

RESPONSIBILITY

I'm frightened of the sacred. I'm frightened of investing in it, in case it's bogus. All that time and commitment wasted. But then, what if the divine does exist? I'll have wasted my life being confused, and judgmental and sceptical. What if the stupid, the poor, the afflicted, the ugly, the timid, the gullible, the feckless, the unlucky, the powerless and the worthless have got it right? What if they are loved equally? What if they are blessed? That thought scares me. What if I am not blessed? That thought also scares me... But if they are right, why doesn't God help them? God should help them... Should I help them? Me? How? How, with no belief? *Me?*

CAN I GET A WITNESS?

Sometimes there is a seagull looking back at you. Sometimes, after all you've been through. All the wrongs you righted or made worse. After all the dread. After absolute denial. After your hand on your heart. After the worst has happened, there's a seagull looking back at you. You're alone on a windswept pier, with a bag of chips, and there's a seagull looking back at you. You're alone on the ferry deck, hiding behind the funnel from the wind, and there's a seagull looking back at you. You're wondering how to turn the boat around. You're wondering if you can ever go home. You're wondering who the fuck you are—and there's a seagull looking back at you. When you're out there! There's only ever a seagull looking back at you.

2,000 LIGHT YEARS FROM HOME

Because of Dark Energy I've begun praying. I never prayed before, because I knew there was no God. So, there was no point! But now I know there's another force keeping us moving out into the universe, when science says we should be falling, collapsing in. Something unknown is tearing the planets and galaxies further and further apart, faster and faster—flying! Something stronger than any other force. So... I have found a belief in that force and I pray to it. Dark Energy. I pray for Uncle Hamish and Aunty Dilly. I hope the biopsy is benign. I pray for my father and mother. I pray for my sister, and Ian and Gemmell. I pray for us and our long long journey. I pray for our deliverance in Dark Energy.

PORTRAIT

I'm no artist, but if I was, I know what my final painting would be... An ordinary window in a dull room. The window open a little, and the thin white curtain in front of it luminous, billowing and falling back... That's the subject. The breeze and the curtain, and the light coming into the room when the curtain allows... The game between them. Just a window in a bland city room, but the curtain lifts, and opens, flickers. And as it sags and loses its vitality, as it sinks, it's caught again by the draught and dances in sunlight. A moving thing among the abandoned furniture and the dead staring ornaments. Moving... lighting... resting... moving. Repeating, but never the same pattern. The movement of light is everything.

ROOMS TO AVOID

Sometimes your whole life is just a room. A small room with a dodgy lock on the door. A very small and dirty window looking onto dustbins or another room. Sometimes the room has been furnished by a colour-blind moron. There are prints of vintage motor cars on the walls. Two prints have slipped their mountings. The furniture is too big for the room. The sofa is puffy and made of a shiny sticky black material. The cushions separate when you sit. You end up with your back unsupported and your arse halfway to the floor. The carpet has all the colours you'd find in drying vomit! There are stains on it from other lives. The coffee table has a cracked glass top. One leg needs two coasters under it to even up the slope. This is not a room to spend a life in. This is not even a room to redecorate. Nothing can flourish in this room. Get out!

ME, MYSELF, I

I don't want you to love me! I don't want your gifts, your thoughtfulness, your attention, your proximity, your contact, your skin, your domination. I don't love you! I just like to spend my money. I just like to drink. I just like to socialise. Party. Be carefree. I don't want you to want me. I don't want you to need me. I don't want you. *Listen*. I just need company. I just need laughter. I just need witnesses. I don't need you. I don't need your perjury.

REBEL REBEL

Sometimes I don't wash. I slop around in dirty underwear. I eat from a tin. I drink juice straight from the carton. I drop food on the floor. Leave the dishes to congeal in the sink. Spill beer on myself. Throw the cushions around. Un-recycle the recycling bins! Deliberately miss the pan and piss on the floor. Pathetic, I know. But the closest I ever get to freedom.

WHAT HAPPENS LATER?

I had a teddy bear called Nimbo. I loved him. At the top of the playground slide he had two eyes but at the bottom he only had one. I still loved him. Took him everywhere. Then a time came when I could let my parents give him away. I loved comics when I was little. Scrooge McDuck was my favourite because he was mean and bad. I could reread the same story countless times and still laugh at the pictures. I built up quite a stack. But then a time came when I could move to another house and leave the comics behind. I loved photography all through my children growing up. I took pictures of all three of them in different stripy clothes. After they left home, I sorted all the pictures into albums. Occasionally, I'd leaf through them and remember. I still love them. Then a time came when I could close the covers and put them away.

THE WILDNESS

I was wild because I couldn't speak.
I was wild because nobody would listen.

I was wild until I found the other side.
I was wild until the wildness answered back.
I was wild until the wildness was all used up.
I was wild when the wildness came back.
I was wild because I made no choices.
I was wild because I only risked myself.
I was wild for you to save me.
I was wild to reach you.
I was wild to take you.
I am still wild.

SATISFACTION

Somehow, without my noticing, I've stopped wanting the big things. The dream job. The dream girl. The lottery win car. Biceps. Abs. Coming home on the bus, I caught myself really looking forward—not to rampant dirty sex, or a plunge in my Olympic sized fantasy swimming pool, but to something much more basic. I was happily anticipating my dinner! Food and eating have replaced my young ambitions. I'm a man that loves his nosh! Ah! Bolognese sauce! Thai Green Curry! Cheese Mashed Potato! Sans Abs. Sans six pack. Sans waistline. I wonder what other undetectable thresholds are just in front of me and about to be crossed...?

MERCY

I believe that God creates, and God destroys. God does nothing else. Things appear, then disappear. There is neither malice, nor love in it. It is action. Only action. Action without a bias towards a positive, or a negative outcome. Either one will do. Either one is a consequence. And, of course, the consequence causes another action. In perpetuity... Punch, or embrace? It is human to see the good, or the bad in it. It is us who see a judgement between giving and taking. A value. That's what being human is. A bias towards an outcome that resolves, completes, ends yearning. We are not God. We hope for the best... We see it fail... We created mercy. Everything else is function.

SOLO ACT

It's better to be alone. There's no argument about what friend, or movie to see. I can have complete control over the TV, and zap from channel to channel, without the moaning and complaining. I can eat what I want, when I want it, without bothering about indigestion, or restless sleep. Much better to be alone! I can see my mates. Get drunk. Have my mates round. Leave the cans and bottles, and mess to the next day—or the week after. Alone is much better than together. I can stay up and play Xbox all night. Don't need to answer calls. I can drive faster. I love being alone. I love it. Alone forever! That's my motto. Leave me alone. I'm happy with my own company. Perfectly content to be by myself. Alone. All alone with a smile on my face. A smile no one can see. A smile no one can change.

THE BEHOLDER

Wonder is the best emotion. Open face. Open gaze. It opens you up right through to your soul. It opens that too. And there you are, with your soul exposed to the world. There's no history. No past tense. There's no future.

Wonder is absolutely now! Now is where nothing is decided. Now has no criticism. Now has no analysis. No filter of intelligence. Now is total contact. Total possibility. No expectation of a negative. The true self, given to the moment... I wonder at you.

THE PHENOMENON

I was driving back from a holiday up north. I was about three quarters of the way home and not expecting anything now in the way of scenery or nature. Then I saw one tiny rabbit. All along the side of the loch—more baby rabbits. They started to hop across the road. I had to slow down because herds of them decided to leap onto the bitumen. Everywhere I looked rabbits bounded about. They only moved away when the car was right up to them. Hundreds! It was wonderful. I was moved. Tears came to my eyes. I felt elated! I was the only one there with all these unafraid rabbits. And then I thought—it's just rabbits. Rabbits aren't that wonderful. They are just a dirty browny grey and they aren't rare. There are lots of fucking rabbits! And I took the wonder out of my brain. I began to speed up again in order to get home to my old dull self.

THE LIAR

All the opinions I espoused to entertain you, you now define me with. I thought you were in on the joke! I thought you knew I would say anything to make you laugh. But now, I see you really do think I have no regard for the brightest and the best. I do not hate the writers, actors, artists and singers I traduced. I'm not jealous of talent and achievement. My political incorrectness was a kind of extended free style jazz, an improvisation on transgression. A riff on foolishness. I'm not a racist. I'm not elitist. I'm not a misogynist. My position on any subject was a pose. Even the personal stuff—the confessions. The vulgar toilet habits. The dinner party faux pas. The comical misunderstandings at work. The sexual disasters. ALL MADE UP! I thought you knew. But now you judge me. You cite the same fictions that had you slapping your thighs. I can tell by your face that your judgment is not a pose... I expected more. I expected you to be as generous to me, as I have been to you... I realise that I've wasted my time and my imagination on you. I truly did not know how valuable time and imagination were.

BAD ROMANCE

I know I'm not the love of your life. Not your dreamboat. You had something else in mind. I know who you still hold a candle for. Too bad about that! That's all gone. I know I'm not THE ONE! But I care about you—for you. I love you... And, well—I'm all right. I'm not a loony or anything. Everything is in working order. I look decent enough. Got an okay job. So... what I'm trying to say, is, is that—I don't need everything, the whole package from you. You don't have to love me with a deep all-consuming love. You don't have to love me at all. Of course, if you could—eventually, but if not, that's—I understand. I can live without it. But if you could be kind, I'd like that. If you could like me—that's important I think, liking. If you could respect me, that would be good. That would be enough. Just liking, and respect. I'd be happy with that. Very happy.

GIFTS

I should have gone to the funeral. It was easier not to, of course. But I should've gone, even though I only liked her intermittently. Even though we lost touch. Not out of respect—I think she had silly values and was mistaken about most things. But she helped me once. Casually, almost in passing. She persuaded me to read a book. Lent it to me. It was by an author I had already turned up my nose at. Dismissed! I was so pig-headed. I read it only because I knew she would ask me about it. I felt obliged. And, well… Well it was stunning! I was so wrong. I loved every page. I never gave her the book back. I couldn't part with it. That's why I should have gone to the funeral.

SELFLESS

I fell off a ladder putting in a light bulb. Woke up in hospital with a hole in my head and no recall. Didn't know my name. Didn't know where I came from or grew up. I had no idea what I did for a living. I didn't even know my address. Didn't know if I was married, or engaged, or divorced, or in love. Did I have children? Who were those faces in my wallet? Didn't know if I liked olives, or shellfish, or black pudding. Was I allergic to nuts? Could I ride a unicycle? Were my parents alive? … I had no idea. But in my mind, I wasn't no one. In my heart I wasn't just a cipher. My identity wasn't infinitely changeable. Interchangeable with anybody else. I was not confused. I hadn't lost my definition. I forgot the context, the attributes, the accumulation of decisions, but I knew myself. I knew, without memory, who I was. There was no panic. My soul was the same.

THEN AND NOW

I never understood it at the time. Why an old couple would invite us to join them on their yacht. They took us out from Kristiansand on midsummer's day. The weather was perfect. High blue skies. We smiled the whole time the wind filled the massive white sail. We didn't have a care in the world. The old man did all the work. We sailed until the stars came out. Plunged past islands where bonfires were lit to celebrate the longest day. Sparks rose into the twilight. We couldn't stop laughing with the pleasure of it all. And that's all the old couple wanted. Nothing else. Just to share a little part of our youth. I'm sorry I haven't given them a thought in all this long while. I remember them now. I remember those bright young things in Kristiansand... If I had a boat today, I would invite them on board.

SCOTLAND

I love my country. I never thought I'd say that. The loch shingle speaks to me. The bruise of shadow crossing the hill makes the hairs on my arms lift. The sunlight sieved through the leaves of birches is all the sunlight I need. I even love the clichés—the heather and the thistle. Look at a heather bell right up close and the cliché disappears. There's light inside. I don't have internal organs, instead I have the geometry of hill farms. The irises of my eyes are damp forest bluebells. Doesn't make sense. Doesn't have to. That's love. My mind is river-bubble and water meeting rock. My imagination is the cloudscape sky—the west coast light. My soul is the—is the—is the way it all moves together. The interplay of it all. I love my country.

IN THE STILL OF THE NIGHT

It's just you and me and the big TV. Sometimes it was just you with the TV. Sometimes it was just me with the TV. But it was never just you and me without the TV. Once you dared me to switch off the TV, but you really didn't mean it. Once I dared you to switch off the TV and I did mean it, but I was relieved you didn't do it. We switched it off once when we had visitors, but we put it back on when we all realised that we wanted to watch Celtic in the semi-final. After, we went to bed and lay there in the dark with no screen between us. I thought you said something, but I was too shy to answer. The next day we went into town first thing and bought a giant screen for above the bedroom mantelpiece. We both got a great view propped up on two pillows.

THE GRASS AIN'T GREENER

You were practising to be generous. You practised on me. I was practising on being caring. I practiced on you. Hard work being caring! I never got it right and quit halfway through. You never noticed the difference. You never felt it. But you practised your generosity until it was ideal. Perfect! Then you gave it to a boy called Josh... I noticed. I noticed the difference. I felt it for the rest of my life!

YOU RASCAL, YOU

You love to shock. Your swearing is always a novel concoction of outrage and possibility. Fuck, you are funny! And everyone says—what a personality! What a larger than life character—what a force of nature! A pusher of boundaries. A breaker of social taboos. What a free spirit, unbound by sexual conventions. A conjurer of toilets in foreign lands without locks! A magician of sexual misfortune. But I say the opposite. I say attention seeker! I say needy! I say desperate! I say a plain dullish sparrow pretending to have peacock feathers. Ha! All that boasting about unbridled humiliation, and an uncontrollable body— from a fastidiously clean timid little virgin. I say the real thing is better kept quiet. Silent. I should know.

TRAVELLING ON

We weren't saying goodbye. We were making arrangements to see each other again. Soon. Sooner than the last time. Voices gushing with goodwill and promises. Eyes stretched open with enthusiasm. It's not so far. We'll keep in touch. Perhaps September. It depends on work. It depends on Lena. September isn't long to wait. We'll be on the phone. I'll give you a call. We were busy, busy with the business of holding on. Then you were a hand waving from the car window. A silhouette. Then you were a darker shadow, shining headlights on the road. Then you were red tail lights and a high beam crossing the bridge. Then you were gone... Later a single spot of light climbing the black hill. It's the one who stays behind that feels it worse. The one who stays behind knows what distance is.

TEMPORARY THING

You held me. But I am forgetting your arms. You kissed me. But I am forgetting your lips. You made love to me.

But I am forgetting your body. You showed me your dreams. But I am forgetting your eyes. Piece by piece, I am forgetting you. All the moments and days of you—forgotten! Soon you will be entirely gone from my memory. And I'll be longing for arms, lips, thighs—all pressed against me. I'll be dreaming of them. Wanting them now, wanting them tomorrow, wanting them new... When the memory of my passion has receded—sound, smell, touch, all faded. All the me that was with you gone—nothing. Longing will be my identity. Longing will be my name.

BENEDICTION

Because I never said, 'bless you', doesn't mean I didn't wish you good luck and all the happiness that life can bring. Because I never said a prayer for you, doesn't mean, I didn't think of you every day and desire your wellbeing. Because I never said, 'God love you', doesn't mean that I didn't love you. Love you through anxious testing times, when one expert after another gave you bad news. I never said the obvious. I don't, that's my pride—but my heart said it all. I want to hug you now, but that would be banal. I want to hug you now...

DAYDREAM BELIEVER

Dolores believes she saw her dead husband out shopping with her half-sister. Willie Thompson believes the world will end on the winter solstice in exactly two years. Devo, at work, believes in reincarnation. Tarik, my best friend, believes that NASA faked the moon landings. My big sister believes in angels. My little sister believes in Santa Claus.

Auntie Lillie believes the Virgin Mary will persuade Jesus to cure her. Uncle Claude believes in astrology. My father believes that coronavirus came from an alien escaped from Hangar 18. My mother believes that if you see a shooting star and make a wish, your wish will come true. And I believe…? And I believe…? I believe I love them all.

THE GUESTS

I love the aftermath of parties. I love all the used-up glasses around my living room. Lipstick smudges on the rims. I think of the fun each gulp gave. I love emptying the dregs into the sink. Each little dribble is the only evidence left of a good time. The plates abandoned under chairs, under beds and shoved in wardrobes, with their spill of breadcrumbs and morsels of cheese, tell me of appetites satisfied. The hard kernels of peanuts and the greasy flakes of crisps left in pottery bowls, let me know I bought the right things. Soiled, screwed up paper-napkins halfway down the sofa, show me how useful they were. Cutlery retrieved from behind the scatter cushions, are my trophies of success. My guests brought their party to me. It's a satisfaction to clean up the squashed Smarties from the polished hall floor. It's a reward to set right the mess my guests have made of me. It's the spillage, the breakages and the stains that make me invite them back.

I CAN SEE FOR MILES

I'm terrific at geography. I've got an excellent sense of direction. A Satnav brain! I remember street names, byways, lanes, dead-ends, even junction numbers. Ask me how to get somewhere and I will tell you. Do you want the shortcut, or the scenic route? Walking, bus, train, tram, bicycle—it's all the same to me! I'll describe the landmarks, what to watch out for. I'll tell you when to indicate, I'll tell you when to change lanes. I'll draw you a route map. No need to ever get lost when I'm around. Just name where you want to go. I'll know where it is. And my reply is always the same—I wouldn't start from here! Near or far, I'll tell you—I wouldn't start from here! If you want to get back home. You don't want to start from here. If you want your heart's desire—you can't start from here. You can't get there from here!

TELL ME WHAT YOU SEE

A small man standing doing nothing at a big bright green shed. As my train passes, he looks up. We see each other. Then what does he do? I don't know. I've moved on. Does he think of me moving on? Does he wonder where I am going? Why do I think of him receding? What is he doing now? Am I thinking of him only as a roundabout way of thinking about myself? What if he is thinking of me, what can he know? What can he decide from a glimpse? Better not to think about me. Better for me not to think about him, either thinking of me, or not thinking of me. Better to be on a train going anywhere, than be a small man just standing there doing nothing at a bright green shed.

DESIRE

I am a toad. I live in the pond of the moon. The moon is half-light and half fresh water. I glisten with romantic notions. My skin erupts with wanting and the fire of lust. But the moon is too far away. My mouth gets wider calling for the moon to swallow me up. My mouth is full of mud. My legs lengthen with trying to leap into a reflection. My legs are prayers. I am luminous with singing. The moon is singing to me. The moon is coming closer. The moon is another toad. Tonight, we will be lovers. Tonight, we will be full. Tonight we will burst!

THE GREAT VALERIO

The show was terrific. It blew me away. I loved the two main actors. They were both jaw-dropping. The poise, the physical control, the subtle layers of power in the voice—spell binding! It's the best thing I have ever seen. It's what I'd love to do. My dream! But seeing it now, for real. Seeing how good you must be, to be, an artist. To be able to lift an audience out of themselves, to show them what it is to be human—to find forgiveness in adversity—wow! To find balance after injustice—bigger wow! The placing, placing of thought, emotion and meaning in and out the words! The sheer skill! That's, that's beyond me. I know in myself I can't be that good. I can't get there! It's a standard I will never reach, no matter how hard I try. So, I've made my decision. There will always be work for plumbers. And my uncle Dale can get me a start. At least I know. No regrets. Just... total admiration...

A FLEETING MOMENT OF INSIGHT INTO THE MEANING OF LIFE

I was thinking I would have a few days to myself, doing nothing. Just stare at the wall. Think about whatever. What it's all about? Ask some of the bigger questions. So, there I was, gazing out the window, about to think about something important, when my nose started to itch. After a few satisfactory scratches, I was about to ask something profound, when the tip of my right ear went hot. Scratching solves everything! I settled back down to contemplate existence, and then, right then, at that very moment—my arse nipped beyond belief! I tried to ignore it and focus on the bigger picture. But it itched worse. The more I tried to ponder existence, the more my arse wanted scratching! Then I had a blinding revelation—Itching and scratching are the gateways to hell and heaven. The Ying and Yang of it all! An itch traps you into reincarnation. A scratch is enlightenment... For a moment I understood it all.

THE GETTING OF WISDOM

People confide in me. I must have one of those faces. I'm a drop-box for confessions. Secret after secret. Terrible things. You would think they would give me sleepless nights. An ulcer! Make me lose faith in human behaviour after hearing all the shocking things ordinary folk have done. But along with the endless stream of wrong actions, bad actions and vile actions—there's the tears. Howling regret. Powerful, soul splitting regret. Facing the consequences without excuses. True contrition. Life changing remorse. And then... a kind of clarity. Something pure. A simple frail goodness. I could tell you true stories.

Make your hair stand on end. But I'm not a gossip. I want to keep all that final goodness for myself.

WHO DO YOU LOVE?

I'm drawn to so many people. Almost everyone. Think of all the possibilities. I could end up in bed with any old scrubber. So, best to put some filters in place and exclude the worst excrescences of humanity. To limit the damage. The desire. So, no piercings, or studs. No tattoos. No one chewing gum. No eating with an open mouth. No one with a logo on their clothing. No one coughing, sneezing, spitting or sniffing. No fatties. No one walking and texting at the same time. No one who cannot speak without mangling their grammar. No one who has no friends. No one who doesn't vote. No one who can't dance. No one who can't cook. No one without good teeth. No one who doesn't read books. No one who votes Conservative. No one with a stupid ringtone. No one who can't sing. No one with a—. No one who—. No one that—. No one—. I want—no one. I don't want... no one.

CRUSH

Your daughter is, how can I say this? Aware of me, becoming sensitised to me. She's, she's developing an, an interest. No that's too much—maybe not. I notice her looking at me, looking at me, looking at me with—interest. So, I want you to know that I, well, I don't know what you can do. It's her age, just a phase but... Perhaps you could have a word. I'm just a bit uncomfortable with, with—the way she looks at... It makes me feel, err, not good—

disturbed—you know? And I wanted to bring it to your attention, in case you thought that, I, that I, had any anything, any interest—ah! I think you—you need to—. After all, she's your daughter and I don't want to hurt her feelings. It's a delicate age to be and I've always been fon— liked her—. So, I don't want to be cruel, or not see her in the future. If there was a way you could defuse—no not defuse—there's nothing to defuse. Maybe it's all in my imagination. Forget it. Oh no, that would be worse! It's not in my imagination! It's not. Just forget it. It's not... Not. Absolutely not... Not!... Got it? NOT!

SELF-HARM

Today I saw a scar on the back of my left hand. Almost invisible but a clear line crossing four blue veins. Forgotten it was there. I had forgotten I put it there one summer afternoon. Now I remember doing it with the point of a compass. Digging in. It took a long time. I did it on a hard-backed chair in the dining room. Nobody was home. I had never heard of self-harm. I remember wondering if there would be a scar. I remember wondering how long the scar would last. I remember challenging time. I look at the scar on the back of my hand now. It is like somebody else's scar. I think about the pain I must have inflicted on my hand. All the pain has gone. I've learned that pain does not stop time.

WAY OVER THERE

I saw her getting the news. She was at the end of the corridor. And the news seemed a long way off. I was two clicks from finishing one section of Angry Birds. She was alone as far as she could be. Then the doctor touching her arm. I saw her fold over. But it was... such a distance. I expected it to happen to her. She looked like she had expected it. She was upset. But I was in a different world. What could I do? So far away. Almost at the lifts. Then she looked at me and suddenly we were in the same world. She was so—so without any... comfort. She was full of grief. Right up close! There in front of me! In my face! And all I felt was ashamed. Ashamed and unable to get to the next level.

BODY AND SOUL

They tried to love. But she had lost her mother young and he had won a war. They tried to love by dancing, but he hated to look a fool, and she wanted to move like an angel. They tried to love by making love, but he made love to other women without love, and she made love to men that liked to wink. They tried to love by drinking beer, then wine, then vodka, but it made him punch his pride and it made her walk into doors. They tried to love through their children but both sisters told lies, took sides and were unable to trust love for the rest of their lives. They tried to love, they tried to love, tried to love. Then he died. The one left remembered everything but could not remember why they could not find love. Even left alone she tried to love. Year after year. It was trying to love that brought her wisdom, not love.

THE HISTORY OF YOUR GAZE

Your first look was in the Lismore Bar—you thought I might have something for you. Outside you looked at me like the sun had just come out. Down the street you gave me wide eyes and a crooked smile. There was lots of that. A summer and another season at least. In a flat without door handles you looked at me like you were hungry. In a garden flat on Wilton Street you looked at me like you had eaten that before. You looked like you wanted to refuse but you were too polite. After we married you looked at me mean. Then you looked at me like I was autumn ripping at the leaves. But you still looked at me for something. Still looked for something now and then. Your last look was like you had startled pigeons. You never liked pigeons. Then you didn't look at me. Then you didn't look at me. Never looked at me again.

A MAN FOR ALL SEASONS

If you've got it sunny, a white shirt is the best advice. A white cotton shirt. If you're slim, tuck it in. Looks good. If your hips are the same width as your shoulders—wear a thick leather belt. Brown or black, doesn't matter. But the buckle must be simple, no words—no icon or symbol. Just rectangular with some weight in it. Looks secure but easily undone. And as simple as that you've got the kit. Now you're a man that can go anywhere. Enter any room. A man who will be liked before he speaks. A man with a three second advantage over any other man. For dull days see my advice on cardigans. If you live further north than Manchester, see the supplementary notes on rainwear.

HOLD ON

I had a hand on my chest once. I think it was resting. It rested me. I had a hand on my shoulder when I was young. I think it was encouraging. I felt an obligation to be enthusiastic. I had a hand on my forehead when I wanted attention. It was never enough attention. I had a hand on my feet. I think my feet were dirty and had been somewhere unpleasant. I had a hand over my eyes. The hand helped me to trust. I had a hand on my thigh. Perhaps it was a fantasy. I had a hand, any hand, many hands upon my sex—but they all had claws for fingernails... And I never had a hand in my hand. A hand to hold on. A hand to join 'done' to *doing*—'doing' to *done*. A hand to place anywhere I wanted... I need a hand to join my hand... To make a union.

THE JOKER

I'm not a serious person. I only have a serious job. Everyone thinks I'm a serious person because I have a serious job. But I just want to fart and laugh at the sound. I want to watch silly trash daytime TV and jeer at the lowlife. I want to eat ice-cream and Haribo's and giant Chocolate Buttons. I want to listen to show tunes. I want to grin at off-guard celebrity pics. Giggle at anything serious—that takes itself seriously. Giggle at my superficial seriousness... I'm going to sprinkle inching powder at the Board Meeting! Put a Whoopee Cushion under the Marketing Manager! Place Dirty Face Soap in the executive loo! When they start to become human, I'm going to spray the bastards with Party String!

BEAUTIFUL LIAR

Because I wasn't honest, I let my father think I was going to be a doctor. He told everyone I was going to be a doctor. I could never stand the sight of blood. Because I wasn't honest, my boss thought I was a totally loyal company man. Until I took his secrets to a rival firm. Because I was not honest, my girlfriend thought I loved her. I just couldn't say no. Because I wasn't honest, my best friend trusted me with his wife on holiday. Well, as I said, I couldn't say no! Because I wasn't honest, I pretended for half a lifetime to have faith in God. I thought prayers were enough. Because I wasn't honest, I tried even longer to believe I was a good man. I am not a good man. I am an honest man, at last. Honesty is not much to be left with.

ALL MY LOVING

I love you. I love loving you. Loving you makes me love my life. I love giving my life to you. I love you you you! I love feeling like this. I love giving this feeling to you. Sharing this feeling with you. That is love, isn't it? Being absolutely certain of what we absolutely share. Sharing all you and all me with each other. Making ourselves different by adding each other. Adding each other's love. I'm so happy to love you. I'm so happy! Thank you for loving me. Thank you for letting me add you to my love. Thank you for letting yourself be loved.

US SOMETIMES

I've got you. There's no parting. There's no distance between us. I've got you in my arms. You could never be separate. We could never be parted. You know I'm with you. You know that wherever you are, you are in my arms. Whoever you're with, you are in my arms. You are not in Dortmund. You are not outside the Ostwall Museum. You are in my tight arms. You are not made of shadows. You don't have to please. You don't have to laugh into the cold night air. You don't have to laugh in pubs with leering sordid faces. I've got you in my arms. I've still got you in my arms. You are here with me, wherever you are. You are really with me. We are complete. No matter who fucked you!

RESURRECTION SHUFFLE

Every year I dig my grave. Every year I choose a new spot. A bluebell wood. A sandy beach. A thistle patch at the end of a garden path. The floor of an abandoned basement. I have a garage full of tools to rupture any surface. Shovels, spades and pickaxes of every size and shape to quarry into clay, or rock. Six feet down! Every year I stand over the hole and stare. I stand there with a gun in my hand. Sometimes the bottom is only mud and slime. Sometimes I see hell waiting. Some years it is heaven. Mostly it's nothing. Occasionally a beetle, or a worm. I stand over my grave until I feel my soul return… If it does—I go on with my life.

RIVER DEEP, MOUNTAIN HIGH

They tested me for lightning.
They tested me for deluge.
They tested me for hurricane.
They tested me for lava flow.
They tested me for avalanche.
They tested me for earthquake.
But I kept my love a secret.
And my love changed everything.
My love changed the world.

DIVINE COMEDY

Edward Hopper's very last painting is of a man and woman, dressed in white Pierrot costumes, isolated on a high bare stage. The man is slightly forward, there is a suggestion of a smile. He is holding his partner's hand, as if to encourage her to approach the audience and receive her rightful applause. There is no scenery. What they did, they did alone. Her other hand is raised in modesty. Her head is slightly on one side. She needs more to convince her than cheers and stamping feet. He touches his heart, or he gestures towards her, it isn't clear. They have finished their act, done their best. For a moment they look unsure. Perhaps another bow? Gratitude is all they have left. Behind them a vast blue darkness is already beginning to descend.

FLAWLESS

You flew above the clouds for hours in bright blue sunshine but did not change your eyes. You lay naked beside another person for half of your adult life, but you did not change your hunger. You changed your hairstyle every second season. But you didn't change your dreams. You changed your breakfast cereal. But you didn't change your energy. You changed your friends. But you never changed your status. You grew old, but you did not change yourself. The whole world changed, but you did not change yourself. The world moved on... You were left alone... You thought the world was wrong for changing. You never changed your opinion. You were always alone. That never changed.

EVOLUTION

I am a monkey. Smart. Quick. Strong. But in between these three things—smart, quick, strong—I wonder... I feel. Feel like I've come from somewhere else. Somewhere dirty, brutal. It draws me back. To be wild—primitive! As I swing from one branch to another, I feel so—released. As if I was about to become something more. Flying over the chasm between trees, I'm sure I'm almost there—gifted, special—complete! MORE! For a moment suspended between absolutes. Behind me jumbled up greed and savage gratification—out there, just a grasp away—something fine standing up full height. I feel unfinished for a whole lifetime.

THE WHOLE STORY

There were four little pigs, not three. Little Miss Moffit became obese and developed type-two diabetes from eating all that curds and whey. Humpty Dumpty trained as a psychotherapist and used the insights he had gained from dealing with his own fractured Ego, to help others. Little Red Riding Hood wrote a self-help book on how to deal with jeopardy, and now runs a company providing assertiveness training for women in work-based environments. A story is information left out. Life is all the rest of it. A story is a beginning, middle and end, with the beginning at the start, then the middle joined on, and the end coming last. A story is one thing leading to another. A story is what you need to know and that's enough! A story is where the final full stop should land. Life is making sense of what you are left with when the story is over.

NOT THAT KIND

I hope I have been kind. I would like to have been kind. I wish I had been kind. I have not been kind. I regret not having been kind. So many people have been kind to me. I have tried to make myself kind. I have been unkind to myself with accusations and punishments to try to change myself into being kind. But this made me unhappy, it did not make me kind. I am grateful though—for all the kindness I have been given. It surprises me to find out that I can be grateful but not kind. I'm so grateful. I'm just not kind.

LAST MAN STANDING BLUES

This is the last blues song ever written. Nobody writes the blues anymore. For the blues you must feel regret. Who feels any of that nowadays? Make a tit of yourself, and you put it on YouTube for the world to gawk at. Today's electronic democracy of embarrassment has no shame.

'Hellhound on my Tail'—I don't think so! I regret contrition passing out of the world. I regret losing the voices that blame themselves for thinking wrong, speaking wrong, wanting wrong, loving wrong! I regret that the boasters and the bullies have stormed the stage to shout their defiance—not to sing. To validate their hatred—not to sing. So, for Muddy, B.B., Bo, Sleepy, Lee, Lightning, Blind Lemon and Howling Wolf, I wrote this song, my final song. I hope they can hear me where they are.

LITTLE BASTARD

When did you become a bastard? Were you born that way? Did a nurse put you in an incubator and set the dial for, let's see... liar? Sneak? No, full on bastard it is! Maybe, it was your parents, they trained you. 'Come in you wee bastard, your tea's getting cold!' Perhaps you did the degree in bastardology, at the University of Selfish Pricks! Eh? Well, you graduated with a distinction, no mistake! Did you top it up with a Ted talk? Get your order in for bastard booster shots over the dark web? I don't know. I don't fucking know what made you a bastard. Right?! But you can't guilt-trip me! It wasn't me! Oh no! How fucking dare you say it was because of me. BASTARD!

PASSIVE BALLET

I am too selfish for a blessing.
I am too angry for forgiveness.
I am too lazy for a sacrifice.
I am too proud for a pilgrimage.
I am too rational for prayer.

I guess it is over to you.
I know I am in your hands.
If your hands are not bored with taking.
If your hands can forgive.
Take me.

CRAZY LOVE

You were frightened of the dark. But the dark was half the world. You were frightened of the sea and all the little splashes it made. But you could swim underwater with your eyes open. You were frightened of half of yourself. Only half. Frightened of half of me. More than half! You were frightened of your pleasure. Frightened before pleasure and frightened after. You were frightened of the music and frightened of the stars. One fear had distance and one fear was loss. So much fear. So much distance. So much loss... But I hung around. Dodging the stars and the sea and the music and the darkness—just to give you my love.

UNION

You had yesterdays, made of sugar and chip-fat under your fingernails. You had a yesterday of West Coast beaches and the seaweed of Ardnamurchan in your armpits. I was attracted despite myself. You had yesterdays scattered in your hair. The usual Dolce and Gabbana breeze coming out of those playful holiday down times. You had yesterdays, instead of eyes. Yesterdays, inside those yesterdays. That's what you gave me when I wanted sunrise. You gave me potential when I wanted the action of your breath. Breathe in! Breathe me in!... Us!

BY THE WAY

Where were we, when the steering wheel was so hot it burnt my hands, and we had to wait staring at a blazing white wall? Where could that have been? Where were we, when I changed that tire on our clapped-out old Ford? There were finches flying in and out a hedge. Why didn't we stop there? Where were we, when the headlights went out and there was nothing to see but some shapes in the dark? Where were we, when the stone hit the windscreen? I pulled into a layby with a view of a deep blue loch. I don't think I could find that place again. Where were we, when the exhaust fell off and I reversed around a bend to get it? Why aren't we dead? Where were we, when the wipers froze? We were frozen too. Not talking anyway. Where were we, when you slept, and I drove on? Who was I then? Where were we, when I turned left instead of right? How did those people get here? How did then arrive at now? How did our love get home?

LITTLE BRITAIN

There are places like real places, but better. Little Italy is like Italy but without the smell of drains, the litter and the graffiti. It's got pizza and brilliant ice-cream. It's even got some authentic looking Italians. But the good thing is they can all speak English. There's a little China with a big Chinese gateway and red lanterns hanging down every street. It's better than having to go all the way to Beijing to cough black spit up because of all the traffic fumes. Everything with the word 'little' in front of it is better. Little Eiffel Tower, Little Sydney Opera House in Legoland. The best thing would be to have Little Africa, Little Switzerland, Little Thailand and Little Russia—places like that, in all our cities. A whole bunch of them. Wouldn't that be great!? Then we wouldn't have to go anywhere! We could just stay home and be little!

SUMMER UNIFORM

We wanted to connect to the landscape. To make it part of us. To make it live in our imaginations. You said, the poplar trees at the edge of the path were flashing their silver swords. We went metaphor, we went military. I said, the horse chestnuts paraded in golden epaulettes. Then you let me kiss you, and the other trees in the meadow put on their bravest medals. You kissed me back, and the light fluttered down in coloured campaign ribbons for the whole afternoon. We saluted each other on the tartan rug, until the rowans did up their gilt buttons and the maples shot the fancy frogging on their cuffs. As we fell asleep to the swish of alders, you whispered that they were slipping on their white gloves. Later, I made you laugh by saying that the sun was polishing its cap badge. You said, I made everything sound dirty. I folded the rug and smirked.

POTENTIAL

All the growing up you did was never enough. You never felt like a grown up. You still weren't grown up when you began to wilt—shrivel. All the fears you lived behind, never kept you safe. All the lopsided judgement you used to push people away, pushed people away. You choose not to remember. All the love you threw out of windows, sent across dance floors, posted in chatrooms, sang between headphones and promised between cotton sheets was never returned... All the love you did not use is ready to use again. All the love you did not use is ready for someone special. All the love you did not use is ready for your reach. All the love you did not use is ready for your embrace. All the love you did not use is ready for growth! Love can reverse decline. I am within reach.

THE PUZZLE

Not much perplexed him. The major upheavals in politics held little interest. His work was a pleasant numbness. His family was mostly a vague irritation. He anticipated death, or retirement, (which ever came first) with mild curiosity but little imagination. He had friends. He was not an unpleasant man. He knew enough about football to pass on a goalie joke with some authority. But the difference between a seagull and a kittiwake remained something he was unsure about for all his adult life. He lived in a midland town and only occasionally travelled to the coast. It was unlikely he would ever see a kittiwake. But this lapse in his knowledge of seabirds troubled him. It niggled until he bought a guidebook to the 'Birds of Britain and of Europe'. Back home he meant to look up what a kittiwake looked like. But he left the book unopened on a shelf. As he aged, he stopped going to the coast altogether. At his funeral no one looked up to identify the squawking birds, high overhead. No one was interested in Kittiwakes.

I ME MINE

Between one guilt and another, I want some Me Time. Time to waste staring at ants. Between the lethargy yesterday and the lethargy tomorrow, I want Me Time. Time to watch a cloud arrive, change my mood and go. Between the dreams of avarice and my fantasies of philanthropy, I want more Me Time. Time to drop my shoulders and ease my breath. Between the craving for friendship and the longing to get away, I deserve some Me Time. Time to remember myself in someone else's photograph. Between the consequences of my carelessness and the consequences of my flattery, where is my Me Time? Time to wait for a revelation. Between the fear of indifference and the terror of being forgotten, I need to gather Me Time. Time to give myself a soul. Here it is... Me Time at last... Uninterrupted Me Time... No one intruding... No one needing a piece of me... No one around... An endless moment... Just empty Me Time...

IT'S GOTTA BE REAL

My compromises are different from your compromises! You wouldn't budge on money or price, but you would give in on terms and conditions. I would reduce the cost, but I would insist on having only top-of-the-range fittings. You would cave on interior decoration and furniture, but you would insist on space and location. I would never give in on wall colours, rugs, curtains, blinds and occasional tables, but I could make do without an extra room, or get upset about how the house looks from the curb. As I said, my compromises are different from your compromises. I couldn't live without love and physical affection, but I could do without dusting, vacuuming and washing up. You want things spick and span and show off showcase, but you can ignore the lips of your servant without any problem! From now on no concessions! No negotiations. No deals! Just my need and your compliance.

THAT SINKING FEELING

A young man throws a stone at the universe. It flops towards a small pond in a public park, hitting nothing but the side of a birch sapling and then grey water. The ripples struggle to matter and then are lost returning to the point of entry. All these events take a lifetime. At the end of the process an old man throws a stone at the young man he used to be... It feels the same.

WORRY B. GONE

All through the pandemic you worried about your far-flung family. Each one vulnerable in a different way. A granddaughter with cystic fibrosis and her little brother Scott with his asthma. Plenty of family to worry about. Uncles Tommy and Frank with diabetes. Auntie Patty with her operation on hold. You hardly slept a wink! Tossing and turning about poor Jessica's blood transfusion. And when the shadow of the virus left and the world started to get back to normal, you still worried. About—about... It was the *worry* that kept you company.

I'M STILL HERE

After the funeral we went back to the son's flat. We were out of the bone-searing wind. We were out of the horizontal rain. But it was more than that... Much more! We were inside welcome. We were inside generosity and central heating. We were inside quips, gags, jokes and friendships. We were inside the tentative but gathering momentum of life continuing. We were where our laughter made its own community. Where we could die and never die! Where we could never die, as long as someone laughed.

TWO OF US

You've changed. You used to be great, funny, a real laugh. Now, I don't know, you look scruffy and a bit hard. A bit grim, to be honest. What are you eating? Look at your skin! It's, it's almost grey. Kinda slack. You know you've got bags under your eyes? Are you sick? Your hair! It's—have you looked in a mirror recently? Looks like it needs a wash. So lank. I can see you're thinner. Certainly lost weight. Where's your energy, that famous fucking cheeky spark? You keep mumbling and fading out. I don't get it. You left me! I was the one you walked out on. I'm the one who should look like death warmed up. Not you. You were the one who said it wasn't working out. What happened? Change your mind? Want me back?... For the goodness of your health.

FALSE POSITIVE

You expended a huge amount of energy convincing everyone that you weren't lazy. You were at it every minute of the day. Helping friends with car engines and installing computer software. Putting in extra, extra shifts at work. Painting your sister's bathroom ceiling. Cutting grass. Walking your neighbour's cockerpoo. Offer after offer! Everyone admired your enthusiasm. Your endless endeavour. You were a force of nature. And all of it pretending. Engaged to the max. 100%! Pretending to be a role model. 110%! An exemplar. 130%! More! Fucking

200%! Why not!? Arithmetic isn't real. It is pretending that makes us who we are. That's who we really are.

LIFE IS GOOD

I invented social distancing. I was born screaming. I screamed when my parents came near me. Fucking howled! Growing up, I avoided team games. Fled from family parties. Didn't trust handshakes, hugs and kisses. Made myself alone in every crowd. I didn't want to be disappointed. Didn't want to disappoint. Self-isolation was my little kingdom. Then you all came running with your big bad viruses. You shut the door on friendship and love and wiped it down with bleach. Lovers disappeared from the streets. Days became slow, quiet. Silent... Time disappeared! Eventually, I left my flat and tiptoed downstairs... The town was gleaming, empty. I touched were you used to lean and sit and cuddle and stroke and fondle and wish. I wept. But you did not come back. I wanted someone to listen to my apology. I wanted someone to just say they understood. I wanted to say sorry to a healthy face. No one found me. No one looked out a window. Then I realised, I was the virus.

FIX ME NOW

I have wasted my eyes. I can only see the worst in people. My friends have abandoned me. I cannot see the point of other people. Then I saw you! I have abused my toes. They bunch together for protection. Anxious. Shoes no longer fit me. Then I danced with you! I have blunted my fingers. They are scarred and ugly from all those times I shook hands with the devil. Then I touched you! I have ruined my tongue. I can only taste sugar and my teeth itch and ache at night. Then I kissed you! I have broken my heart on city girls and country music... Then I fell in love with you.

ANYBODY'S HEAVEN

While the sunlight's still on me, did I mention steppin' barefoot on grass? Oh! Before the light goes out, I should tell you about swimming naked in the naked big blue. Oh! While I'm still warm and my eyes are bright, I invite you to dance with me in your beautiful new bought clothes. Oh! At the same time as summer breaks my windows, here's a bubble lifting from the kitchen sink. Oh! When the summer holidays come at last, I want to sing those high Lennon & McCartney notes, as we drive past Loch Lomond. Oh! While the sun jumps from tree to tree, I remember a dusty foreign street where you crushed a Bay Leaf and held your hands to my nose. Oh! While there is still shine in my memory, I see my childhood running through a ticking water sprinkler. Oh! Before the moon takes me from you, remember I said Oh! That was the only important thing... OH!

A BEGINNER'S GUIDE TO THE BLUES

This song is for the jilted, the betrayed, the broken-hearted. The fools who loved too well and were kicked in the nuts! This is for all those who know how to bear a grudge. This song is for what you did to me and what I did to you. This song is for all those who knew better but couldn't resist temptation... This song has no official title. When I sing it,

I call it by my own name. When you sing it, you call it your name. And so the truth goes on. Personal and universal at the same time. The whole song is unusual. It only has one line. I'm going to sing it loud and clear—I would go back and do it all again! I would go back and do it all again! I WOULD GO BACK AND DO IT ALL AGAIN.

LEAF BY LEAF